finding Joe

Lynn Lovene Publishing
Morgantown, West Virginia

Vicky,
Hope you
enjoy the book.
Becky

© 2018 Rebecca Hunn

Visit my Facebook page at facebook.com/rebeccahunnbooks
or email me at hunnbooks@gmail.com.

ISBN: 978-0-9993984-0-1

Cover design: Belinda Miles, Dragonflies Design

Production by Populore Publishing Company, Morgantown, West Virginia

Something's Up

I know them better than my own family. Who begot whom, who died young, who bequeathed the family heirlooms to one daughter leaving nothing to the other. I know who never married and who tried it two or three times. I have their dates of birth, dates of marriage, dates of death. And since they aren't mine, I'm free to imbue them with personalities, often based solely on their names. A Katherine was aristocratic, a Myrtle quite down to earth! I paint portraits in my head of people towering or diminutive, stout or lanky, stylish or dowdy. I imagine happiness and tragedy, riches and poverty, see family quarrels emerge and peacemakers triumph. And, in the final analysis, none of these musings is at all relevant to my work. I need the names and dates and legal documents to prove who is the legitimate heir of whom. The rest is just my imagination run amok, but it's such great fun.

I'm an oil and gas rights leasing agent—part sleuth, part genealogist, part salesperson. My name is Donna Cain, and I think I have the best job in the world. The rest of my life isn't bad either: thirty acres in the West Virginia countryside, a cabinetmaker/musician husband, a deputy sheriff son making the area safer for all, and an older brother in a cabin on the property.

It was early morning, still dark outside, and I was just trying to wake up. Months before, a bad case of insomnia had sent me to the back bedroom to escape my snoring husband, Sam, and a very noisy cat door. There was a small deck off our second-floor bedroom with a cat door that, on some nights, saw a lot of traffic. Our little orange tom loved to bring in live critters as presents.

As I lay in the dark, I heard Sam coming down the hall. But, before he could get to the back bedroom to make sure I was awake, there were three loud, raspy blasts and it was definitely close by. Sam's approach got faster.

"What was that?"

"Not sure," I whispered. "Turn on the light."

He did, and I rolled to the side of the bed away from the door. My glasses were still on the bedside table so I was at a definite disadvantage in my survey of the corner where I thought the sounds had come from. Finally, my eyes focused in on the source of the noise. Peeking out from under the rounded end of a violin case propped in the corner, was a frog. A large frog. My little tom had brought me a bullfrog.

"It's a frog, Sam. Go get your pitcher and I'll keep an eye on him."

Sam had become quite the critter catcher. He uses a rectangular plastic pitcher that makes it easy to get into corners and scoop things up. The hard-to-scoop include mice and chipmunks, both very fast. Moles are easy and frogs are a breeze. Sam returned quickly, picking up the unresisting amphibian and plopping him down in the pitcher. He covered the opening with one arm to prevent any high-jumping escapes, and our unwilling, but perfectly fine, visitor was back in the creek in a flash!

Sam and I live in an old, medium-size farmhouse, not exactly plumb anymore, but cozy, warm, and inviting. At least to us. The start to my workday mornings is pretty much the same except for Wednesdays when I have a 7:00 a.m. Rotary meeting twenty-five minutes from my house. Every other day of the workweek I take my shower, enjoy coffee and breakfast, and then do a quick kitchen cleanup. After that I march up the stairs (or the wooden hill, as Sam's father always called it), make a left into what was once a bedroom, and I'm at work.

"So, what's on your agenda today?" Sam asked, as I ate my eggs.

For some reason, I have always eaten breakfast standing up at the kitchen island. I sit for every other meal, but wouldn't dream of doing that for breakfast.

"I'm starting a new tract," I told him. "That's always fun and, from the property's title, this one looks interesting. I'm just hoping I can get in touch with one of the current owners quickly to get the ball rolling."

In this age of cell phones, I was finding it harder and harder to get good phone numbers. I often had to resort to knocking on doors, or writing letters and asking people to call me. They usually did, but it slowed the process down.

"What are you up to today?" I asked.

"Helping the guys finish a kitchen installation and getting started on a couple of estimates. I like doing the jobs, but hate doing the estimates."

Most of what Sam's cabinet shop produced was high-end. They did a lot of kitchens, built-in bookcases, and entertainment centers, much of it in newly constructed homes, but upgrades in older homes were a significant part of his business too. Sam gathered up his laptop, reading glasses, and phone, and gave me a hug and a kiss, then went out the door.

I tidied up the kitchen and headed up the steps, ready to tackle another workday. As an oil and gas leasing agent, I review the title that the courthouse crew gives me. Once I understand it and agree, I begin contacting the oil and gas owners the title has identified. I talk to them about leasing their oil and gas rights for the company I'm on contract to. I live in Monongalia County, but my leasing activity is in Taylor County about a forty-five-minute drive from my house.

So, on this sunny Monday morning in April, I was getting ready to call one of the four great-grandchildren of Barrett Tredloe, all brothers and sisters, and each one owning a one-fourth interest in two hundred forty-seven acres of oil and gas. After four generations, I'm usually dealing with at least twenty people and, often, well over fifty. But the Tredloe clan had not been at all prolific. With only four living descendants, I thought, this one would be a piece of cake. Time would prove me very wrong on that count!

I'd just dialed the phone number of the first Tredloe heir I'd been able to find contact information for. Her name was Miriam Baxter, and the phone was ringing. I had no idea what I was getting myself into.

"Hello."

"Hi. Mrs. Baxter?"

"Yes."

"Mrs. Baxter, my name is Donna Cain and I'm a leasing agent working for Dean Oil and Gas. Do you have a few minutes to talk?"

"I do," she answered in a no-nonsense way.

"Mrs. Baxter, are you at all familiar with Dean?"

"I think I've heard the name," she says with some hesitation. "Maybe from someone at church."

"Well, Dean is an oil and gas exploration and production company, and we're leasing and drilling in your area. Mrs. Baxter, I'm calling because my company has run the title, that's the ownership history, on two hundred forty-seven acres that were owned by your great-grandfather, Barrett Tredloe. Our research shows that the oil and gas is now owned by you and your siblings."

The silence on the other end of the phone tells me she has no idea she owns this. And here I was coming out of the blue to tell her she has something that's potentially very valuable. All I'm hearing from Mrs. Baxter right now is silence.

Finally she responds. "That doesn't sound right. Why do you think we own this?"

From her tone of voice, I can tell she's backing up fast!

"You know," she continues, "times were tough back then and our family didn't have money. I'm fairly certain that Great-Grand-dad died with just the family farm and that wasn't very big."

"Mrs. Baxter, we have full title on this property going back to the eighteen hundreds. Barrett Tredloe reserved the oil and gas rights when he sold the land, and it never got on the tax rolls. I had a feeling you might not know anything about it and, believe me, that's not uncommon. However, I feel very certain that your family owns this."

I explain how, over time, Barrett Tredloe had bought a total of two hundred forty-seven contiguous acres in seven pieces. But then, after a few years, he started selling them piece by piece. However, in each deed there was a rock-solid reservation for the oil and gas. Barrett Tredloe reserved the oil and gas under each and every one of the two hundred forty-seven acres. And that ownership had descended to his four current heirs.

"Mrs. Baxter, this tract was adjacent to your great-grandfa-ther's sixteen-acre farm, what I'm sure you know as the home-place. But the two hundred forty-seven acres was an entirely separate piece of property. Our title definitely shows that the oil and gas has passed down through the generations to you and your three siblings."

After a short silence, she says, "Two siblings."

"Oh . . . I thought there were three. The title shows you, Harold David Tredloe, Debra Christine, married name Little, and Joseph Morgan Tredloe."

"Joe's gone," she replied.

"I'm sorry. I had no record of him passing away."

"Neither do we, but we haven't heard from him in twenty years. I still don't understand how we could own oil and gas and not know it."

I noted the rapid change of subject from the missing Joe and knew to leave it alone for the time being.

"It's kind of complicated," I told her. "I'd really like to sit down with you and explain more about this. I'll have the full title with me and we can review it together. Would that be okay? Could we talk sometime tomorrow?"

She hesitated, but then said she would be free around two o'clock. She gave me good directions and we said good-bye. That was my first contact with the Tredloe family, the beginning of a journey that would shock, teach, amuse, and, most of all, change a few lives.

Kids and Kingfishers

A glance at the clock told me it was noon. I decided to grab a quick sandwich and go for my daily walk at lunchtime rather than wait until after work. The sun was shining and I just wanted to get out in it. I'd made a firm commitment to walk at least five days a week. And so far, so good! Of course, I'd just started my walking program four days ago, but still, my recent jaunts did show some degree of dedication.

I headed out the door and up the road which, for the first quarter mile or so, follows a good-sized creek that I always watch like a hawk. I get glimpses of muskrat and water snakes, see deer drinking and ducks floating downstream. And I always enjoy the dive bombing kingfishers who sit on the utility lines and fly headfirst towards the water at high speed only to pull up at the last second with minnows in their mouths. What timing and execution.

After a quarter mile, though, I have to make a decision. I can stay on the paved road and follow the big creek, or I can turn left up a one-lane dirt road and, after another quarter mile or so, take one of two picturesque, and even smaller, side roads. It's a maze back there.

I turned onto the first dirt road bordered by a steep bank and woods on the left. On the right is a very small, spring-fed creek and several houses in a meadow on the other side of that. It was a sunny day with a nice breeze and I was just passing under a tree throwing dappled light on the road, when a little voice said, "Hello."

I jumped. Just a few feet away from me, standing in the shadows, was a young boy.

"I'm sorry. I didn't see you standing there." What a cute kid.

He laughed and said, "Want to see something?"

"Sure!"

He turned and walked to the wee little creek meandering willy-nilly through the edge of the yard. I followed as he pulled on a thin rope and up came a minnow trap.

"Look at all these minnows. Dad and I are going fishing later!"

"Whoa, fishing! Do you like to fish?"

"I sure do!" This kid was all energy and enthusiasm.

"How old are you?" I asked.

"I'm six."

"Six? You sure are tall for six!"

He just grinned and told me his name was Justin. I said good-bye, noticing the truck parked in front of the rental house. It sported Texas tags and had a commercial welding unit bolted down in the back. Ten to one, Justin's dad was working on laying one of the many gas pipelines crisscrossing our area. In fact, the lack of finished pipelines was holding back gas production throughout the region. But it would catch up.

I decided to veer left at the next fork in the road. That choice takes me through a canopy of trees with woods on either side and no houses in sight. I always walk quietly and watch the dark woods to my left. The road is cut into the side of a hill, almost at the bottom. That leaves a shallow ravine on the left, and then the hill going up the other side with mature hardwoods and very little underbrush. The trees on both sides of the road meet in the middle creating about a thousand feet of cool, shadowy tunnel to walk through.

I'm always hoping to see a bear. We know they're in the area, but I've yet to spot one. I will admit that, in my pants pocket, I keep my police-grade, Fox pepper spray at the ready. A bear sighting is what I want, not a close-up and personal meeting.

This walk was sans bear. I turned to make my way back home and noticed that Justin was nowhere to be seen when I passed his house. I waved at a couple of other neighbors, came upon a bird taking a dust bath in the road, and watched the turkey vultures soaring on the thermals above our valley as I emerged again onto the paved road. There's so much to see if you just pay attention.

I arrived home feeling refreshed. The dogs were napping in the sun and only gave me a couple of weak thumps of their tails on the ground to acknowledge my presence. I grabbed a glass of ice water and headed straight to my desk to do some prep work for my meeting with Mrs. Baxter.

Prior to calling her, I had thoroughly reviewed the title on the two hundred forty-seven acres. While a title is the ownership history of a piece of land and the minerals beneath it, it often provides a fascinating peek into a family as well. With this title, I had the distinct feeling I'd come upon, if not a mystery, at least a very interesting story. The title was solid and I didn't doubt its conclusions. But, the way the seven tracts were bought and then sold was very odd. What happened was laid out as clear as could be. It was the why that had me intrigued.

The oil and gas I needed to lease was in Birch District, Taylor County, West Virginia. Mrs. Baxter, her sister, and two brothers were the current heirs listed on the information sheet. Mrs. Baxter and her brother Harold lived in Taylor County, Debra was in nearby Marion County, and the missing Joe had a name but no address. I wondered if Tony, our lead abstractor and the guy who ran the title, had noticed any other information about Joe, so I dialed his cell.

Tony had two years of law school under his belt when he decided he had the brains, but not the desire, to be a lawyer. While still deciding what he really wanted to do, he'd gotten a summer job with a law firm running title. After a few hours' training, he was on his own in the courthouse. To run title, you start with the current owner of a piece of property and then follow deeds, wills, intestate descent, tax sales, etc., back as far as you can go. Along the way, you make note of any oil and gas reservations and then run those forward to see who the current owners are. It takes a very analytical mind, which Tony certainly has. He chucked law school, and got a job full-time with Dean Oil and Gas. Tony was quite well-paid for his service, which, in addition to abstracting, included managing our courthouse crew. We were lucky to have him and we knew it.

"Hey, Donna," Tony answered in a whisper, "give me a minute."

Abstractors "run title" in the county clerk record rooms in courthouses. These days, they're crowded, as more and more oil and gas companies race to get title done before someone else beats them to a lease. Courthouse etiquette is important, so Tony was getting out of the record room so he could talk to me without disturbing anyone.

"Okay, I'm in the hall. That place is a zoo today and I'm about ready to pull the earbuds off a couple of guys' heads and stomp on them! They're dancing in place and keeping the beat on the counter with their pencils. It's annoying!"

"Will you be stomping on the earbuds or their heads?"

"The earbuds, but now that you've mentioned it . . ."

We both laughed.

"Tony, when you did the Tredloe title, did you notice any-thing more about Joseph Morgan Tredloe than what you put in the title? I talked to his sister earlier today, and she said he's miss-ing and has been for twenty years."

"That kind of missing sounds like dead, don't you think?" Tony said. He was never one to mince words.

"Maybe, but it's hard to say. His sister didn't say much, and quite honestly, I don't think she meant to say as much as she did."

Tony had a certain vocal ritual when he was thinking. He was doing it now. A series of sighs, hmmms, huhs with a question mark. I kept quiet and let him cogitate.

"Well, I don't remember anything else. I couldn't find an address for him, but that's not unusual if the oil and gas isn't taxed. No, Donna, I don't remember seeing anything."

"Could you do me a favor, Tony, and look at the records we don't normally look at. Look in the Miscellaneous books, check his name in the circuit clerk's office, things like that. I don't really care if it doesn't pertain to the oil and gas. I'm just looking for any clue whatsoever over the past twenty years or so."

"Sure! You're saying the family doesn't know anything?"

"That's what his sister said, but maybe they do and maybe they don't. I have an appointment with her tomorrow and I'd like to know as much as I can before we meet. I'm going to hit the Internet."

"No problem. If I find anything, I'll scan it to you tonight."

"Thanks. That will help."

Tony had kind of made a left-hand turn from law into title, but I'd done an outright U-turn. After thirty years in radio sales, I had totally changed careers. Around 2007 the Marcellus shale boom was just emerging in West Virginia, and I found out what a "landman" was. I immediately knew that was my future. It was a gut feeling, and a very strong one at that. I had a lot of sales under my belt; however, I was clueless about the oil and gas business.

My timing couldn't have been better. Anyone who had even a tiny bit of oil and gas experience was already on the job. The well was dry, so to speak, and the companies had no choice but to train inexperienced people like me. My years in sales got me an interview with a very good brokerage and, within a few weeks, I was on the job.

Their theory was that you can't lease oil and gas if you can't read and understand title. And you can't understand title if you've never run it. I started my career in a mountain-county courthouse, learning the ins and outs of deeds, wills, chancery suits, and vital records. Did that experience ever serve me well!

I liked title work, but I made it known to my boss early on that I wanted to lease. That's what a landman does. I wanted to get out into the West Virginia countryside, meet the prospects face-to-face, and negotiate.

There weren't many women in the field, but after six months in the courthouse and a little prodding on my part, my broker gave me a shot at leasing with one warning. "There is no such thing as a landwoman! You're a landman and that's that!" But it didn't take long for the ranks of women to grow, another barrier falling away.

My phone rang and the caller ID told me it was Tony. If he was calling back that fast, he'd found nothing.

"I couldn't find anything, Donna. I ran his name through the computer. I looked in the indexes. He's not showing up over the last twenty years with real estate or personal property in this county. He hasn't sued or been sued. Nada!"

"That's okay, Tony. I knew it was a long shot but I had to check. This one's going to be interesting and a challenge."

"You know, Donna, it was really strange the way Barrett Tredloe bought and sold his property," Tony said. "Here was a guy with a sixteen-acre farm, not much in those days. And then about 1908 he starts buying the farm next door in pieces. The owner, a guy named Hagen, had died, and the farm was partitioned so each of his kids got a piece. Somehow Barrett Tredloe was able to buy all seven pieces, almost two hundred fifty acres. I mean, you'd think one of the seven Hagen kids would have wanted to keep a piece of the family farm. Mr. Tredloe had to be offering some decent money to get it all, don't you think?"

"I noticed that too, Tony, and I agree. It takes him several years to buy the whole thing and then, a few years later, he starts selling it off, piece by piece, but keeps the oil and gas. And, according to Miriam Baxter, he didn't have money, so how did he fund those purchases."

"I don't know. Land was cheap in those days but it still took some bucks to buy that much property. By the way, Donna, we should have the title on Barrett Tredloe's sixteen-acre farm soon. It's on the schedule to be run."

We said our good-byes, each wondering if we would ever know the real story behind the Tredloe oil and gas.

Entertaining the Dearly Departed

Tony's comments had piqued my interest, so I was rereading the early parts of the title when my musings on the matter were interrupted by the phone.

"Hey, Josh."

"Hi, Mom."

Josh is our deputy sheriff son, our one and only child. He's a conflicted twenty-eight-year-old who grew up in the country with liberal parents. Many of his other influences were more conservative. He sorts things out for himself, sometimes coming down on one side, sometimes on the other. But it's left him with a knack for being comfortable with almost anyone. And, while school just wasn't his thing, he's bright, learns fast, and has a very good work ethic.

When Josh finally set his sights on law enforcement, he went full speed ahead. He's a good cop, tough when he has to be but with a lot of empathy too. And sometimes he keeps us entertained with amusing stories.

"What's up, kiddo?"

"I have a good one for you. There's a little country church out Morgan Run with a graveyard on a hill. The caretakers asked me to patrol up there when I was in the area because people have been driving up at night."

"Looking for ghosts and goblins?" I asked.

"Not exactly. Last night it was kind of warm out and I was

just cruising, window down, Lynyrd Skynard on the radio and, since I was going past it anyway, I turned into the graveyard."

Josh kept stopping to chuckle so I knew it was something good.

"So, I was heading up the hill and I saw this dim light up under a little grove of trees. I realized it was a car dome light so I turned the radio down and killed my lights. When I got closer, I could see what looked like the back side of a white jeep with the rear gate open. Mom, I may never get this picture out of my head. A very large, very bare male butt and it was a butt in motion!"

"Not a pretty sight, huh?" I commented.

"Oh no! And I'm getting closer and closer and they don't show any signs of knowing I'm there."

"They were preoccupied, Josh."

"Pretty much! So I got within about twenty feet and hit the lights. They lit up in red and blue and they still didn't stop right away!"

"Weeell . . . that could be a little . . ."

"Yeah. I know. They finally got loose and she flew over the back seat and he just stood there looking stupid."

"What'd you say?"

"Put your pants on, buddy!"

Josh and I both had a good laugh.

"Did you arrest them?"

"No. I just lectured them. It was pretty good, too. All about the sanctity of a graveyard and the abomination their deed was to those who chose it as their final resting place. But man, was it ever hard not to laugh."

"Good grief, Josh. You think they learned a lesson?"

"I don't think they'll get naked in a graveyard again."

I'm always glad when Josh's encounters are on the lighter side. Like any cop's mother, I worry.

"Hey, Mom. One more thing. Be careful walking. Don't forget that pepper spray I got for you. Bo Lightner is out of jail and he lives over on Derby Pike, which isn't all that far from you. He spends his time running the back roads just looking for easy break-ins. He's a druggie and just plain stupid on top of it. Be careful. I worry about you."

"I don't leave home without my pepper spray, Josh, and I'm always careful. I'll be fine, but it's nice of you to worry about me."

"Mom, why don't you take your cell phone when you walk? That would make me feel a little better."

"Actually, I usually do have it. I like to take pictures of wild-flowers as they bloom and sometimes I find new ones to identify. I'll make sure I take it all the time, okay?"

"What I'd really like you to do is pack your pistol, but I know you won't."

"Josh, I'm not a good enough shot, and I'd probably never pull the trigger anyway. Besides, I don't have a license to carry. I'll be fine!"

We said good-bye and hung up. I was left shaking my head and thinking that it was just a few short years ago that I was constantly telling Josh to be careful. Not that I still don't.

I finally hit the computer, looking for some trace of Joseph Morgan Tredloe. In my job, you get very good at Internet searches, but I'm usually looking for people who aren't trying to hide. Finding someone who apparently didn't want to be found was different and an interesting challenge.

The first place I always start a search is with the SSDI, the Social Security Death Index. I want to make certain I'm not searching high and low for someone who isn't even above ground anymore. So I searched for Joseph Morgan Tredloe, Joseph M. Tredloe and just Joseph Tredloe and I found nothing. If Joe was dead, the government hadn't recorded the fact, although that doesn't mean for sure he's not deceased. He could have legally changed his name, died a John Doe and was never identified, or simply been the victim of a recording error. In all likelihood, though, Joe was still among us.

Next I hit Google. When I'm doing a Google search, I always hope my subject has some level of either fame or infamy, and it doesn't take much of either. I've found people because they had their picture in the paper with the Little League team they coached. I've gotten a hit because someone was published in a journal most of us never heard of. But at the end of a solid hour of searching, I had nothing but tired eyes and a dry throat, so I pronounced my workday done. It was time to go outside and kick the partially deflated soccer ball for the big yellow lab that loves to chase it.

Tredloe Family Lore

The next day dawned in a thick, foggy haze, and I was happy to be in my home office, a cozy respite from the bleak scene outside. It's really just a spare bedroom in our old farmhouse, totally inefficient, but I like it anyway. There are four floor-to-almost-ceiling, oak bookcases courtesy of my woodworking husband, Sam. Another wall has lower shelves under the window, and there's an old mantel sporting family photos. Add my desk with a credenza, a big map-covered work table, lots of file crates, two printers, soft lighting from a couple of lamps, and at least one lounging cat, and you've got my office. It's a space I always feel comfortable in.

This particular morning I arrived with a steaming cup of coffee. I wanted to be well prepared for my meeting with Mrs. Baxter, so I sat down to review the Tredloe family tree and commit the names to memory. It really wasn't too difficult. Not only had the Tredloes not been good at producing offspring, there was also a lot of tragedy in the family history leading to early deaths. It was almost as if fate had guided this family through time single file. Like I've said before, rural families in the first half of the nineteen hundreds were usually large, but not the Tredloes.

Great-Grandfather Barrett and his wife, Anna, had two children, Delos and Delia. Delia died at age thirteen. Delos didn't marry until he was in his mid-thirties. He and his wife, Marilee, had one son, Avery, the only child born before Marilee passed away a couple of years after his birth. Tony had noted that her death certificate listed drowning as the cause of death.

Delos and Marilee's son, Avery, however, did a little better job of siring Tredloes before the family genes withered and died. Avery had married Elizabeth Morgan, and I was guessing that was the source of Joe's middle name. Avery and Elizabeth were the parents of the four Tredloes I needed to lease. They were the four great-grandchildren of Barrett Tredloe, and I hoped all four of them had gone forth and multiplied as well. A family dying out is just plain sad.

I finished memorizing the Tredloe family tree, then spent the rest of the morning putting together leases on other tracts. As noon approached, I changed into nicer clothes for my meeting with Mrs. Baxter and left the house to grab lunch at my favorite hole-in-the-wall restaurant. They'd gone upscale on the day's special, and I was treated to a spinach-cheese quiche and salad.

It was then on to Miriam Baxter's house in the hopes of successfully explaining what I was up to, what it meant to the family, and why we needed to find Joe. The first order of business, however, was to earn her trust.

Mrs. Baxter lived in the country, first down a narrow, paved road and then onto a dirt road with just four or five houses before it dead-ended. It was my favorite kind of place! Her house was the second on the left, uphill on a long, gravel driveway. It was a small, wood-framed, two-story house, white with green shutters and a great front porch. I didn't know how great until I climbed the steps and looked out. Woods surrounded most of the driveway but, as you approached the house, you emerged into a clearing with a meadow dropping down from the yard. The view from the porch was spectacular.

Miriam Baxter answered my knock. She was an attractive woman who did little to accentuate her good looks but didn't really have to. She was wearing casual brown slacks, a tan knit top, and a burnt orange cardigan that had the worn look a favorite sweater often gets. Her hair was light brown, speckled with gray, and cut short but stylish. She suggested we sit on the porch. It was only April, but the sun was providing enough warmth to make it very pleasant, at least for a while.

"Can I offer you some coffee?" she asked. "It's made and ready."

"I'd love some. Black, please."

"My brother Harold wanted to be here," she said, as she headed in the door, "but he's working on a pipeline job and they're behind schedule."

Her comment told me that Harold was in the oil and gas business. That was a good thing. He'd have an understanding that most people wouldn't.

She came back with two steaming cups of coffee, and I asked her if Harold was on a local job or was working far from home.

"He's in Marion County now, but I think the line cuts up through Monongalia and ties into lines in western Pennsylvania. None of it's too far from home and that's good. Sometimes Harold's gone for weeks at a time, and it's hard on his wife, Kathleen. Hard on Harold too. They have a small farm, just a few head of cattle and some chickens, but even that's tough to keep up with when Harold's gone and you work full time like Kathleen does."

"I have trouble keeping up with two dogs and three cats! It's amazing how much work they can be," I said, "but I'd never want to be without them."

Mrs. Baxter agreed as a gray tabby walked up the porch steps and jumped to the railing to observe me. Quickly deciding I wasn't a threat, she proceeded to take a bath, yawn, and then lie down and somehow maintain her balance while dozing on the banister.

I liked Miriam Baxter. She was obviously intelligent and a straight shooter. She told me she was divorced, had three grown children, and worked from home as a medical transcriptionist. Her youngest, Thea, had moved back in while working on a master's in education at West Virginia University. The condition of Mrs. Baxter's house, yard, and garden, where I could already see lettuce and peas poking through, portrayed an organized, hard-working woman. We chatted some more and then got down to business.

Mrs. Baxter asked me the question everyone asks when you tell them they own oil and gas and they don't know it. "Please explain to me why you think we own this."

"Well, the surface of a piece of land and the minerals below it can be bought and sold separately," I told her. "One is called the surface estate and the other is called the mineral estate."

I continued with my explanation hoping it would make sense. "Since they're two separate estates, when someone sells their land and they own the oil and gas as well, they can reserve the oil and gas in the deed. So they're selling the surface and keeping the oil and gas. That's what Barrett Tredloe did."

Mrs. Baxter still looked puzzled. "But how did we get it?"

"You're his heirs. It has simply flowed down through the generations to you. And, if your generation doesn't sell your interest, or leave it by will to someone else, it will keep right on going to your heirs."

"But why didn't we know we owned it?"

"Because there was nothing to tell you the ownership existed. When your great-grandfather sold the land and reserved the oil and gas, it should have gone on the county assessor's books as a separate tax assessment. If it had, you would be getting tax tickets on it. But it didn't. That happened a lot back then. Mrs. Baxter, I assure you that there are thousands of people suddenly finding out they own oil and gas because an oil and gas company has run the title and determined who the owner or owners are."

"So, I guess you talk to lots of people who are surprised."

"I do. But please understand that Marcellus wells are very expensive and the last thing we want to do is get the ownership wrong. That can be a very costly mistake if you've already started drilling. It can hold you up in the courts for a long time and literally cost millions. We do a very thorough job when it comes to determining ownership."

Miriam Baxter was still looking puzzled. "And you think my siblings and I own it?"

"I'm certain you own it. No one in the family had a will. Not your great-grandfather, your grandfather or your father, so everything passed according to the intestate laws of West Virginia. I know that might seem shaky, but it's really not. In the absence of a will, those laws provide where the ownership goes," I told her.

"The Tredloes weren't big on wills," Mrs. Baxter commented.

I could see she was thinking so I remained quiet.

"After I talked to you on the phone, a lot of things came back. I do remember references to 'the land.' These are things I haven't thought about for a long time and that never seemed important to me, so they're hazy. Besides that, I was pretty young and uninterested when I did hear them. But, I remember Delos, our grandfather, being angry with Axel. He would say that Axel was the reason that Barrett bought the land and he never should have done it. In retrospect, I suspicion this is 'the land' we're talking about now."

"Who was Axel?" I asked, thinking maybe I'd find a clue to

the mystery Tony and I both believed was lurking below the bare facts in the Tredloe title.

"Axel was Barrett's older brother. He left home as a very young man, still a teenager really, and headed south, ending up in Central America," Miriam Baxter replied.

"So he would have been your great-great uncle?"

"Yes. There were lots of stories that came down about Axel, but you were never sure what were true and what weren't. Axel lived a pretty action-packed life, which may be a nice way of saying it. Aunt Maud talked about Axel, but I also remember Grandpa Delos and Dad talking about him, and never too kindly. I was young and, from what I overheard, I thought Axel sounded exciting."

"What did they say about him?" I prompted.

"Well, I remember them saying that Axel spent a lot of time in Honduras and Guatemala. He liked to call himself an adventurer, but Dad always said he was really a hired gun."

"Sounds like they were on to him."

"They were. When my dad was young, just a kid really, his mother was killed in a flood. It was just he and Grandpa Delos, with a house that was too big for them. So Grandpa talked his dad, my Great-Grandpap Barrett, into moving in with them. My great-grandmother had died so he was alone in his house too."

"So your great-grandfather sold the farm?" I wanted to get this story straight.

"I don't think so. In fact, I think the farm got sold after Great-Grandpap passed away. I can remember my grandfather saying Barrett still kept a garden out there and went back a lot in the summer to tend it. People get attached to their land. It was probably hard for him to sell it."

"So then Delos sold the farm after Barrett passed away?"

"I'm pretty sure that's how it happened. We still call it the homeplace even though it's been out of the family for a long, long time."

"So your great-grandfather moved in with your grandfather and your dad, Avery, who was very young at the time."

"Yes. And, Dad could remember their conversations about Axel. They talked about him coming back every couple of years or so in the early nineteen hundreds. As the story goes, Axel always had pockets full of money and he would speak Spanish to impress everyone. And, apparently, Axel claimed he was the reason they had bananas to eat."

Mrs. Baxter smiled.

"Dad always said that didn't make any sense to him because there were never bananas at their house."

Mrs. Baxter was gazing out over the meadow her eyes fixed on what I've heard people call the middle distance, a kind of mental projection screen into the past.

"You see, I guess I did know about the property, at least in a very vague way. I think most of my memories come from Dad relating all of this to Aunt Maud."

"You've mentioned her a couple of times but I don't remember any Mauds in the Tredloe family tree."

"Aunt Maud was a Morgan, my mother's youngest sister. Mom's family and the Tredloes all grew up around here. Maud was an amateur writer and historian, and she was always sitting on the porch talking to Dad and to Grandpa Delos, when he was still living. Maud would take notes, write them up, and put them in a three-ring binder."

"And you were there with them for some of those conversations?"

"Yes, especially with Dad, but I remember sitting on the front porch with Aunt Maud and Dad and Grandpa Delos, too. Maud would get them talking and she'd take notes. But it wasn't just the Tredloes Maud was interested in. She started writing about lots of families in the area. Aunt Maud always told me to pay attention because truth was stranger than fiction. I remember her telling Dad one day that she was going to write everything up and give a copy to the library. But Dad said not to. He wasn't sure the statute of limitations had run its course on everything Axel was guilty of. He would laugh and say maybe they could hold Axel's heirs accountable and that wouldn't be good!"

"As family histories go, this sounds like a good one," I commented.

Miriam laughed and continued.

"From what I remember, the story was that Axel would give Barrett a lot of cash and tell him to invest it in property. When Grandpa Delos got old enough to understand what had happened, he always said his dad should have given the money back to Axel and refused to buy the property. He said the money had to have been stolen and that Barrett had put the whole family at risk by accepting it. But, apparently Barrett did buy the property with it, just like his brother asked him to do. I never knew where the property was though. They may have said, but it just wouldn't have been important to me back then. I'm surprised I'm remembering this much."

"Well, I can fill you in on the location." I pointed to the file on my lap and suggested we head for a table inside, so I could show her exactly where the property was. It was breezy on the front porch and not conducive to laying out papers.

We gathered our cups and the file, and Mrs. Baxter held the door for both me and the cat who sauntered slowly in, settling in a spot of sun coming through a window. Mrs. Baxter and I pulled out chairs at a country-style table, whitewashed and pleasantly worn. I pulled the tax map from the file and set it in front of her. Tax maps are produced by each county to reflect the boundary lines on each and every parcel of land.

"This is tax map ten," I told her. "And right here, parcel thirty-two, is the sixteen acres that was the original Tredloe farm. I've highlighted it in yellow. And next to it, on the southwest side, I've highlighted in blue the parcels that make up the two hundred forty-seven acres."

She peered at it a while. Most people never look at their land or their ancestors' land on a tax map. It's interesting to see the positioning of the tracts relative to close-by roads and creeks and rivers.

"And you're saying Great-Grandpa Barrett bought everything highlighted in blue and then sold it?" she asked.

"He did. When it was all one piece, two hundred forty-seven acres, it was owned by Artis Hagen. When Mr. Hagen died, his seven children fought like crazy over who got what. We know that because it had to be partitioned in court, and there are depositions that pretty much lay out the disagreements. Anyway, the judge divided it, giving each of the seven kids a piece of the land. Over the course of a few years, Barrett bought all of that farm piece by piece from the seven Hagen heirs. And, from what you're telling me, it sounds like he did it with the money that Axel gave him."

While Mrs. Baxter was digesting all this, I had another question.

"Axel never came back here to live?" I asked.

Mrs. Baxter chuckled. "He may have intended to, but Axel apparently departed this earth rather abruptly. There's more than one story of Axel's death but Grandpa Delos did some investigating when Axel hadn't turned up for five years or so. He finally got confirmation that Axel was dead and buried in Guatemala. He was convinced that Axel was murdered, and he always figured it was by someone he'd swindled."

"Did he ever marry, have kids?"

"No marriages that we know of, although Grandpa always figured Axel had kids scattered from here to Central America. As you've probably gathered, Grandpa Delos didn't hold Axel in very high regard. As he got older, he talked about him a lot. I do remember a lot of what he said then because it always made me wonder about this outlaw relative we had. At least that's what Grandpa Delos made him sound like."

I kept quiet because I wanted Miriam Baxter to continue talking. She did.

"Axel was a rounder, and very good looking in a rough sort of way. I've seen old photos and he could strike a pose! Before he first left this area, he had a girlfriend. Axel went off to who knows where and told her he would marry her when he came back. Her name was Sallie and she waited for him. It took him about eighteen months to show up again, and then he avoided her." Mrs. Baxter smiled and shook her head.

"As the story goes, he was packed and ready to leave, but just as he was saying good-bye to the family, she walked out from behind a big silver maple and pointed a forty-five at him. Axel started sweet-talking and moving slowly towards her. I guess he thought his charm wouldn't fail him. It did. Sallie wasn't much of a shot, but when Axel was about ten feet away she pulled the trigger and he lost two fingers on his left hand."

Well now, this was turning out to be a good family tale.

"Dad said Grandpa always grinned when he told the story. According to him, Sallie turned and walked home like she was out for a Sunday stroll. There was no going to the law and she knew it. Axel had made himself known to local law enforcement over the years and not in a good way. Grandpa Delos said the cops would probably have arrested Axel and given Sallie a reward."

"So what did they do about the wounds?" I asked.

"They patched him up, kept him a few days to make sure he was on the mend and then said their good-byes for a second time with family members posted as lookouts around the property and two armed cousins to escort him to the train."

"You remember a lot about this story!"

"Aunt Maud loved to tell it, so I heard it more than once. And, like I said, Grandpa Delos talked a lot about Axel as he got older. I heard him tell this story too."

"So why do you think Barrett sold the land off but reserved the oil and gas?" I asked.

"Oh my, I never heard anyone talk about that. I remember Maud saying Axel could be rich one day and poor the next, so who knows. I mean if it was Axel's money that bought the land, maybe he needed it back. He was no stranger to trouble. I do remember Dad and Grandpa Delos saying that when it came to Axel's personal business, Great-Grandpa Barrett wouldn't talk. For whatever reason, he was loyal to Axel."

Miriam Baxter smiled and continued. "You know, some of the things you told me on the phone got me to thinking. At first, I didn't think I knew anything about this, but then memories started seeping in. It's funny how memory works. But I sure didn't know anything about the oil and gas being reserved or that I might own a piece of it. And really, I'm not sure my dad or grand-father knew about the reservations either. What's it worth?"

"Well, the ownership is divided four ways, a fourth each to you and your three siblings. We'll pay a thousand dollars an acre to lease for five years and you each have a net of just over sixty acres, so that's sixty thousand plus. And then, if it's developed, you'll be paid royalties," I told her. "And royalty on a little over sixty acres for each of you could be pretty significant."

"That's a lot of money to just fall out of the sky all of a sudden."

"Well, Mrs. Baxter, to make it all work, we have to have Joe. Or, if he's deceased, we need evidence of that. Under intestate law, he still gets a share, missing or not. Would it be a problem with you and your siblings if I tried to find him? But please understand, I honestly don't think I can do it without your family's help."

Again, a long pause, followed by carefully measured words. "It wouldn't be a problem with me, but I can't speak for the others. Let me talk to them and I'll get back to you."

I handed her my card, thanked her for her time, and headed down the driveway.

Ham Bone

I took about forty-five minutes to get home, enough time to think about what Miriam Baxter had told me. And I marveled about how much she had been willing to divulge. But that's not really uncommon. People love to talk about old family stories to someone who actually knows who's who in the family. When you have title that goes back to the eighteen hundreds, you know all the players.

The whole story about Axel was fascinating. And his tie to Central America was especially intriguing to me. Miriam had mentioned Guatemala and Honduras. It just so happened that I'd made two trips to Guatemala in recent years. In the early nineties, my Rotary club began working in a mountainous region inhabited by indigenous Mayan Indians. We were originally asked to buy a one-hundred-dollar bag of seed, but our involvement eventually turned into much more. It wasn't long before we'd discovered a well-run and very respected Catholic Mission in the village of San Lucas Toliman, and began channeling our efforts through them. Over the years, we'd been involved in and supported many projects, but our current focus was on the village's dental clinic.

I'd been on two of the dental missions over a four-year period and had become rather proficient at aiming flashlights in gaping mouths and suctioning without snaring tongues. We had two professors of dentistry in our club from the West Virginia University School of Dentistry, so one, or sometimes both of them,

30

would lead a team of seven or eight third-year dental students as well as other dentists they'd recruited for the trip. There was usually room for a couple of Rotarians to tag along, so I did.

Over a three-day period, about half of the dentists and students would see patients in the dental clinic. The rest, however, would head out to the "fincas." The fincas are small communities with very basic, and often very insufficient, housing. The workers used to be housed on big ranches, but the ranches had gone away decades ago leaving the villagers to fend for themselves. These were people unlikely to ever come to the clinic for dental care, even if it was free. They would, however, be waiting in line, and usually in pain, for the dentists to come to them. Some of them endured toothaches for months, banking on our yearly trip to end their misery.

The setup in the fincas was limited but as clean as we could make it. We headed out from the clinic in the back of a truck. In Guatemala the beds of pickup trucks are commonly used to transport people, and almost all have a tall rack made of pipe affixed to the bed so that you can stand up and hold on, thus packing more people in. We'd load up clean pans, clean water, sterilizing solutions and all of the other equipment and supplies. And then people who hadn't ridden in the back of a truck since they were kids, if then, would clamor in and begin the bumpy trip to whatever finca we were heading to. This was not OSHA approved!

On my two excursions to the fincas we worked in open-air, outdoor pavilions, using wooden tables and rickety chairs brought in from nearby homes. There were chickens and dogs and little kids running around our feet, the animals scavenging for food and the children hoping to be given the blue latex gloves that we had in great supply. They were fascinated by them, each and every one of them huffing and puffing to blow them up like balloons.

There was only one option when you were working in the fincas—pull teeth. Lots of teeth. My first day there, the dentists and third-year students did sixty-one extractions, many of them multiple teeth from the same mouth. Given the conditions they were working in, they really couldn't go beyond that, and these were teeth that definitely needed to come out. And yes, we did have anesthetics.

Pulling teeth is hard work, and when you're doing it with very basic instruments, while working on people in an old wooden chair leaning back against a wall, it's even harder. I saw two things very clearly; first, how incredibly grateful the Guatemalans were for what we consider very basic dental care, and second, I saw dental students grow immensely as human beings, with a better understanding of the world beyond their borders. Those two trips had a huge impact on me as well. Spending time in a third-world country guarantees that you'll never look at the world quite the same as you did before.

So I think my travels probably made me a little more interested than most people would have been in what Axel might have been up to in Honduras and Guatemala. But, bottom line, whatever he was doing a century ago didn't mean beans to the leasing process. It didn't matter whose money bought the property. When the tracts were purchased they were put in Barrett's name and, when he sold them, he reserved the oil and gas. I had no doubt it was solidly in the hands of Barrett's living heirs, being Avery's four children. My real issue was Joe, and I'd gotten no information to move me ahead in that department. However, when dealing with family issues, I've learned to move slowly and listen closely.

I turned on NPR, but the news was depressing, so I switched to my now favorite CD. It was the first and only recording, so far, by Ham Bone Music. What an entertaining group! And I swear I'm not biased by the fact that Ham Bone is my husband, Sam. He's a cabinetmaker who's been playing guitar since the obligatory high school band. For decades after that, he only picked it up occasionally. But then, in his mid-fifties, he started playing every evening. And singing! He never sang before, at least not seriously, and for a while, it was a bit trying. I kept thinking he'd get over it, but he fooled me and got better. A lot better!

He eventually started going to open mics at a local coffee shop where, unless you're really good, the audience doesn't pay much attention anyway. He played and sang, and the audience chatted all the while, which was a perfect way to get over stage fright. But once he found his confidence and sang with conviction, it became very apparent that he could sing. The audience sat up and paid attention and, the next thing you know, he'd formed a band.

When I pulled in the driveway, I was happy to see my stone crew was there. Our house is built into a hill and we'd always had landscape timbers holding everything back at the end of the driveway. There was a small, decorative garden cut out of the hill behind the house so Doug was replacing the timbers with cut stone and laying stone steps up to the garden with a rock path going through it.

I got out of the car and admired their progress.

"You got a lot done today, Doug."

Before Doug could say anything, his newest helper, "Dang" (I kid you not), said, "Hey, I've done a lotta walls in my time, and I can get those buggers in solid and real quick. Saves you money, don't it!"

Doug was standing behind him, his face a contortion of expressions as he fought the urge to give the guy a good whack on the head. I was trying to get my mouth closed and wipe the look of incredulity off my face.

It was Dang's second day on the job. The day before, I'd heard Doug repeatedly saying, "Dang, come help me lift this stone!" And Dang's answer was invariably, "Dang, these things are heavy!"

And as to saving me money, I wasn't paying by the hour. Doug had given me a price and that was the price. Dang wasn't saving me a dime, but I figured he was costing Doug quite a few.

Most of Doug's helpers seemed to be quite averse to a five-day workweek. One would be there a few days, get paid, and you'd never see him again. Pretty soon, Doug would have another one in tow. I came to realize that "see you tomorrow" really meant "some tomorrow," but maybe not the one attached to today. I was just glad Doug had a helper and the wall was almost done.

My big yellow lab, Daytona, however was not at all happy with Doug and Dang. He thinks we've hired them to kick one of his five soccer balls, all of which are partially deflated so he can get a good hold on them with his teeth. The guys eventually get tired of him putting balls at their feet and barking, so they gather them all up and put them on top of the woodshed. That was the dilemma Daytona was in when I arrived, so I invited him, along with our hound, Buster, into the house for a treat and a nap. That worked, especially for Buster! Food and sleep are right up his alley.

My retired brother, Dennis, was in the living room. He lives in a one-bedroom, log house on our property, but is usually camped out at our place since the TV is bigger and the fridge is well stocked. But he earns his keep as a doorman for the dogs, and they keep him pretty busy.

He pointed to a package from FedEx.

"Huh. Wonder what that is?"

"Beats me," he said, with absolutely no interest. He was watching the Pirates and the Reds, and neither I nor the package were on his radar.

It was addressed to my husband, didn't rattle, and wasn't heavy so I figured it was the new white suit he'd ordered on eBay. Ham Bone Music plays songs reminiscent of the nineteen thirties and forties, and they like to dress the part. He's found some amazing period-style suits on the Internet, designer names at a fraction of the price. Pair them up with a spiffy fedora and the right shades, and back in time he goes!

I headed to my upstairs office to make a few phone calls and check my email. I went through the motions, but my mind was really on Joseph Morgan Tredloe. And the more I thought about it, the more I realized that I was at the family's mercy on this one. Without their input, my chances of finding him weren't good.

Sam pulled in the drive, so I decided to end my day. Sam is a good and very creative cook. He prepares meals; I clean up. Well, I do have salad duty most days. I headed downstairs to see what was on the menu. Pasta primavera. Woo-hoo!

After we got dinner moving along, I said, "Sam, I met with Miriam Baxter today. Remember, I told you about the odd title and the woman who told me on the phone they hadn't seen their youngest brother in twenty years."

"Yeah, I remember," Sam replied. "Did she elaborate?"

"No. In fact, she didn't mention him at all. But I told her we had to have him to move forward. I could tell she was thinking hard about it, and she finally told me it wouldn't be a problem for her, but she would have to talk to her brother and sister."

"Well, Donna, she didn't say no. So far, so good."

"I agree. Mrs. Baxter said he disappeared twenty years ago. That's about when their mother, Elizabeth Morgan Tredloe, died.

Joe would have been in his late teens."

"Maybe it had something to do with her passing, Donna. Losing your mother at that age is never easy."

"True. I just have to step very carefully. I think Mrs. Baxter regretted telling me about Joe so quickly. It was just a knee jerk reaction to something I said when I first called her. I can tell the whole thing is pretty sensitive."

"Twenty years is a long time to be gone. Could be dead."

"Maybe. But dead or alive, I have to find him if we're going to get one hundred percent of the oil and gas on that tract under lease."

Sam chuckled and said, "You sound like a B movie about the Wild West. Can you put the strainer in the sink?"

We ate some very good pasta primavera and watched the end of the Pirates–Reds game. My brother's been into baseball forever, but Sam and I just signed on last year. We're still saying, "I can't believe we just watched a whole baseball game and enjoyed it!" Last fall we went to a game at PNC Park. The Bucs didn't get one hit, but we still had fun. Go figure!

The Boss Says Go Get 'Em!

The next morning, I was up early, got showered, and came down the wooden hill intent on coffee and breakfast. Sam was reading the paper at the kitchen island and complained that his new reading glasses weren't very good. He buys them at the dollar store because he loses or breaks them at a pretty quick clip. He continued to read while I got my eggs together. I heard him say "Huh!" and turned just in time to watch him pull the plastic protective layer off the lenses.

"Can you see better now?"

"Quite a bit!"

But that didn't end my morning entertainment from Sam. A little later I was at my computer, and he was heading down the hall in his birthday suit on the way to the shower. Just seconds later he came back up the hall holding something small in his fingers.

"I just felt something on my butt and thought it was a tick. I pulled it off and it's a sticker that says 'inspected by 92.' I must have passed!"

Oh my. Sam had just bought new underwear. He sure can get my day off to a light-hearted start.

I decided it was time to bring my supervisor up to speed on the Tredloe situation. I'd never before had a real "missing person" so I thought I'd better see what she wanted done before I went too far. Joanne was a little more concerned than I expected.

"You know," she said, "we just got a lease from a coal company on a ninety-four acre tract on the northwest side of the Tredloe land. There's a good access road cut in from when they mined a few years back, so we wouldn't have to do a lot to get the road in usable shape. No one lives on it, so it makes a perfect drillsite, but we really need the two hundred forty-seven acres or we can't do the southern legs."

"Understood," I said, "but what's our plan of attack on finding a person who has intentionally dropped from sight? I'm good at finding people who aren't really hiding but this is a whole new ballgame."

I could tell Joanne was thinking, so I kept quiet.

When she finally broke the silence, it was to say, "I'm clueless. I've never looked for someone intentionally missing either. The family must know something!"

"I'm banking on it at this point, but I don't even know yet if they'll help. And it could be a sensitive situation. I've talked to one sister and she said she wouldn't mind if we tried to find him but she wants to talk to the other two. I don't know yet how much cooperation we'll have from them, but I hope to meet with her again next week. If we make them mad by trying to find their brother when they don't want us to, they're not going to sign a lease. I'll keep going forward with the family and let you know when I see where we stand."

"I think that's all we can do at this point," Joanne said. "And if they're cooperative, you have to take this as far as you can take it. If we have a company detective, nobody's told me."

"Okay, but you realize it could be very time-consuming and costly."

"I know, but we need the tract. You've found hard-to-find people before. Besides, I know you're dying to do this!" Joanne knew me better than I thought.

"You have me there. Let's just hope the family comes to the table. I can't do it without them," I said.

We chatted about some other issues, and I came away from the conversation with exactly what I wanted, a mandate from the company to go find Joe. Now if I could just get the same go-ahead from his sisters and brother.

Many people don't understand the nature of a Marcellus well. Joanne had just identified the coal company tract as the drillsite. That's where the vertical well shaft would be located, going down about a mile and a half to hit the Marcellus shale. However, prior to hitting it, the drill bit would begin a very slow, very gentle turn until it's horizontal and in the middle of the Marcellus shale seam. From there the drilling continues in a horizontal direction, usually for a mile or more. There are typically three or four horizontal legs going in a southeast direction and three or four more going in a northwest direction. In this unit, it would be southeast legs coming off of the coal company property that would go under the two hundred forty-seven acres.

I spent the rest of the morning doing leases to put in the mail to out-of-town lessors whom I'd recently talked to. For some reason, my little orange cat, Bubba, was feeling needy and insisted on camping out on my side table, holding down all the files I'd put there.

Bubba had arrived one cold January day sound asleep on the floor of a sheriff's department cruiser. It was a Sunday and my son, Josh, had called about two-thirty saying, "Mom, I need you to watch a cat for a couple of days." We were down to one cat, having lost an all-white tom named Shaq a few months before to old age and high thyroid. Our cat population was usually two or three.

"What do you mean, watch?" I asked.

"Well, I just came to pick up my cruiser to go on shift and this little orange cat jumped in," he said. "It's only about six months old. Somebody put it out here on a Sunday and the pound isn't even open!"

The sheriff's department motor pool is beside the county pound. We're all animal lovers and Josh wasn't about to just leave that cat sitting there. He and his fiancée have three dogs who have never lived with cats, so taking it home wasn't an option.

"I have to go pick up a ride-along at the office and then we'll be out."

It was quite a while before they pulled in. Just as Josh got the ride-along in tow, he got a call that there was a man exposing himself in one of the city parking garages. I guess the ride-along entertained Bubba while Josh corralled the exhibitionist.

Bubba is the cutest, most affectionate cat we've ever had. He arrived on a Sunday and headed to the vets to get fixed on Tuesday. According to the vet, he was a year, not six months. He's a little guy, just six and half pounds and all orange and cream with a raccoon-striped tail. But don't let that size fool you. Bubba is an intrepid hunter, with moles being his prey of choice. For now, however, he was sleeping like a baby on two of the files I needed.

I slipped one out with minimal disturbance and continued doing leases. Bubba's tail was hanging over the side of the table, twitching to a drama only he was in on. He was off in kitty dreamland probably chasing big game. I decided to break for lunch and then head to the courthouse to try to solve some title issues.

The Sisters Get On Board

A little over a week passed and I hadn't heard from Miriam Baxter. I finally called her and asked if she'd been able to talk to her brother and sister yet.

"I'm sorry I haven't called you, but I've had one deadline after another for work. I'm not sure why it's so busy," she said. "My sister would like to be here when we meet. Is it possible to do it in the evening?"

"Absolutely. What day works for you?" I asked.

"How about next Monday around six-thirty?"

"That's fine. Are we meeting at your house?"

She said yes, and after we hung up, I hit the Internet again thinking there had to be something about Joe. I went at it from new angles, but again, I came up dry.

Monday rolled around fast and I was headed to Mrs. Baxter's for the meeting. I was thinking hard about how to approach them, and was also wondering if Debra Little would be as nice as her sister. I'm sometimes amazed at the totally different personalities I run into when dealing with siblings.

I pulled in and Mrs. Baxter had the door open as I walked up the steps.

"I had to go out this afternoon, so I grabbed some Chinese on the way home," she said. We just ate, but there's some left if you're hungry."

I thanked her but declined as she ushered me in and introduced me to her sister who went by Chris, a shorter version of her middle name, Christine. Chris was just a couple of years younger than Miriam Baxter. She was a pretty woman with short, curly blond hair and a bubbly personality. My immediate thought was that, of the two, she would be the talker, the one who would give me the most information on her brother. She was dressed business casual so I asked her if she'd come from work.

"Yes, but I'm not supposed to say who I work for or what I do," she responded with a knowing smile.

"Ahh, the FBI!"

She laughed.

The FBI Fingerprint Division had moved to Harrison County in the nineteen nineties, courtesy of West Virginia's much-loved and longtime senator, Robert C. Byrd, now deceased. Many of the employees who transferred from Washington came kicking and screaming. Turns out most of them liked it here. It wasn't long before the FBI transferred more divisions. They employ a lot of people and, according to the rules, no one is supposed to say they work there. However, not telling was telling, and everybody was on to them.

I asked Chris about her family, and she said her husband was an insurance agent and they had two children, a boy who was a sophomore in high school and a daughter in the eighth grade. Mrs. Baxter had put out a plate of oatmeal cookies and offered iced tea or decaf. I took iced tea, they had decaf, and we settled down to business.

I explained to them that their tract was important and why. Still no promises of a well and royalties, but the prospects were looking positive. I also told them that my company had okayed my going forward on searching for Joe, but that I wanted the blessing of the family as well. Most of all, I wanted their help.

"So, if you don't find Joe, they can't drill, right?" Chris asked.

"There's an option through the courts if we don't find him, but it's rarely used. You have to prove to a court that you've made a sincere and thorough effort but have been unable to find the person you're looking for. If the judge approves it, the missing person is leased in absentia and a well can be drilled with their royalties going into escrow once production starts. At least, that's how I understand West Virginia law."

"But," I explained further, "we really don't want to do that. The courts can be slow and expensive, and you don't know if the judge will approve or not. The best solution is to find Joe."

Miriam Baxter was looking down at the table, deep in thought. Finally, Chris said, "Joe left. He just left! One day he was there, the next day he was gone. I don't know how much help we'll be."

There was silence, and I could tell the sisters were torn. I put myself in their place and realized that after Joe left, it probably took years for them to deal with their feelings. If they really didn't know what had happened to him, looking for him might just bring new heartaches. We might find a Joe who'd died long ago, a Joe in prison, a Joe still angry over whatever it was that made him leave. We might find a Joe who didn't want to be found. Given all of the possibilities, I'm not sure what I would have said in their position.

But the sisters knew what had to be done and why. Miriam Baxter put it in words. "You know, Mrs. Cain, I've always been a firm believer in things happening for a reason. When you're young, everything seems so black and white. You're so sure of your beliefs and you're willing to draw lines in the sand and stand behind your convictions no matter what. When Joe left, all three of us, Chris, Harold and I, did that. We knew Joe was wrong for leaving and that was that. We kind of backed ourselves into a corner with each other."

Chris was nodding her head in agreement.

"None of us wanted to be the one to weaken," Miriam continued. "I think you know that age has a way of making you question some of your youthful convictions. You start to see the world is more gray than black and white, and I guess you start to soften a little."

There was a pause, and I didn't move to fill it. We all just sat there listening to the calling of the birds as they prepared to settle in for the evening. Miriam finally broke the silence.

"And something else comes into the picture. Death! If we all die and we never know what happened to Joe, we'll regret it. All three of us were thinking that, although Harold isn't quite admitting it yet. You laying this in our laps forced us to talk about it. We haven't mentioned Joe to each other in years. That's the real reason I didn't call you back too fast. We had to have time to deal with each other and get some of the emotions under control before we really could talk about it. But I think we're okay now. We do want to go forward. At least Chris and I do, and Harold hasn't said no."

Mrs. Baxter's words had been heartfelt but measured. I knew she was holding back some strong emotions. Chris wasn't doing as well. There were tears streaming down her face. Good grief! If anyone in a room cries, I'm right there with them. Doesn't matter why or even if I know why. So Miriam Baxter handed Chris and me tissues, and I apologized for my sappy behavior.

I told them both that I would be as sensitive as possible to their feelings, but that I would certainly be honest about whether or not I found Joe.

"But," I cautioned, "there's one thing I've realized and I have to make it very clear. My job is to find Joe and to lease Joe. If I find him, and he doesn't want his whereabouts revealed, I can't tell you where he is. I hope that's not the case, but I think we all know it could be."

"Don't you file something in the courthouse if you lease?" Chris asked.

"Yes. A memorandum of lease will be filed and it will have an address. It could be a post office box, but it is a matter of public record."

"That would be far more than we have now. And," said Miriam, "I don't think Joe would let you put that much on record if he was determined not to be found."

With that said, we made plans to meet again the following week. I said I would think about how to get started and hopefully they would do the same. We said good-bye on the front porch, looking out over a peaceful country scene. I was pleased with their willingness to at least try.

I awoke the next morning to Sam wiggling my big toe back and forth through the covers, saying, "Time to get up!" I do my best sleeping in the morning, so getting up is sometimes rough. He's up and at it early at the first whimpers from the dogs. They're crying to get out for a quick pit stop and then right back in to gulp down breakfast. By the time I get a shower and head downstairs, the coffee is made and the newspaper is on the counter. What service!

"So anything new on Facebook?" I asked, as I walked into the kitchen.

He's totally into Facebook, and I'm just a casual observer. However, I do check in once a day or so to see cute animal videos and get any major friend news.

"I just defriended someone for making stupid Obama remarks," he said.

"Oh well. I guess you'll have that!"

We had a leisurely breakfast followed by a short concert. Sam always plays a few tunes on the guitar before he heads out the door. It's a fun way to start a day for him, and I like it too.

"I'll be at the courthouse this morning," I told him after a quick hug.

"Okay. Catch you later."

We always say good-bye on Sam's first leaving, and then I kid him when he returns at least once, sometimes twice, for something he forgot. Sam's the creative sort.

I tidied up the kitchen, grabbed my stuff, and headed to the courthouse to check in with Tony. He was leading a crew of three title searchers, and they were all busy churning out title reports on tracts that I needed to lease. We met at a local coffee shop to catch up.

Tony was one of those long and lanky guys who appears to walk slow but takes big strides. If I was walking with him, I had to do double time to keep up. He came ambling in and set seven new title files in front of me.

"You guys have been busy!" I said.

"We keep it moving. There's a couple of tough ones in there."

"Tough to run or tough to lease?" I asked.

"Probably both. One of them has fourteen owners identified but some of them died in the twenties and thirties and there's nothing on file here. Good luck with that," he said with a grin. "I think you might find something on them in Marion or Harrison. The families seemed to have some roots in both counties."

"Well, thanks. I guess you can call it job security," I commented, taking a quick look at some of the info sheets.

"And, Donna, the one on the bottom is the original sixteen-acre Tredloe farm."

"You mean the one they lived on? The only one Barrett didn't sell and the one that his heirs didn't reserve the oil and gas on?"

"Yep," said Tony, "that's the one."

I pulled the map from the file and looked at it.

"Tony, that's directly beside the coal company acreage where our drillsite is planned. To do all of the southern legs, we'd have to have it. You're showing that the current surface owner, Earl Crofton, also owns the oil and gas, right?"

"The oil and gas has flowed with the surface all the way. Never reserved," Tony replied.

"Okay, I'll tackle this one before any of the others. With this tract and the Tredloe heirs' interests, we'd have a straight shot going south."

"By the way," I continued, "I met with two of the Tredloe heirs last night, the two sisters, and they've agreed to help me find Joe. That's a big relief. Without them, I don't think it would happen. Might not happen with them, but I think I have a fighting chance."

Tony and I got some coffee and I told him the stories about Axel Tredloe that Miriam Baxter had told me in our first visit. Tony was fascinated.

"So this guy was hanging out in Guatemala and Honduras during the early part of the century? And he was kind of a rough character. Not too honest, maybe?"

"Sure sounded like it. Why?"

I could see the wheels working in Tony's head, and he started to smile.

"So the family doesn't know what he was doing down there?" he asked.

"From the stories they heard he was up to no good. He died there and his brother and nephew figured he was murdered. What are you getting at?"

"Axel was in the right place at the right time to be part of the Banana Wars," Tony said.

"I've heard of the Banana Wars but don't know much. Miriam commented that Axel told his family they had bananas because of him so maybe you're on track with this Banana Wars thing. This sounds interesting, Tony."

"It's a sordid piece of American history that gets swept under the rug. Let me read up on it and see what I can find. And, one more thing, Donna."

"Yes?"

"Remember Barrett Tredloe sold the surface of the tracts he bought?"

"Yes, but he kept the oil and gas."

"Right. All of the people he sold the seven tracts to were in Louisiana. You know how they usually put the lawyer's name and address on the deed, you know, the lawyer who prepared it and who they're going to mail it to once it's recorded? Same lawyer on all seven deeds. Address was in New Orleans. I also looked up the addresses on the tax rolls for each of the people who bought the seven tracts. They were all going to Louisiana addresses. Odd, don't you think?"

"That is odd. And it's in each of those deeds that the oil and gas was reserved to Barrett. That seems strange as well. People in Louisiana knew the value of oil and gas so you have to wonder why they let it go, don't you?"

"Maybe it was Barrett Tredloe's reward for acting as an agent and buying all that land. I really think that was his role in all this."

I agreed wholeheartedly with that. And, even though it was a mystery that didn't affect the oil and gas ownership, I knew Tony would pick at it until he came up with an answer. He showed me some things to watch out for in the title files he'd given me, and I headed home to review.

A Little Peace and Mayhem

By the time I got home my body and my brain both needed a break so I put on my walking shoes, stuck the pepper spray in my pocket, and headed up the road. It was a cloudy day with the sun occasionally peeking through the grayness. I spooked three mallards who made a hasty and noisy lift-off from the creek, wings beating frantically as they climbed skyward. As my eyes followed their path, a sunbeam shot through a thin cloud. It created one of those shimmering shafts of light that Josh always called "angel light" when he was little. It was a fleeting mirage appearing and disappearing right before my eyes.

I waved to a neighbor and stomped my foot and yelled at her two-pound, seemingly ferocious little dog who always came out to threaten me. A car was coming, and I didn't want to see him squashed. I'd never yelled at him before, and when I did his little eyes bugged out and he turned tail and ran. So much for his bravado.

I turned onto the dirt road and was making good time until one of the Berrys' horses caught sight of me. He and his buddy were in the lower field, and he always had to have a nose scratch and check me for treats. He hung his head over the fence, and we communed for a few minutes. I was going to have to remember treats.

I was soon under the cool canopy of trees you enter on the left-hand fork of the road, that long, inviting tunnel of shadowy peacefulness. It was always a pleasant part of my walk, but I soon emerged into the sun on the other end, turned around, and headed back. We'd had some rain so the little stream in the shallow ravine on my right was running, though barely. Up ahead, two turkey vultures descended from a branch in the trees, landing in the ravine next to a fallen tree. I stopped because that was odd.

Turkey vultures are large birds with wingspans up to six feet. And, while they have amazing soaring abilities, endlessly riding the thermals without beating a wing, they're not at all pretty when you see them up close. They've evolved to have red heads and long necks with no feathers on them. They're carrion eaters and often dine on large, dead mammals, extending their heads well into the carcasses. Having no feathers means it's much easier to keep their necks and heads clean and free of infection. But I was used to seeing them in open spaces like roadways where it's easy to spot the dead and dying from the sky.

They seemed unaware of me so I stood still and watched. I wasn't close enough to see much, but I could tell that one of them was tugging on something under a tree that had fallen across the ravine over the creek. Whatever he had was breaking loose and, as he pulled it from under the branches, I thought I saw some blue. He pulled it out a bit more and then began tearing at it with his beak. And that's when the queasiness started. Even from a distance, I knew I was looking at a blue shirt on a human arm and the lighter thing I could see at the end of it was a human hand.

I started yelling and running and the birds took off. I slowed only long enough to make certain I was seeing what I thought I was seeing, and there was no doubt about that.

I ran another six hundred feet or so to just past where the road forks and a yard begins on the right. It's the home of Justine Bennett, a sixty-something widow. I didn't know her well, but we'd chatted a few times when she was on her porch. Her car was there, and I started yelling her name the minute I hit the yard. She came to the door looking confused and scared, and I told her what I'd seen.

She motioned me in and locked the door. It's a funny reaction to a dead body, but I was happier with it locked as well. I was breathing hard and, while getting me a glass of water, she told me to catch my breath before telling her more. The house was a small cottage, with an inviting kitchen that couldn't have possibly been cleaner. It literally sparkled.

The windows were open; I heard a loud muffler and then someone yelling something. Justine heard it too and we both froze. The sounds were coming from up the road where the body was. I summoned up my courage (or foolishness, maybe, since I often have trouble distinguishing between the two) and went out the door and to the very far end of her yard. It ended at the point where the road turned slightly, and when I peered through the trees, I could see an older black truck stopped near the body, about five hundred feet from where I was.

The driver was yelling, "Get in here!" as another guy came up out of the ravine and jumped in the truck. The driver gunned it and came down the road fast. I didn't have time to run back to the house, but I was able to jump behind a shed where they couldn't see me. I peeked out, but they went speeding by so fast I wasn't able to see anything on the license plate. I could, however, tell it was an old Ford Ranger with rusty fenders and a tan gate when the rest of the truck was black. At least the side I could see.

While I was outside, Justine hadn't waited for the rest of the story. She'd called 911. They told her to get me inside, lock the doors, and stay put.

"Here," she said thrusting the phone at me as I ran in, "It's 911. They want to talk to you."

I took the phone, breathlessly asking, "Did she explain where we are?"

"She did. Units are en route. Now what's your name?"

I managed to say Donna Cain between ragged breaths. I really hadn't run that far, and I sure hoped I wasn't going to hyperventilate.

"Donna Cain? We have a deputy from out that way. Are you rela—"

"He's my son."

"Josh Cain is your son."

"Yes."

"Well he's on his way. Now tell me what happened."

Oh, great! Josh had repeatedly warned me about the dangers of walking these back roads by myself and now I'd found a dead body. Well, it wasn't my body, so he couldn't say too much.

I proceeded to explain everything I'd seen, at least what I remembered, to the 911 operator. I could hear her broadcast the description of the vehicle. She stopped dealing with me long enough to pull Marion County in as well. We were very close to the county line and when the guys in the truck hit the paved road they would have lots of options no matter which direction they turned. They could be in another county in a flash. Of course, they didn't know anyone had seen them or that police were converging from several directions.

It didn't take long for us to start hearing sirens. And, of course, the first guy on the scene was Josh. He jumped out of the car and ran to the door yelling, "Mom!"

I opened it and said, "Josh, I'm fine! How'd you get here so fast?"

"I was only a couple of miles away serving a protective order. Mom, I tried to tell you. Not everybody is out in these woods to enjoy nature!"

"I know, I know. Come up here, and I'll show you where the body is."

I thanked Justine for the help and told her I'd keep her informed. Josh told her to keep her doors locked, but I don't think he had to. I jumped in the cruiser, and we drove about three hundred feet and stopped well short of where the body was.

"We're staying in the car," Josh commanded, as I reached for the door handle. "You're sure he's dead, right?"

"There were two vultures pecking at him, Josh, so I have to assume so. I didn't hear him object!"

"There's a detective and crime scene specialist on the way. This is going to be a delicate scene. There's a thin layer of wet mud on the road so those tire tracks won't last long and I don't want to run over them. We'll get the best ones where they stopped. With all that leaf litter on the bank, the footprints probably won't be that good, but maybe."

"What about the guys in the truck? Shouldn't someone be chasing them?"

"There's five or six units running them down. State's on it, we're on it, Marion County is on it. We'll find them. Did you get a look at them at all?"

"The passenger had light-brown hair, kind of a shaggy, dirty, curly mess that came below his ears. He had on a ball cap. Oh, and he looked skinny. His arm was out the window kind of pounding on the truck door the way people do when they're excited. I really didn't see the driver at all. Do you think they're the killers, Josh? And why would they go back to the body?"

"I don't know, Mom. Maybe they forgot to check all his pockets for identification. Maybe he wasn't dead when they left him and they wanted to make sure he'd died. It's hard to say. And Mom, could the tree have fallen and killed him?"

"No, Josh, that tree's been there for a while. I was watching some squirrels running across it one day and that was months ago."

"How long had you been at Mrs. Bennett's house when you heard that truck?"

Darn, I was afraid he'd ask that.

"Oh, sixty seconds. Maybe a minute thirty."

"Odds are those are the killers in that truck. What if they'd seen you there. Do you know what a close call that was?"

"It's beginning to sink in, Josh. It's beginning to sink in."

Josh gave me the same look I'd given him a hundred times or more. It was that "maybe now you'll listen to me" look. How in the world had the tables turned so fast!

Grilled Cheese and Fresh Ink

The next few days passed by quickly and quite uneventfully. For that, I was thankful. I'd get the occasional call from Josh with any updates on the investigation. Amazingly enough, they hadn't caught the two guys in the truck. With all the cops converging on the area, that meant they had gone to ground somewhere close, probably after hearing the sirens. Odds were, at least one of them lived nearby where they could hide the truck in a barn or garage. As a result of the suspects not being found, I'd been grounded by my own son. Luckily, I had no desire to walk until someone was safely behind bars.

I spent Wednesday calling potential lessors and processing several out-of-state leases that came in the mail. On Thursday morning, I decided to finally tackle the title for the sixteen-acre farm that Barrett Tredloe had lived on. It was the one referred to as "the homeplace" by his current heirs.

On this tract, the oil and gas traveled with the surface up to the present day. None of the owners of the land had ever reserved it when they sold the land. And Miriam was right. It was Delos who sold the tract after his father passed away. As Barrett's only living heir, he'd inherited a one hundred percent interest in it.

I started thinking about how these tracts fit together in our unit. Marcellus wells are all drilled on a northwest to southeast angle. The ninety-seven-acre coal company property was our drillsite, and it set northwest of the two-hundred-forty-seven-acre

Hagen farm. Tucked in on the eastern side of the unit, bordering both the drillsite and the Hagen farm, was the sixteen-acre Tredloe farm. In order to drill all four southeastern legs off of the well pad, we needed all three of those oil and gas tracts.

The title on the sixteen acres looked solid, and it was time to contact the oil and gas owner, Earl Crofton, who was also the surface owner. But why did I have such a bad feeling? I put that behind me, went online to the Assessor's site and got the address they were sending the taxes to. But I came up empty-handed on a phone number. Nothing in the Taylor County phone book; nothing I could find online. Apparently, Mr. Crofton only had a cell phone. I hate it when that happens, especially when the person I'm looking for lives at the end of a little dirt road!

I finally laid the sixteen-acre title down and turned to a more pleasant task. It was about nine-thirty on Thursday morning, and I had an eleven o'clock appointment to get signatures from the Randall brothers, both in their eighties. I got dressed, checked to make sure their leases were in my satchel, and jumped in the car.

I knew from my phone conversation with one of them that it would be an interesting meeting. Harlan seemed quite the character. I had sent the leases in the mail so that Harlan's son, an attorney, could go over them. He'd called me, asking for some changes. Some I could do and some I couldn't, but we reached an agreement and he gave his dad and uncle the go-ahead to sign. His last words to me were "Good luck!"

I arrived at eleven o'clock in the middle of a downpour. It seemed like one of those spring storms that comes out of nowhere and leaves in a hurry. The Randall brothers lived in a traditional, two-story, white farmhouse surrounded by pastures and a barnyard. There was a wraparound porch on two sides, with a very inviting-looking porch swing, at least on a sunny day.

Harlan and Lewis Randall owned seventy-two acres inherited from their parents. The title told me that much. It was a working beef cattle farm, but from what Harlan's son had told me, a nephew who lived on the adjacent property did most of the farming these days.

It was raining hard so I moved fast from the car to the porch and knocked loudly, hoping their hearing was good. The rain hitting the metal roof made quite a racket. Harlan threw the door open and looked startled.

"What are you doin' out in the rain?"

"I'm Donna Cain, the leasing agent. We had an appointment today," I replied.

Harlan turned from the door and yelled, "Get dressed, Lewis, the gas lady's here!"

I'd never been called the "gas lady" before.

Harlan invited me in, keeping me in the hall for a minute while Lewis had time to "skedaddle" as he put it. That was an old-timey word I hadn't heard in years.

"Come on in to the kitchen," Harlan said. "We'll sit at the table. What's your name again?"

"Donna Cain, Mr. Randall. Remember, we talked a few weeks ago, and you had me send the lease to your son."

"You talked to him?"

"Yes sir. We agreed on some changes, and he said you and your brother were ready to sign."

Lewis came in, and I don't have a better word for him than "ornery." You could just see it in those sparkly eyes.

"So you're the gas lady, huh?" he said, and then cackled.

"I guess that's as good a label for me as any," I replied, not really agreeing with my words.

Lewis sat down, and I began to tell them what was in the

lease. They both listened for about thirty seconds when Harlan said, "Whoa there! That's what I sent my son to law school for. Tell you what. We'll sign if you'll fix us each a grilled cheese sandwich."

"Now you're talking!" Lewis said. "Harlan always burns 'em!"

Oh my! Now I was seeing why the son had said, "Good luck." These two guys were playing me for all I was worth, but they were grinning like two ornery boys and I figured they were just happy to have some company.

"It's a deal. Where's the pan?"

Lewis got the pan, and Harlan rummaged through the refrigerator for cheese and butter. I found the bread on the counter. Lewis was pouring a can of tomato soup into a pot and said he'd watch that. I called a halt to everything, and said we had to sign the lease before everyone got buttery fingers.

"You won't run off then, will you?" asked Lewis.

"You have my word. Two sandwiches coming up before the ink's dry!"

They signed and I grilled sandwiches (one for me too), and we had a very tasty lunch. These two guys were sharp as tacks even though they'd have you believe otherwise. Harlan had been an accountant and Lewis an engineer. Harlan had lost his wife a few years back, and Lewis had never married. They told me great stories about growing up on the farm. Sometimes I can't believe I get paid to do this job.

Getting to Know Joe

As a private contractor, if you don't work, you don't get paid. There's no paid vacation, no benefits. But, to offset those things, you get paid a better rate than if you were an employee. And there are advantages, the primary one being, you're in control of your schedule and your time. I had told Joanne that I was taking Friday off. Sam and I were heading out on a three-day weekend to Gettysburg where we were meeting his cousins who lived in Pennsylvania.

It was a break we both needed and proved to be a very enjoyable as well as interesting weekend. But, as happens with all pleasant trips, they go way too fast.

Before I knew it, it was Monday again and back to work. I was actually anxious for it to come because it was my next scheduled meeting with Miriam and Chris. I figured this was when I'd finally get some information on Joe.

I arrived at Miriam's house at the appointed time. Chris was already there and, after the usual pleasantries which included iced tea and some killer chocolate chip cookies Miriam had made, we got down to business.

"What can you tell me about Joe and why he left?" I asked.

Chris sat up straight, took a deep breath and began. "I guess the first thing we should tell you is that we really don't have hard facts. We're going to explain the situation as we saw it, but maybe someone from the outside can make more sense of it than we have. You need to know that Harold is the oldest, next Miriam, next me, and Joe was an 'oops' baby."

I chuckled saying I'd never heard it called that.

"Well, he was eight years younger than Chris," Miriam offered. "We first three were all, more or less, two years apart. We thought that was that, the end, and then along came Joe. Mom was thrilled, but I'm not so sure about Dad. He loved Joe, no question about that, but he was probably looking forward to the end of parenting. Dad was a mechanic and he worked very hard to support us. There were some lean times but we never did without. I think by the time Joe came along, Dad was just kind of tired."

"What kind of a kid was Joe?" I asked.

"He was a wonderful kid." Chris smiled as she talked about him. "I think you have to call his disposition sunny. At least when he was young. And that really didn't change overall, but as he got into his teens, there just seemed to be something bothering him."

"One way Dad dealt with Joe was to make him his helper in the shop. Dad was usually working for a car dealer, but he did small, under-the-table jobs in the garage at home. Brakes, oil changes, things like that. He had Joe in the garage from the time he was about eight years old, and by the time Joe was fourteen or so, he could do most of the jobs on his own. And he did too, but he never seemed to enjoy it."

"What did he like to do?"

Neither sister answered quickly, but finally Chris said, "He liked to help Mom. Joe could cook and he could bake and he always looked happy in the kitchen. That bothered Dad, but Mom defended Joe and she kept telling Dad to think about chefs. 'They're almost always men,' she'd say. Dad wasn't buying it."

"And then," Miriam added, "Harold came home. Joe was sixteen and in high school, I was married and out of the house, Chris was living in Morgantown, going to school, and Harold had just finished two three-year tours in the marines. Harold had a very narrow view of what made a man a man, and Joe wasn't fitting the pattern. Mom was always running interference, but shortly after Joe turned seventeen, Mom died. It was very sudden and very devastating to all of us. But it was hardest on Joe. He was at home with Harold and Dad. They were three men all grieving in different ways, and it wasn't working out well."

"Joe kind of took over Mom's role in the household, even though he was still in school," Chris said. "He could cook, he could do laundry, he could shop for groceries. He was doing things that helped Dad and Harold, and for nine months or so, there was kind of an uneasy truce. Nobody was happy, but they weren't hassling Joe for doing things they both considered women's work. They wanted to be fed, so they backed off a little."

"But then something happened, and we truly don't know what it was," Miriam offered. One Friday night the lid blew off, and the next thing we knew, Joe was gone. Dad and Harold said we girls didn't need to know. It was better that Joe leave and not come back. Our anger was never at what Joe did, whatever it was. It was at Joe leaving without talking to us. That's always been our issue, and we've never really been able to resolve it."

"And Harold never told you what happened? Never at least hinted?" I asked.

"Harold Tredloe is one of the most stubborn men you'll ever meet. To Harold, something is either right or wrong and there's no in between. And, no, he never told us anything. Harold thinks we're better off not knowing."

"But you must have some idea of what went on. You've speculated, tried to come up with something that made sense."

"We have," said Chris, "and we both think that Joe was probably gay, but we don't think that would explain such a long absence. He would have to figure that over the years, we would have become more open to that. 'We' meaning Miriam and me. He probably wouldn't expect Harold to change. It's a far different world than it was twenty years ago. Surely he doesn't think we're incapable of ever understanding or accepting him."

My heart went out to Miriam and Chris. Their expressions and tone of voice told me just how much Joe's disappearance had hurt them.

"We just can't understand why he's never tried to talk to us," Chris continued. "Why he's never sent a letter or made a phone call just to see if there's a chance. After all, Miriam and I were never negative towards him when he was at home. We never told him he shouldn't be helping Mom or that he needed to get back in the garage with Dad. He had no reason to abandon us. That's what hurts so much!"

I could fully understand their anger and frustration. I agreed. You don't leave for twenty years because you're gay. The problem was, I didn't have any better ideas. And really, we were all just speculating. I trusted the sisters' instincts though. They knew him. He was their brother!

"Is there any logical place Joe might have gone when he left?" I asked. "And did he have money? How could he possibly support himself? And for that matter, how old was he?"

"Joe was eighteen. He had just graduated from high school, and he wanted to go to college. Joe was smart. He had good grades," said Chris.

"Was he starting in the fall?"

Miriam explained that their mother had died in late September of Joe's senior year in high school. And, with that happening, Joe said he'd take a year off after high school and work and help out around the house and then go to college. She said it was the summer after Joe graduated from high school when he left, and he couldn't have had more than a few hundred dollars, if that.

"But," Miriam continued, "we've always thought that he might have gotten some help from Aunt Maud."

"You mentioned her when we first talked," I said. "She was the one so into family histories. Your mother's sister, right?"

"Yes. Aunt Maud was Mom's sister. She was also the progressive one in the family. Maud was well educated. She had a teaching degree and taught high school English for several years. She married a well-to-do businessman who, it turns out, never stopped dating after he got married. Aunt Maud had a good lawyer and, apparently, a sympathetic judge. She came out of that marriage in good shape financially. That was before 'no fault' divorces. Aunt Maud decided to go back to school and become a licensed counselor. She worked primarily with young adults with all kinds of issues. Chris and I have always thought Joe might have turned to her. She could have helped him both emotionally and financially. When Joe ran off, Maud was living in Pittsburgh. That might be where he went.

"Did you ever ask her?" That seemed like the obvious course of action to me.

"Yes," Chris replied, "we did. Quite a few times actually. And she was always vague. She would say things like 'I don't know why you girls think Joe would come to me' when it was quite obvious why he would. They'd been pretty close before Aunt Maud moved to Pittsburgh. But she never gave us a straight answer, and we finally quit asking."

"Is Maud still living?"

"No, she died in 2008 after a very bad bout of pneumonia."

The sisters had given me a lot to think about and it was getting late. I told them they'd been extremely helpful, and I needed to do some more thinking. I had to figure out what the most logical first step would be in setting out to find Joseph Morgan Tredloe.

"There's something I've been thinking about doing for a long time," Miriam said.

"What?" Chris and I asked in unison.

"Going through Aunt Maud's papers."

"Oh good heavens! Miriam, I completely forgot we had them. We carted all those boxes back, and we both said it would probably be good reading in our retirement. Do you know where they are?" Chris asked.

"Yes. They're up in the rafters over the garage. We may not find anything, but we've always suspected that Maud knew something."

"You're right! And Maud always wrote things down."

"That she did!"

I left the sisters thinking about how they were going to tackle Maud's papers and wished them the best of luck. We agreed to meet again in the next week or two, and I was happy to see a sense of excitement in them. I knew there would be ups and downs throughout the journey, but for now they were focused on finding Joe! I realized that, in this meeting, I hadn't seen the hesitancies I'd seen in our prior get-togethers. They were engaged and moving forward. Thank goodness!

Bits and Pieces

I have a once-a-week date with the alarm clock. It goes off every Wednesday morning at five forty-five so I can get to my 7:00 a.m. Rotary meeting in Morgantown. I'm about ten miles out of town, so I have forty-five minutes to wake up, get showered, dressed, and headed down the road.

This Wednesday morning, it was a little tough. I'd lain awake far into the night figuring out ways to begin the search for Joe. I agreed with the sisters that Pittsburgh was a good place to start. Joe would have needed a job. He might have lived with Maud or rented, if he had enough money. It was before cell phones were much in use, so he might have had a landline in his name if he rented. He might eventually have gone to school part time and, at some point, he might have owned a car. Even a junker requires registration so there might be some trace of that.

I would also find out where Maud had lived and see if there was anyone in the neighborhood who'd been there a long time. If she was in an apartment, an owner or the management might know something. I'd learned that when it comes to finding people, you just have to keep plugging away. Sooner or later, something turns up.

I dished up my weekly Rotary breakfast of fruit and sweet rolls and sat down beside Harris, one of the two WVU professors in the Dental School who leads the trips to Guatemala. Harris has a law degree as well. Needless to say, he has an analytical mind, so I told him what I was up to and asked for any suggestions.

"If I were looking for an eighteen-year-old male who'd left home under bad circumstances, I'd check the daily report," he said.

"You mean the police records?"

"Yeah. I don't mean he was necessarily a bad kid, but look at the facts. Eighteen-year-old male suddenly on his own. He was probably angry. Probably a bit desperate. Eighteen-year-old males do lots of stupid things when they have good support, let alone when they're suddenly free to do what they want. Just something to think about."

"No, no, you're absolutely right. I call them stupid boy tricks. My son, the cop, did his share of them when he was younger. Now he says that's what makes him a good cop. Been there, done that sort of thinking. That's good advice about the police records although it might be like finding a needle in a haystack. If you think of anything else, let me know. This could be a difficult hunt."

I realized I hadn't told Harris anything about Axel and the Guatemala connection so I gave him a brief summary, which he found interesting. But our conversation was cut short when the bell rang, so we stood to recite the Pledge of Allegiance, bowed our heads for the prayer, and settled down to business. The speaker was the director of a local social service agency, yet another organization serving too many people with too little money and resources. I didn't mean to be inattentive, but my mind kept wandering to Joe. A plan was starting to emerge in my head, and a call to the office was the next logical step.

After Rotary, I headed home, intent on running my plans for finding Joe past Joanne. She spends a lot of time in the field, so I was happy when she answered the phone on the first ring.

"You know the missing guy we talked about on the Tredloe property? Well, I met with the family, at least the two sisters, and they say to go forward and they'll help as much as they can," I told her.

"That's great! Did they have any input?" she asked.

"A little. They think he headed to Pittsburgh because that's where their Aunt Maud was. They think she would have been inclined to help him, although she never admitted it. Aunt Maud died in 2008, and one of the sisters has her papers packed in boxes in the garage. They're going to start going through them to see if there are any clues. Aunt Maud was an amateur writer. She did a lot of family histories—stories and stuff—and they think she might have written something down that would be useful."

"I hope she did. It would sure make it easier," Joanne commented. "In the meantime, what are you going to do?"

"I think my best bet is to head to Pittsburgh and start digging." I explained to Joanne that I'd start with Aunt Maud's neighbors and the building management if she'd been in an apartment. I wanted to see if anyone remembered Joe being around. I'd also check school enrollments and personal property records for Joe. Things like that.

"That's going to take more than a day. You're what, an hour and a half away?" she asked.

"About that, but I have an aunt in Oakland near the Pitt campus. I think she'll pull the rollaway out of the storage closet and let me sleep there for a couple of nights. And realistically, I'll try and do as much as I can on the computer before I even go. I'll get Aunt Maud's last address from the sisters and scout the area online," I said.

She agreed to the plan and told me to keep her posted on my progress. We hung up, and I started a list of things I needed to do before heading north.

I was busy writing out my list when my son, Josh, called. He was telling me about finding a fifty-six-thousand-dollar excavator the night before that had been stolen in Pennsylvania. He'd been working the case for a while. He knew who stole it and knew it was being hidden in the area he patrolled, but he needed the evidence.

"So how'd you get the guy?" I asked.

"Easy. He was moving it down the road on a flatbed at night! Nobody with any sense moves heavy equipment on narrow roads after dark. I had just answered a call on a domestic and it was pure coincidence I was on that road. I was driving towards him and figured that had to be the machine. I slowed down and looked up at him in the truck cab and he just freaked. I don't read lips that well, but there was no mistaking, 'Oh shit! A cop!' was what he said."

"So did he just stop?"

"Yeah. I hit the lights and he knew he was fried. He sure couldn't outrun me hauling a few tons on a flatbed. He gave me three bogus stories. I cuffed him and told him I was taking him in, and he just caved. Once he gave me the real story, it all coincided with what I already knew."

"Well, I guess a confession is as good as it gets."

"Yep. He'll do time in Pennsylvania for this one."

I'd been thinking about Harris's advice to check the police reports in Pittsburgh on Joe Tredloe, and I figured someone with legitimate access to computerized archives could do that a lot faster than I could.

"So Josh, if you wanted to run a guy's name through Allegheny County in Pennsylvania, would you get everything on him down to traffic citations? I'm talking old stuff, like back almost twenty years."

"Maybe. Is this about your missing guy?" he asked.

"Yes. But I'm not even sure he went to Pittsburgh yet. Let me try to confirm that one way or the other and if I need you to run him, I'll let you know. I don't want you to do something you shouldn't though."

"It should be all right. I was working with an undercover P-A cop on the excavator case. He could probably run it. Let me know."

"I will. Thanks!"

We said good-bye and I went back to my list.

Critters without Legs

ver the next two days I leased three local people on other
tracts, answered about a zillion questions from someone
in Nevada who had no idea they owned oil and gas in
West Virginia, and, in between, compiled facts on Joe and Aunt
Maud to get my search started. The sisters had given me Maud's
full name, Maud Marie Trimbly, and her address in the Shadyside
section of Pittsburgh, which is right next door to Oakland where
Aunt Betty lives. Shadyside is an older neighborhood known for
its trendy shops and good eateries. It's a well-respected address in
the Pittsburgh metro.

Maud had lived in the same building for a little over fifteen
years. I googled the address and clicked on Zillow. Between the
information they offered and the aerial photograph, I learned it
was a three-story apartment building on a street scattered with
private homes, possibly some duplexes, and other small, older
apartment buildings.

And, when the mail arrived, I was very happy to get an envelope from Miriam and Chris with copies of three pictures of Joe
shortly before he left home. One was his high school graduation
picture so it was a good close-up. There were a couple of other
snapshots that showed a brown-haired guy of medium height
and medium build wearing nondescript clothing. He was good
looking in a quiet, understated sort of way. In other words, Joe
was a guy who could disappear in any crowd and not be noticed.

I would have preferred a six foot three behemoth with fiery red hair and tattoos!

They sent me a couple of pictures of Maud as well, along with a list of some of the things she was involved in. She loved the theater, the symphony, and the arts in general. They said she often talked about going to shows at Heinz Hall and the Benedum Center as well as stage productions at Pitt and local theater companies. I wondered if Aunt Betty might recognize her. My aunt had been going to symphonies and operas and live theater productions for as long as I could remember. Wouldn't that be a stroke of luck.

The sisters said that Maud also volunteered at a local shelter for battered women and, at Maud's funeral, close friends had revealed that she usually had one or two people she was quietly helping on the side. She was a social worker by trade and at heart, and she kept at it even after she retired. It was all information that could prove helpful.

I was studying the photos when my brother, Dennis, yelled my name as he came in the back door. "Watch out! Bubba just went up to the deck with something in his mouth."

I could see the cat door off the deck from my desk. Just as I turned my head to look, I caught a streak of orange coming in followed by a pounce and a sideways jump in the air. Ahh geez!

Bubba loves to bring critters in live and turn them loose. I think it's part entertainment for him, part gift for us. This particular critter, however, came minus legs. I grabbed my pitcher and scooped up about ten inches of garter snake off my bedroom rug, a little fella compared to the last one Bubba brought in. Garter snakes tend to play dead when in danger, and that makes them easy to catch.

"Snake!" I told my brother as I came down the steps. That's his cue to open the front door so I can keep my captive secure with both hands. I turned him loose on a rock at the top of the creek bank, apologized for his harrowing experience, and off he slithered. For the hundredth time I threatened Bubba with losing his cat-door privileges. We both know it's a bluff.

I went back to my desk, called Aunt Betty, and booked in for the following Monday night.

Good Grief—It's Harold

Sleeping in on Saturday morning for me is getting anywhere past seven. I rolled out about seven twenty-five and had just had my first drink of coffee when the phone rang. A quick glance at the caller ID got me awake fast. Harold Tredloe!

"Mrs. Cain?" he bellowed in a commanding voice.

"Yes sir!" Darn! I shouldn't have called him sir. Now he'll have the upper hand.

"About this oil and gas. There's something wrong here."

"Mr. Tredloe, I'd be happy to answer any questions over the phone or meet with you if you have time. Your sister said you're working a pipeline job and I know that's long hours."

"We're down for a few days with equipment issues. You know, this isn't making a lot of sense to me, you saying we own all this oil and gas. You get clear back to Great-Grandpap Barrett—he didn't have any money! You got the wrong answer here."

"Mr. Tredloe, I'll admit to you that it's odd, the way your great-grandfather bought and sold those tracts. More went on than meets the eye in the documents. But there's no mistaking, based on the deeds on file in the courthouse, that you own this. Those documents don't say where Barrett Tredloe got the money to buy the properties, and they certainly don't say why he sold them. But they do confirm that he did buy them, that he was given clear title, and that when he sold them, he reserved the oil and gas."

"And you're sure of that!"

"Very sure. And since that time, the ownership has flowed from generation to generation."

"My sisters told me they'd heard something about the property but not the oil and gas. I don't know where they got that story from."

"Your sisters did know a little about it. Not much, and they were skeptical as well. But they think the money might have come from Axel Tredloe based on what your father and grandfather said and stories that your aunt told them."

"Aunt Maud! Now there was a . . . well, I'm just not gonna say anything except Aunt Maud could tell a tale and most of them were just that. So you need four Tredloes to make this work?" Harold Tredloe's questions were more like statements of fact that he was commanding me to agree with. There was never an uptick in his voice to indicate he was asking me something.

"Yes, I do need all four. In the state of West Virginia, you have to have one hundred percent of the oil and gas owners under lease before you can drill. There's one or two ways around that, but they're complicated and certainly not the routes we want to take."

"You're gettin' into something here that maybe shouldn't oughta be gotten into. I think the girls said go for it, and I've never been able to talk sense into them. I'm too busy right now to deal with this, so I'm going to sit back and see where this buggy goes. I'm guessin' in circles."

"That's very possible, Mr. Tredloe. I know the odds are against me here. I'd be happy to call you once in a while with a progress report."

"I'm hard to get, and I'm thinking no news is good news on this deal. Let's see how it plays out. Thanks for your time." And with that, he hung up.

I was ecstatic. Harold Tredloe had just given me a go-ahead. I've dealt with more than a few Harold Tredloes. Honest, hardworking, hardheaded men of few words and no give. Much of their communication is based on what they don't say, rather than what they do. Harold Tredloe did not tell me not to try to find Joe. He was telling me I'd fail and, at the same time, I had a feeling he was hoping I wouldn't. I figured Harold would still throw some rocks in the road, but maybe he'd hold back on the boulders.

I was wide awake and ready to go now! Josh and his fiancée, Lindsay, were coming over for dinner along with our friend Jill.

"So Sam, what's on the menu?"

"Ribs."

"Mmmmm!"

Sam's ribs are killer. A couple of hours in the smoker, a couple of hours in the oven, and then finish them off for a couple more hours on the grill—low heat all the way. So tonight it was Sam's ribs, Josh's special recipe mac and cheese, my salad, and Jill's barbecue sauerkraut, which I was very skeptical of the first time she brought it. It's delicious.

It was a day of running to the store and cleaning the house for me. Sam tended the ribs and did some trimming while my brother mowed the grass. By late afternoon, house, yard, and people were all fairly presentable, and the ribs were smelling heavenly.

"Where's the fruit?" Jill had managed to get to the front door without the dogs detecting her, so now the hound was howling in alarm and Daytona, the lab, was making a flying leap toward the bowl of sauerkraut in her hands. She sidestepped him, and my brother shooed him out the front door.

"I've got two bags of fruit and lots of fruit sauce," I told her.

"Good. It's been one of those days!"

Fruit is kind of a euphemism with us. Jill went through the kind of divorce where you're really glad to be rid of the narcissistic, egomaniacal, pain-in-the-butt man, but other things happen that aren't so good. We'd get together for a bit of sangria therapy, sangria being the fruit sauce, the fruit being frozen and quite delicious after thirty minutes or so in the sauce.

Josh, Lindsay, and the lab came through the back door with Daytona doing all he could to wrestle the mac and cheese to the floor. My brother ushered him out the front door again.

"Ahh geez. They're hitting the fruit!" Josh loved to kid us.

"You want some, Lindsay?" I knew better than to offer it to Josh. He called it a "chick drink" and totally unfitting for a cop.

"Yeah, I like it." We'd brought Lindsay into our fruit circle before. "But why do you guys call it fruit?" she asked.

"Blame my mother for that." Jill rolled her eyes and launched into another Mom story. "My sister and I took her out to dinner for her eighty-fourth birthday and she ordered sangria. I couldn't believe what I saw the waitress coming with. It was in a glass as big as Mom's head with about half a pound of frozen fruit floating in a pint of sangria. Mom belted that thing back like a pro, and after every drink, she'd say 'I love fruit.' 'This is just the best fruit.' 'You girls should eat more fruit.' She was fruit stuffed and quite happy at the end of it. If you asked her what she had for dinner, she didn't have a clue."

After that, Jill called me and said, "Hey, we need to put frozen fruit in our sangria," I added. "So now we do. And boy, do we love fruit!"

Josh just shook his head, and Sam rolled his eyes as he got a couple of cold beers from the fridge. We always congregate around the island in the kitchen, so, while I made the salad, Josh settled on a stool and told us yet another cop story.

"Last week I got a call from Mr. Tucker. I went to high school with his son Paul. Anyway, he said someone had made off with his scrap heap, and he asked me to come out and talk to him."

"Scrap heap?" I said, rolling my eyes.

"Yeah, junk pile, you know. There's a lot of money in those piles. Iron, steel, aluminum. Anyway, I went out wondering how I was going to track this one down, but it turns out Mr. Tucker knew exactly who had taken it. He had three witnesses and one of the best pieces of evidence I've ever seen." Josh was chuckling when he said that.

"Mr. Tucker lives up a dead-end hollow. So, Harley Haney and a couple of his bone-headed friends drove Harley's truck up the road, still daylight, mind you, and loaded the junk pile in the truck. But here's the thing: Everybody in that end of the county knows Harley. He's a bowlegged, four foot eleven, goofball who drives a sixty-something Chevy with one gray fender, one green fender, and a tailgate made from two-by-fours. It's not like it could be anybody else's truck.

"So, anyway, they come flying out onto the paved road and there's two neighbors standing in their yards talking and looking right at them. Mr. Tucker was at his sister's birthday party, but one of the neighbors called him when they saw his truck go by later.

"Well when I got to Mr. Tucker's, he said 'get in the Gator,' and we headed for the scene of the crime. He was smiling all the way and kept saying, 'You're gonna love this, Josh.' We stopped where the junk pile used to be, and Mr. Tucker got out and pointed to the ground. I swear, it was the best impression of tire treads I've ever seen!"

"In mud?" Sam asked.

"Nope. Cow shit. And it was perfect, which, of course, I documented with my phone.

"You know, if you got it right in the middle of the curing pro-cess between fresh and leathery, that would be a perfect medium," Jill pointed out. She was a horsewoman and knew a thing or two about manure.

"Anyway, Mr. Tucker told me that was his rainy-day pile. He said if he was short on cash, he could sell the pile and always be several hundred to the good. But, it was also kind of a commu-nity pile. He said they used it once to get old Mr. Moore's car in shape to pass inspection. And another time, his nephew talked him out of it so he could rent a limo and take his prom date to a really good restaurant. Mr. Tucker said that in his day it didn't cost a whole scrap heap just to go to the prom."

"Times change," I said.

"So, I headed over to Harley's place. Harley's about thirty years old and probably hasn't done an honest day's work in his life. He lives in a ramshackle travel trailer way out a dirt road. I pulled in right beside his truck and, sure enough, the tire treads were a perfect match to my cow pie pictures. I was still squatting down chuckling when I felt Harley breathing down my neck. He's a sneaky devil.

'What ya doin', Josh?'
'Well, well, well. If it isn't the junk pile bandito!'
'I don't know what you're talkin' 'bout.'
'Harley, before you say anything else, let me ask you a ques-tion. Do you really want to be known as the guy who got con-victed based on cow shit?'
'That'd be pretty crappy evidence, Josh.'

"Well, Harley thought that was hysterical. He had a beer in his hand and tried to drink it while he was laughing and got choked. I whacked him on the back, probably a little harder than necessary, but it got his attention."

'Harley, look at this, buddy. This is a picture of your tire tracks in a nice big cow patty. Said cow patty is located at Mr. Tucker's farm right next to where his junk pile used to be. Looks like a perfect match to me, Harley.'

'Lot's a tires out there with that tread, Josh.'

'You are aware of the two neighbors who saw you as you pulled out, aren't you, Harley?' "

"So what did he say?" Sam asked.

"He just stood there looking goofy as usual. But, he finally admitted he'd dumped the junk a little ways behind his house. So, I told him he had two choices: load up the scrap and take it back now, or get in my cruiser and head to jail. Harley actually stood there and thought about it a while. I suggested he load it up or I'd charge him with everything he was guilty of and a few things he wasn't. He finally said he'd load it up and take it back. But, of course, I had to stand there and watch him, and then follow him over so he didn't make a break for the scrapyard and sell it. The whole thing took the better part of my day."

We were all laughing.

"I'll guarantee you one thing, though," Josh said. "Doing all that work made a bigger impression on Harley than a few days in jail would have. He was one tired and achy boy when it was all said and done!"

Sleuthing with Aunt Betty

I spent Sunday evening packing and thinking. Where should I start and what should I do? It still wasn't clear, and my online searches had yielded little. I finally decided to start with footwork. I'd head to Maud's old address, 223 South Myer in Shadyside, and hope there was an owner on-site. If not, I was hoping for a long-term resident who would remember Aunt Maud and the young man who was, hopefully, hanging around in the nineties.

Monday morning, I ate a hurried breakfast, called my brother next door with a couple of reminders, hugged Sam and the animals, and headed north. I was excited. It was a new adventure, a treasure hunt.

I hit Pittsburgh traffic at entirely the wrong time and crawled to the Fort Pitt tubes. It's a totally amazing sight as you emerge from the tunnels onto the bridge—a breathtaking vista featuring downtown Pittsburgh, the North side, and the Point, where the Monongahela and the Allegheny Rivers come together to form the Ohio.

Aunt Betty had recently chastised my cousin and me for going all the way to Oakland to get to her place on Bigelow. Turns out, it's a lot quicker to zip up Grant Street through downtown. But, years ago, when she'd moved from the heart of Oakland to Bigelow, we just got directions from her old place to the new, and that's how we'd always gone. I took the Grant Street route, which was none too quick on a workday morning.

Aunt Betty's apartment house is an eight-story, art deco treasure perched on the side of a hill. It's always a treat to go there. The architecture is fascinating, and I never tire of the panoramic view of the Pitt campus from her fourth-floor living room window.

She greeted me with fresh orange juice and coffee cake, and I started telling her what I knew so far about Aunt Maud.

"Aunt Betty, I know it's a long shot, but Maud loved theater and music and the arts. Her nieces say she went to productions at Pitt and Heinz Hall and the Benedum Center. I have a feeling that the two of you were in the same place at the same time more than once," I told her.

"Oh, wouldn't it be a stroke of luck if I recognized her?"

"Here's a picture, but it's not a very good one. It's probably twenty or thirty years before she passed away. Her nieces are digging through her things though. They might come up with something more recent."

Aunt Betty took a good look at the picture, but it didn't spark any recognition.

"You know," she said, "I have a couple of friends who live in the same general area that she did. They're big music lovers too. They might remember her."

Aunt Betty was having as much fun with this as I was. She'd been a visiting nurse and knew Pittsburgh like the back of her hand. She made a few notes and, with pictures in hand, we set out determined to put our best investigative skills to work. I drove and she directed. Shadyside wasn't far away, so within ten minutes we were parked in a central location and ready to roll.

I may not have mentioned that Aunt Betty is my father's youngest sister. There were five siblings, and she's the only one still with us. Aunt Betty is eighty-seven, but we rarely notice because she refuses to act her age. She has a mind like a trap and moves at a very sprightly pace.

Once parked, we had just walked around the corner onto South Myer and were scouting the duplexes and apartment buildings for street numbers. Aunt Maud's building, 223, was in the middle of the block. From the outside, it appeared to be six apartments, two to a floor, three stories high. It was an older, red brick building that had obviously been well maintained. I loved the windows. They were oversized, double hung, mullioned windows, and they were all sparkling clean.

As we stood there looking at the building, a woman came out the front door. She was looking at us skeptically, so we thought we'd better explain ourselves.

"Hey, say, I wonder if you could help us?" Aunt Betty said. "We're trying to find someone who knew a woman who, we're told, was a longtime resident of this building. She passed away in 2008. Maud Trimbly."

"Well, I've only been here a year, but there are some tenants who've lived here quite a while, and I think the owner has had the building for maybe fifteen years or so."

"Does the owner live on-site?" I asked.

"No, I believe he lives in Lawrenceville right now. He'll buy a place that needs work, live in it while he fixes it up, then rent it out and do it all over again," she said.

Aunt Betty and I both realized our bad manners at the same time and introduced ourselves. Her name was Beth and she was on her way to the bus stop. She gave us the owner's name and his rental company name before she bid us good luck and hurried down the street. It was progress.

I was carrying a small notebook, so I wrote the information down. We figured the mailboxes for Aunt Maud's apartment house were inside the front door, and decided to go in and see if there were names on them. It wasn't a secure building and the door into the hall was unlocked. The mailboxes were there and had last names and apartment numbers, but no first names.

"Do you think we should just knock on doors?" I asked.

"I don't know. People are skeptical anymore with so many scams going on. Maybe we should find the owner and talk to him."

She was right and I knew it, so we decided to call the owner. If he'd talk to us this morning, we'd head that way and have lunch in one of Lawrenceville's many new eateries afterwards. It's an old working class area where renovation is all the rage right now. It's eclectic, counterculture, and very interesting. We'd been there a few months before on a trip to an old and well-known shoe store. I was saving up to go back. I had my eye on two pairs of oxfords, and they weren't cheap!

I googled the rental company's name and a number came up. A quick dial and three rings and I was talking to Tyrell McClain.

"Mr. McClain, my name is Donna Cain. My aunt and I are standing in front of 223 South Myer, and—"

"I don't have any vacancies and probably won't. That building stays full."

"No, no, we're not looking for an apartment," I explained. "I really need to talk to you about Maud Trimbly, a tenant of yours who passed away in 2008."

He hesitated, wondering what in the world I wanted, but finally said, "I remember Mrs. Trimbly."

"Mr. McClain, I know this seems odd, but I can assure you it's all legitimate. And it's nothing negative, but I'm going to need a few minutes to explain it. Would it be possible to talk to you for ten minutes or so this morning? Or maybe early afternoon? I'm only in town for a couple of days."

There was another hesitation but his curiosity got the better of him, and he agreed to see us around eleven. He gave me the address of the house in Lawrenceville he was rehabbing, and I assured him we'd find it.

Aunt Betty and I congratulated ourselves on our forward progress and headed for the car. It was ten fifteen and it would only take twenty minutes or so to get to Lawrenceville, but we wanted to make sure we could find the address. Aunt Betty was my GPS. I have a strong aversion to the real things and refuse to let them in my car.

Traffic was pretty light, and by ten thirty-five we were headed down one of Lawrenceville's main streets. She directed me to go left up a hill and then decided we'd turned too soon. We cut across a couple of blocks, went up the hill to the next corner, and there was our street. We turned left and quickly spotted the house we needed. There were sawhorses in the front yard and a long, orange extension cord coming out of an upstairs window. We found a parking place and spent the next twenty minutes lining up our strategy.

The houses in this area were almost all wood frame, two or three stories, with the height of each level proclaiming nice high ceilings inside. Some had been recently redone, most were just well maintained over the years, and a few were true fixer-uppers.

It was almost eleven, so we hopped out and climbed the four steps up to Tyrell McClain's current project. The front door was open so I stepped inside and yelled, "Hello!"

"I'll be right down," a voice shouted from upstairs.

Tyrell McClain came down the stairs in paint-spattered bibs with a ball cap on backwards and tools in each hand. I hoped he'd put it all down and really give us some time. I needed to pick his brain, but I might have to do it in more than one session. We introduced ourselves all around, Tyrell displaying two very dirty hands and apologizing for not shaking.

"Come on back in the kitchen," he said. "It's not nearly so dirty, and there's actually chairs."

We all sat down and I started explaining. "Mr. McClain, I'm an oil and gas leasing agent working on a project in Taylor County, West Virginia. That's where Maud Trimbly grew up and where some of her extended family still live."

"So Mrs. Trimbly owned some oil and gas? Is this Marcellus?"

The Marcellus was very much in the news in western Pennsylvania. Everyone was aware of people making lots of money on bonus payments and royalties.

"Actually," I told him, "Mrs. Trimbly didn't own any that I know of, but her nieces and nephews do, and that's why I'm here. I have three of them located but I need the fourth, and they don't know where he is."

"Are these all brothers and sisters?"

"Yes. The youngest one, Joseph Morgan Tredloe, left home almost twenty years ago and hasn't been heard from since. His sisters think he might have headed this way and that Aunt Maud might have helped him. She was a social worker so she would have been supportive. And they think she would have kept quiet if that's what he wanted her to do," I told him. I handed him the best shot of Joe I had.

He studied the photo for a moment. "I'm afraid I don't know anything that could help. I don't ever remember seeing this guy, but then, I probably wouldn't. I was only at the building occasionally to make sure everything was okay. If repairs were needed, sometimes I did them, but sometimes I got somebody else."

Aunt Betty chimed in with the really important question. "Who in the building has been there the longest? Or do you know who knew her best, and do you think they'd talk to us?" she asked.

Tyrell McClain smiled and said, "That would be the 'Good Professor,' Dr. Arnold Wilson, retired. Former sociology professor at Duquesne. I'm smiling because I think he and Mrs. Trimbly were pretty good friends, but they were always arguing. That, I do remember. And yes, Professor Wilson will talk to you. He'll talk to anyone who will stand still and listen. He's quite a character."

"So you think he and Maud were close?"

"A few years ago there was a water leak on the third floor of their building and it ruined the ceiling and part of the floor in the second-floor hallway. Mrs. Trimbly had one apartment on that level, and Professor Wilson still has the other. I spent a couple of days drying and painting ceiling plaster and dealing with the floorboards. Mrs. Trimbly and Professor Wilson were my entertainment. They argued, but they were enjoying themselves. They were good buddies. I'd start with him."

Tyrell McClain had given us just the kind of information I'd hoped he would. Aunt Betty and I thanked him profusely, and then headed out to find lunch.

And we found a good one: a new deli in a former hardware store. They'd kept some of the former store's vintage wooden shelving and bins. The bins were filled with artisan breads and the shelves stocked with olives, relishes, mustards, etc., all from names I'd never heard of. Definitely not supermarket brands. The food was good and the patrons interesting, but our minds were on Professor Wilson. We ate faster than we should have and headed back to Shadyside.

"Do you think we should call first?" I asked.

Aunt Betty thought about that. "To be polite, yes. To accomplish the task, no."

"I think you're right. He can put us off on the phone. But in person, he probably won't. And besides, how threatening are we?"

She agreed and we walked down the street once again to 223 South Myer.

A quick look at the mailboxes told us Apartment 202 was Wilson so we started up the stairs. The building had a quiet elegance. It was early twentieth century, well-built and well-maintained.

Professor Wilson's apartment was on the right at the top of the stairs. Aunt Betty knocked and in just a few seconds we heard footsteps and then silence as the Professor peered through the peephole. We must have passed muster because the door opened, and I knew we were in for an interesting visit.

Arnold Wilson had curly white hair, a bit long, that stood out in every direction. He was wearing baggy, brown cargo pants, an old white dress shirt, and a tartan plaid vest. His feet were bare and in one hand, he was clutching a bunch of leeks.

"It's not often women appear at my door," he said. "I do hope you're not selling anything."

We laughed and told him we'd gotten his name from Tyrell McClain.

"We need to talk to you about Maud Trimbly," I told him. "Mr. McClain thought you might be able to help us."

"Maud was a dear friend, and I miss her. I bet you're here to tell me another will has been discovered and she left me her millions!"

"No, no, nothing like that," I assured him.

"Okay, well come in anyway. You don't look dangerous and maybe one of you knows how to make leek soup. I'm attempting it for the first time," he said.

Aunt Betty said she loved leek soup and had made it a time or two. I was useless! We followed Professor Wilson to the kitchen where he put the kettle on and we began explaining our interest in Aunt Maud. I've always found that a good story, especially a mystery, intrigues people and gets them involved. Professor Wilson was no exception.

"So you think Maud might be your key to finding the missing brother," he said, when I was all done.

"His two sisters think that might be the case. They feel he would have turned to his aunt. She would have been supportive, and she could have helped him financially if he'd needed it," I told him.

As we talked, Professor Wilson was busy putting a loose tea, a very aromatic, flowery-smelling selection, into three tea balls and placing them in good china cups. He'd actually not asked us if we'd like tea, but it did tell me he was willing to spend some time with us. It didn't take long for the kettle to begin whistling and the tea to be poured.

"Maud moved in here in the late nineties," he said. "She'd probably been in Pittsburgh fifteen years or so by then. I didn't know her early on, but I think she'd always lived in the Oakland–Shadyside area. I can't say I remember a young man being around, but I can't say that I don't either. Memory's not that good these days. What if this boy doesn't want to be found?"

"That's a fair question and something I've thought about," I said. "I've already told the sisters that if I do find him and he doesn't want his whereabouts known, I can't tell them. And if he really doesn't want to come forward, he won't sign a lease, since if he did, it would be recorded in the courthouse and his address would be on it. I'll certainly make sure he knows that. The ball will be in his court."

Professor Wilson was shaking his head in agreement and I could see he was mulling things over. After a few seconds, he said,

"I'll make some inquiries. I think I know where to find some of Maud's early friends. Let me think about this."

And with that, he ushered Aunt Betty to the stove to examine his broth and help him add a few herbs. They fiddled with the soup and discussed an upcoming opera performance, and I drank tea and considered the possibility that Arnold Wilson knew more than he was telling, at least for now.

That Was Odd of Maud

I t was Wednesday morning, and I'd just returned home from my 7:00 a.m. Rotary meeting and walked in the door to a ringing phone.

"So did you learn anything?"

It was Miriam Baxter. I poured a cup of bottom-of-the-pot, seriously strong coffee while considering what to tell her.

"Nothing concrete, but I have a feeling we sowed some seeds that might bear fruit."

"Tell me about it. Do you have time?"

I could hear excitement mixed with anxiety in Mrs. Baxter's voice, and I felt like I was walking a tightrope between handing her hope or disappointment. It was a fine line.

"I have plenty of time. We talked to a man in Aunt Maud's apartment building. Oh goodness, I hope you don't mind me calling her Aunt Maud. I really shouldn't, and I'm not trying to be too familiar. It's just that, after all you've told me, that's how I think of her."

Mrs. Baxter laughed and told me it was quite all right.

"Okay. Well, we talked to the building owner, and, he suggested we talk to Professor Wilson, Arnold Wilson."

"She talked about Arnold Wilson. I would never have remembered if you hadn't said his name. Chris and I teased her sometimes about him, but she'd always shush us and say he was a friend and that was that. I'm sorry, I interrupted."

"No, no, please do interrupt. I'm hoping some of the things I say will trigger memories. You never know what might be useful. Anyway, Professor Wilson lived just across the hall from your aunt. He's still there. It's just a hunch, but I got the feeling that the Good Professor might know more than he was telling us. And, even if he doesn't, he said he'll make some inquiries among some of Maud's other friends."

"Do you think he will?"

"Yes, I do. He seemed to take a real interest in what we were telling him. We, being my aunt and I. I enlisted my aunt's help. Aunt Betty's lived in Oakland right next door to Shadyside for over fifty years. She and your aunt had many of the same interests. Opera, the symphony, and even volunteer work. She's going to ask around as well. I just have to think they had at least a couple of acquaintances in common."

"You know, Chris and I were talking about the possibility of Joe leaving and never contacting Aunt Maud. We know it's possible, but neither one of us think it's likely. And we've been thinking about Maud's behavior towards us after Joe left. Most of our contact was on the phone or Maud came down here. She never really invited us to visit her."

"That is odd. You'd think she'd invite you up with your kids to go to the museums or wherever."

"Exactly, but when she came she would bring us stuff. She gave Chris and me both sets of very nice china that she had in storage. And she gave Kathleen some pretty valuable cut glass. Kathleen has a nice collection on her own and loves the stuff. She also gave us each an old family quilt from the Morgan side. Looking back on it, it seems a little odd. We didn't think about it then. We were both really busy with families and jobs and all the other things life throws at you."

I agreed that life can get busy and, when relatives aren't close by, we don't always pay attention like we should.

"But there's something else that's odd," Mrs. Baxter said. "A couple of years before Maud died, sometime around the holidays, she sent a check for twenty-five thousand dollars to each of us: Chris, Harold, and me. She said she'd done well in life and wanted us to have some of it now. She joked that she might live to a hundred and, by then, we'd be old too. It came out of the blue. We all thanked her profusely. Well, Chris and I did. Harold grumbled, and Kathleen did the thanking for him. He said he didn't want any of it, so Kathleen remodeled the kitchen! It's a very nice kitchen, and Harold complains about it to this day!"

Miriam and I both laughed at Harold's hardheadedness.

"Well," I said, "Maud's possible connection is still the best shot we've got, so we need to work it for all it's worth. By the way, Aunt Betty and I spent a few hours yesterday afternoon at the Carnegie Library going through old Pittsburgh phone books looking for Joe's name. We didn't find a thing. I'll go back soon and start on city and county records."

With that, Mrs. Baxter told me she and Chris would continue to dig through the last couple of boxes containing old papers and mementos from Aunt Maud and we hung up.

I sat for a few minutes wondering about the relationship between Aunt Maud and Professor Wilson. Had they just been good friends, or had there been something more? Could it be possible that Maud asked Professor Wilson not to disclose anything about Joe if he was ever asked? Of course, I was presuming that the Professor actually knew something in the first place.

Miriam had just told me that her aunt had somewhat distanced herself from them in her later years. Or, at the very least, not encouraged the family to visit her. Maybe I was reading too much into it; but, more and more, I felt Maud was a part of Joe's life after he left, and Professor Wilson was our key to unraveling the whole thing.

I continued to mull things over as I filled the cat bowls, gave my brother a rundown on leftovers in the fridge for his lunch, and then headed to the Taylor County Courthouse.

It was a beautiful, late spring day with trees in bloom, newly blossomed wildflowers bobbing in the breeze, and birds singing their little hearts out. I hit the road and went through my usual list of pros and cons on why or why not to get a low fat, French vanilla latte at McDonald's. This morning, the pros won, so I made a speedy trip through the drive through.

From my house to the front door of the courthouse in Grafton, county seat of Taylor County, it's about forty-five minutes (without the latte stop). It's mostly a winding, narrow, two-lane road that's light on traffic and heavy on scenery. I always enjoy it. A visit to any other courthouse in the immediate area means finding a parking space, calculating your time, getting enough money deposited, and remembering when your time is up. I'm always amazed at how efficient their meter people are. In Grafton, I park free on the street with no hassle, no money. I always park about half a block away so the really good spaces are left for courthouse patrons, many of whom are elderly.

The Taylor County Courthouse has the nicest crew in the County Clerk's office of any county I've ever worked in. I've been in and out for three years so they know me well, and it's always a warm welcome. After saying hello and chatting, I made my way to the basement record room. Tony was up to his elbows in landbooks, which means he was into a problem. When you can't unravel your issue any other way, you start digging through the big, dirty and often crumbling land books in the hope someone

one hundred years ago made a note that will help you. Amazingly enough, you often find something.

"Hey, Donna!" Tony looked downright relieved to have a diversion. He closed the books, returned them to their shelves, and sat down with me at a small table near the copy machine.

"I have some new title for you, but first I have something I want to tell you." Tony's eyes were sparkling as he said this, and I wondered what was up.

"You remember telling me about Axel Tredloe and how he spent his time in Central America?"

"Yes."

"Well, Donna, I've been doing some research. You mentioned Guatemala and Honduras, and you and I talked a little about the Banana Wars. I mean, based on what you told me, this guy, Axel, would have been there when all this was taking place."

Tony was definitely excited.

"Donna, I've got somebody working on this in Louisiana, and I should know more soon, but I think Axel Tredloe might have been a mercenary working under a guy named Lee Christmas. Christmas was a ruthless thug who pretty much ran the dirty side of the operations for Sam Zemurray."

"Wow, Tony, you are losing me big time. But back up to somebody working on this in Louisiana. What do you mean?"

"I have a buddy from law school whose wife has a master's in library science. Her specialty is research. They live in Louisiana now, and she works for the state library system. I told her the story and she got interested. She's already found Axel Tredloe's name connected to Christmas, and she's seeing what else she can find."

"Good heavens, Tony. Now explain the rest to me. I'm totally lost!"

"You've heard of United Fruit, right?"

"Yes, but I don't know much except I have the impression they were bad actors," I said.

"That's putting it mildly, Donna. Well, Sam Zemurray ran United Fruit from the early thirties to the mid-fifties. But long before that, he had a company called Cuyamel Fruit importing bananas from Central America to the United States. Bananas were kind of new to this country in the early part of the nineteen hundreds and people loved them. The market was big. Zemurray was determined to take advantage of it, and that meant getting lots of land in Guatemala and Honduras to plant banana trees on, and lots of low-wage workers to make the operations a go. He was pretty ruthless, even to the point of overthrowing governments that wanted to nationalize some of the thousands of acres he literally stole."

"So you think Axel Tredloe was part of all of this?" I asked.

"It's very possible. I know it has absolutely no relevance to what you need, but it just sounded interesting and I wanted to see what I could find."

"So you mentioned someone named Christmas? What an odd name."

"Yeah, it was Lee Christmas, and he was no Santa Claus, believe me. Lee Christmas scoured the less savory areas of New Orleans looking for guys who craved adventure and had very little in the way of scruples. They basically acted as mercenaries for Zemurray's operations, strong-arming peasant farmers into giving up their land. They were not nice guys, but they were paid well by Zemurray for their services, and they found lots of ways to make money on the side."

"Like what, Tony?"

"Blackmail, theft, prostitution. You name it, they had a hand in it. Some of their illicit operations were on the isthmus and some were back in New Orleans. They'd go back and forth on the banana boats since staying in one place too long wasn't such a good idea. There was always someone who wanted a piece of them."

"Good grief. Do you think that could explain why Axel had the money for Barrett to buy the land?"

"Possibly, and it also may explain why the land had to be sold. Axel could have been paying gambling debts or he could have needed protection money, who knows. These guys lived a lifestyle where money came and went pretty fast. And remember, the buyers of the land were from Louisiana, which was Axel's base of operation. Maybe he owed some bad actors money and didn't have it, so he gave them property."

"I'll be very anxious to hear what your researcher finds. We sure are getting some good stories out of this one, aren't we, Tony?"

Tony grinned. "I'm enjoying it!"

"Speaking of research," I told him, "I have to get back to Pittsburgh and dig through some records on Joe and look for Aunt Maud's will."

"What kind of records for Joe? Property?" Tony asked.

"I think personal property records, rather than real estate, are the most likely. I'm hoping Joe had a car. It would have had to have been registered, and that would at least give us an address on the tax records."

"That won't work. Pennsylvania doesn't levy personal property taxes on cars."

"Darn. That was the record I felt I was most likely to find. Oh well, I'll check real estate. For all we know, Joe is alive and well and living in his own house in Pittsburgh. I really have to make time to get up there again."

"Donna, I've worked Allegheny County and I know my way around there. The company wouldn't even have to pay for a hotel. My brother lives in South Hills and I've been thinking about going up for a weekend. I could head up on a Thursday night, search the records on Friday, and spend the weekend with my brother. You think Joanne would okay that?"

"I don't see why not. It would take me a lot longer than it would you. I'll talk to Joanne and let you know," I said.

With that settled, I brought Tony up to speed on what Aunt Betty and I had done in Pittsburgh, and then we finally got to our title review. It wasn't nearly as much fun as our speculation on the life of Axel and the whereabouts of Joseph Morgan Tredloe!

Meatloaf and Silicone

For May, it was unusually hot and humid, and it had been that way for three days. Sam was at his weekly Tuesday night soccer game. However, on an evening like this, I figured the game would be short-lived. They play on private property so afterwards there's always a fire, hot dogs, and a cold brew or two. I call it the "liniment league"—a bunch of guys in their fifties and sixties who just won't give it up, and that's great! They play indoors in cold weather and outdoors in warm. Keeps them out of trouble.

I had eaten some leftovers and was parked on the front porch, hoping for a breeze and trying to get the dogs to not pant on me. Hot, hot, hot! The phone rang and it was Josh. He works three to eleven on Tuesdays. "Hey Mom, do you have any meatloaf left?"

"I do."

"Well Brian's coming out to see my office. He's never been here. He told me he'd pick you up. How about if you make me a sandwich and ride out with him? It would be fun."

"You know, that sounds like a good idea. I'm not doing anything anyway."

"Well hurry and get ready. I'll call Brian to let him know."

I changed fast, and threw two sandwiches together, just in case Brian wanted one too. Brian is a friend of Josh's from high school who lives nearby. He's a big boy, about six feet three and husky. He has a degree in criminal justice and works as a prison guard in a maximum-security facility. I don't know how he does it because he's a very easygoing guy.

I was just finishing up when he pulled in the drive. Brian has a really cool Jeep Wrangler Sport. The top was on but the windows were down, and a nice breezy drive was just what I needed.

"Hey Brian. I made a meatloaf sandwich for you, too."

"Sam's meatloaf?"

"No, mine. It's one of the few things I do well."

"You sure?" he said grinning.

"Yes, I'm sure!" I said, with fake indignation. Brian is well aware of my cooking skills or lack thereof. He held his hand out, though, and made quick work of the sandwich.

It's about half an hour from our house to Josh's office in the other end of the county. We were nearing our destination when I noticed Brian looking in the rearview mirror more than seemed normal, but I didn't think much about it. We hit a long straight stretch, a rarity in West Virginia, when all of a sudden there was a lot of girlie whooping and hollering and a sporty red convertible, top down, went flying past us. In the passenger-side seat, we were treated to an exceptionally well-endowed young woman, upright on her knees in the seat, turned towards us, with absolutely nothing on from the waist up. She had her top in one hand, waving it like a flag while she twirled her boobs like a pro. And those were professional boobs, make no mistake about it. The biggest money could buy, it looked like.

It was quite a show, but it got even better when she lost her grip on the shirt about the time a state police cruiser came into sight from the other direction. Oh my! The shirt flew by us at high speed, and Brian and I burst out laughing in unison. By this time, the convertible had pulled in front of us, and she pivoted towards the back so the show could go on. Good grief!

Our happy exhibitionist was totally unaware of the cop, but the driver wasn't. She was trying to pull her friend down into the seat, all to no avail. The trooper hit the lights, and he pointed their vehicle and ours to the side of the road as he drove past. He screeched to a halt behind us, did a quick U-turn and was on us in a flash. They usually park behind you, but he pulled in front of the girls. A blocking move, I guess.

"Brian, this should be good. She's lost her shirt and here comes a cop."

Brian just kept saying, "Oh my God!"

"You don't think we're in trouble, do you, Brian? I mean, we didn't do anything."

"Nothing I know of. I wasn't even over the speed limit!"

The trooper was on his radio as he approached the car so I knew he was calling for backup, and that backup would be Josh. He was only about a mile away.

I was guessing Josh was going to have to do traffic control. We were in the country where trucks are big and high off the ground. There sure were a lot of guys suddenly hitting their brakes and peering down into that convertible. In fact, Brian and I were afraid someone was going to swerve into us. He slowly pulled us further off the road, and that's when it happened. A nineties-something truck, the driver's head stuck out the window and looking bug-eyed at the show, veered off the road and over a bank.

That was when I just totally lost it and started rolling with laughter. I couldn't help it. The trooper was trying to talk to the girls while keeping his eyes to the skies and waving traffic on at the same time. He seemed quite embarrassed, but the naked one was fine. She was leaning back in her seat with one arm on the window. You'd have thought she would at the very least have her arms across her chest. I figured with an attitude like hers, she was used to working a pole with a bunch of ones stuck in her G-string.

The truck had gone over the bank just before Josh pulled into sight and the trooper pointed him over to deal with it. As Josh got out of his cruiser, he saw us and gave us a "what did you two do?" look. That's when the trooper headed our way. I was still a pile of giggles, and it was getting worse. I would get it stopped for about five seconds and then break out in a noise that sounded like a donkey braying.

The trooper looked in Brian's window and suggested we stop laughing. I answered with a bray.

"So where are you two going?"

"To see Deputy Cain, sir."

"What does Deputy Cain want to talk to you about?" he asked, in a very accusatory voice, probably thinking we were being hauled in for questioning.

Brian held up the sandwich in a baggie and said, "This is his mother. She made him his dinner and I just wanted to see his office out here, so she was just riding out with me. Josh and I are friends from high school."

I brayed again.

And that's when the trooper lost it. He tried to hold it back but a smile slowly took shape and then got bigger and bigger until he started shaking. He turned his back to the convertible and worked very hard to get it all under control.

Josh came walking over and said, "That woman keeps telling people she's my mother. Not true."

The trooper wasn't buying it.

Josh said Bob, the guy who ran over the hill, was fine, just embarrassed, and there was a tow truck on the way to haul him out. Josh was trying to talk to us, but had to keep waving traffic on, and it was getting heavier all the time.

The trooper was trying to figure out what to do with the girl in the car. "I can charge her with indecent exposure, and will, but I really don't want to put her in the back of my cruiser like that," he said, explaining to Josh that she'd lost the grip on her shirt and it was somewhere down the road.

That's when Brian reached into the back seat, and pulled out a tee shirt. "Hey, this might work. Kind of big, but it's clean. I'm a guard at Henline."

The shirt was an XXL and said "Henline Prison Ball Boys."

Brian grinned when he saw our expressions and said, "That's our softball team's name."

The trooper took it, but it didn't help him quit laughing.

"I don't know why those girls thought that was a good idea," he said.

That's when Brian came clean. "They may have misunderstood what the slogan on my back window means."

The trooper walked around to the back. I was trying to read it backwards, which wasn't all that hard. "I'll take mine off if you'll take yours off!"

"Brian, you were baiting them!"

"It's a Jeep thing. It means I'll take the top off my Wrangler if you'll take the top off yours."

We howled some more, and the trooper told us we were free to go. I gave Josh his sandwich, and he told Brian he'd show him the office another day. And Josh told me he had more info on the body I'd found, and said he'd call me with an update.

As we pulled out, the trooper was handing the shirt to the naked one, and Josh was threatening to arrest two bozos in a truck that had come to a complete stop in the road to watch her put it on, the source of their entertainment slowly disappearing.

Well, that was far more fun than a night on the porch!

Liquor and Loose Lips

Sam is always up before I am. The dogs are confined to the kitchen and dining room and they start making noise about five thirty. They were up and at it, wondering where Sam was. He's the one who lets them out, and I was wondering the same thing.

I rolled over and poked Sam in the arm.

"Hey, are you okay?" I asked.

"No. My shoulder hurts, and I have a sinus headache," Sam grumbled. "I'm not getting up yet."

"Go back to sleep. I'll take care of the dogs," I told him. I was glad it wasn't the middle of winter. He's far better at facing the cold in the morning than I am.

I made my way downstairs as Buster began the insanely loud hooting and howling he goes through in anticipation of some wild animal still being in the yard for him to chase. I opened the door and watched the dogs burst through. All Buster ever finds are scent trails, but he follows each and every one, nose to the ground, volume up full blast. The lab is all about lifting his leg on anything close and then running right back in for food. Sam makes him wait on Buster and that never sits well.

I put the coffee on, then headed out to feed the birds and the ducks and get the morning paper. There's a sizable creek about forty feet in front of our house, and every spring the mallards and wood ducks show up. There are always considerably more males than females, which leaves what I call "duck boy gangs" roaming the yard. They don't seem to have mates, but maybe someday they will. I hope, anyway.

A gang of six ran from under the bird feeder and took wing, landing in the creek. They've made a muddy path up from the creek to the place on the bank where we dump the corn. The boys were paddling in place waiting for me to go away so they could waddle up and have breakfast.

The dogs came back in with me and I fed them, watching their chow disappear far too fast. I poured a cup of coffee and began gathering what I needed for my usual two eggs with peppers and onions and toast. My eggs were unusually good for some reason, and just as I was taking the last bite and finishing the paper, I heard Sam's feet padding down the stairs.

"Feel better?" I asked.

"Yeah, my head doesn't hurt so much now."

He got a cup of coffee and went back up the stairs for a shower. By the time he emerged, I was at my desk thinking about the lunch I'd scheduled for Saturday with Miriam and Chris. I was hoping they'd found something in Aunt Maud's papers.

Sam and I said our good-byes, and it wasn't long before the phone rang.

"You're up early," I said to Josh. He works an afternoon shift getting off most days at 11:00 p.m.

"Yeah, I have to be in court at ten, and I'll bet you anything, the guy I arrested for beating up his girlfriend won't show up for his hearing. I recommended no bail, but hey, what do I know? This guy's got really bad anger issues, and he's going to kill somebody someday. But that's not why I called. Mom, we have the two guys you saw in the truck in custody."

"So who are they?" I asked hoping my walks were now back

on the schedule. "Did they live close? Have they confessed?"

"Hold on, hold on! They both live in Lewis County. They're brothers and they have, well had, a cousin not too far from you. He lived up Skinner Creek Road. You turn up a long dirt driveway off Skinner and the house is way back there, probably a quarter mile or so, in the woods. His parents started building it and never had the money to finish. They both died, and he'd been living there, pretty much in the basement with what amounts to a flat, tar-paper roof over it."

"So it's the cousin they killed? That's the guy I found?"

"Yes to both. The two guys you saw in the truck probably heard the sirens and got to the cousin's property before any of us could catch them. It wasn't far away. Their truck was hidden in a big old barn that was probably there when the parents first bought the place. The barn was being used to dry their marijuana crops. There's not much in it now—last year's crop is gone. But the smell was overpowering, and there's plenty of seed and residue. And, on top of that, we found some precursors to meth."

"Was there a meth lab there?"

"No, but we'll find one close-by once we search the area."

"So how did the brothers get back to Lewis County, Josh?"

"Somebody picked them up. They knew they couldn't drive that truck around since it was pretty identifiable with a black body and tan gate. There was a big dent on the driver's side that you couldn't see when they went by you, and the front fender on that side was green."

"How did you unravel all this?" I asked.

"Well it's like this, Mom. The two of those guys together added up to about four hundred fifty pounds of stupid. You mix that with some alcohol and you get wagging tongues."

"So, they got drunk and spilled the beans?"

"Yep. The two brothers got arrested night before last in Lewis County. They were in a bar, both drunk, and one of them started mouthing off about the perfect crime. His brother told him to shut up and they got in a fistfight, so the bartender called the cops. They were still pretty drunk when they hauled them in, and they didn't have the good sense to ask for an attorney. Apparently, during the interrogation, one of them commented on how stupid those Mon County cops were. From that, and other things they said, the detective knew they'd been up to something up here, but he didn't know what. He sent his report, along with photos of them, to our department, and we realized one of them matched the description you'd given."

"Wow! So I helped, huh, Josh?" I couldn't help commenting.

"Yes, Mother. It was a good description. Anyway, we ended up talking to the parents of these two in Lewis County to see if there were any Mon County connections. They told us about the cousin up here and described him. Sounded a lot like your corpse!"

"Yuck. 'Your corpse' has a very unpleasant ring to it."

"That's how I refer to it around the office, 'Mom's corpse.'" Josh loved to tease me.

"Anyway, the parents of the two guys who were arrested told us where the cousin lived, and another deputy and I went out. I'm glad we did. There was a skinny, scared, and totally clueless girl-friend living there. She wouldn't report the victim missing because of all the drugs and stuff around. I really don't think she realized he was dead. We found a good bit of cash and some illegal guns, too."

"I'm pulling up Google Earth right now. I want to see where it is."

"It's off to the right, maybe half a mile up Skinner. Anyway, this girl needed help. She had run out of food; the dogs were out of food. It wasn't good. We brought her in for questioning and she pretty much told us what we needed to know."

"Which was?"

"Well, the two brothers and the cousin had some pretty sizable marijuana patches on four or five different tracts, all within a half a mile or so of the house. Late last summer when the last patch was ready, her boyfriend harvested and sold it without the two brothers. She knows this because he needed help and took her along to help bundle. He had a buyer willing to dry it I guess. He told his cousins that someone had come in and stolen it. That happens a lot so it wasn't totally unbelievable."

"Sounds like they found out, though."

"They knew all along. Turns out the brothers had a deer cam trained on the patch. They'd never trusted their cousin, and with good reason. Not that they were trustworthy either."

"And they killed him for that?"

"I don't think we have the whole story yet. The girlfriend told us most of this and, when we confronted the brothers, they clammed up, but you could see in their faces it was true. We know from the girlfriend that there were more patches, but we're not certain where they were. We don't think she really knows either. She said they didn't talk in front of her much and never took her with them to the other sites. She's from Ohio, and she just wants to get out of this and go home. That's why she's singing like a bird."

"So where was the patch?" I asked. "I think I see his place, at least there's two structures visible."

"The patch he cut down was on a piece of coal company land."

"Why would a coal company allow that, Josh? That doesn't make sense."

"Mother, probably half of the marijuana grown in this state

is on coal company property. They've got thousands of acres they no longer use, and they don't really pay that much attention to it. If you're a grower, it's perfect. And now, the meth makers look for the abandoned sheds or they haul in old travel trailers. If they blow them up, who cares. Problem is, they're leaving behind very toxic sites."

"You know, Josh, I bet the oil and gas is with a lot of those tracts. Makes sense the companies would hang on to them for potential royalties in the future. In fact, there's a unit I'm working on right now, and the projected drillsite is an old strip job. They're perfect. No one lives on them, you're not taking good farmland, and the surface owner is completely on board. So do you have enough evidence to charge these two guys?"

"Yep. The girlfriend pretty much did them in, and the forensic evidence from the crime scene will be in soon. They're working on the truck right now, and it will turn up some evidence, I guarantee you. These two weren't masterminds and it was a long way from the perfect crime. What we really need to find are the other sites where they were growing. I need to get an ATV out there and follow the trails. I guarantee you I'll find evidence of meth as well as other grow sites."

"No charges on the girlfriend?"

"We could make some stick but nothing major. She's more valuable as a cooperating witness."

"So, Josh, what about the other guy that you told me was out of jail and to watch out for?"

"Bo Lightner? He's back in jail on a gun charge. A trooper stopped him a couple of nights ago and found two loaded rifles in his car. He's not allowed to have guns, period. The magistrate set his bond pretty high, and his family refuses to post it. He should be there at least until his court date."

"So I can start walking again?"

"I suppose so, Mother, but stick to the main road and carry your pistol."

"I don't have a license to carry."

"Get one!"

Oh my! We'll never agree on that one.

That's Not a Nice Welcome

The rest of my Tuesday was filled with title review including another look at the sixteen-acre Tredloe tract. I really needed to pick this one up and run with it, but for some reason I didn't want to. It was just a feeling.

I was quite happy when Sam came home early, and I talked him into walking with me, both of us unarmed! I took the opportunity to recount the story of the brothers and cousin for Sam, and he was as relieved as I was that the culprits had been found.

The next morning, Joanne called. While things were settling down for me, our field crew wasn't quite so lucky.

"Three of our guys went out yesterday to inspect the drillsite next to the Tredloe property. They went about five hundred feet and turned around," she said.

"Why?"

"It was literally booby trapped. They were walking up an old service road, kind of grown over, but you could tell there was some recent use, and one of them stepped on a strip of wood with long nails in it, all pointed up. Luckily he had on thick boots, and he pulled his foot back when he realized he was on something."

"It was meant to puncture tires?"

"Apparently. The guys realized they were into something and started looking around pretty carefully. The sun was out, and, not far ahead, Mike saw light glinting off of something across the path they were on. At first he thought it was a spider web, but he took a closer look and it was a thin, woven wire that would catch someone about neck high if they were on an ATV. At that point, they just turned around and made their way out."

"What a coincidence, Joanne. I got quite an education yesterday on what old coal company tracts are being used for now."

"The guys figure it's to protect a marijuana patch."

"Josh tells me half the marijuana being grown in the state is on coal company property, and there's meth activity, too."

I proceeded to tell her more of what I had learned. I was on the computer looking at the county's aerials as we talked, and she brought them up on her computer as well. Modern technology is amazing. I can enter a tax map and parcel number and up comes a line map with all kinds of information. The owner's name and address, the appraised and the assessed value, and lots more. Plus, with a click of the mouse, I can go from a line map to an aerial photograph and zoom in or out depending on what I want to know.

Looking at the aerials, I could see that the old road the guys had used to enter the coal company land was on the opposite side from the sixteen-acre Crofton tract I needed to lease. Looking down on the farm where Barrett Tredloe had lived was interesting. It was isolated, and I could just imagine the issues getting in and out in the early nineteen hundreds. I realized that the people living there now, namely Earl Crofton and whoever else occupied the house, would be the first you'd suspicion if you were trying to find out who was booby trapping our potential drillsite.

"Have you talked to the coal company?" I asked her.

"One of the guys called Brake Mountain this morning. That's the name of the company. They said they would send one of their security crews out later this week, but I don't know if they'll just assess the situation or clear it or what."

"Joanne, I've asked one of the Taylor County deputies, actually he's the chief, about certain people or places a couple of times. He's given me some good advice. You remember when I couldn't reach that man who owned the seven acres at the end of one of our outside legs on the Wooley well. Turned out the guy was totally unbalanced and paranoid, and the chief said not to go there. I took his advice and I'm glad."

"Yeah, I remember. We ended up just stopping the leg short so we didn't go under his property."

"Well, he was arrested last week for attacking someone who knocked on his door about a lost dog. There are just some places you shouldn't go. They've told me to ask whenever I have doubts about someone. Why don't I ask them about Earl Crofton. He's at the end of a very narrow, poorly maintained dirt road. I really shouldn't just drive back there without knowing something anyway."

"Have you tried to contact him by phone?" Joanne asked.

"I can't find a landline number. But, in the age of cell phones, that's not uncommon."

"Go ahead and talk to your contact at the Sheriff's Department. Just tell him that it's remote and you can't get a phone number and you just thought you ought to check."

"Will do."

"Don't mention our problem with the drillsite yet. Maybe you should, but I'm just not sure. I'd rather see what the coal company security guys come up with first."

"Understood. But, Joanne, one more thing. Turns out, Tony has worked the Allegheny County Courthouse and knows his way around. He wants to go spend some time with his brother who lives close by, so the company won't have to pay lodging. I think it would be a lot more efficient if we have him do the searches I need on Joe."

"Sounds like a plan to me. Can he go soon?"

"I think so," I told her. "I'll talk to him."

With that, Joanne and I hung up with me feeling as if we were making progress, at least in terms of getting a plan in place.

You Can't Fool Your Wife

I t was Wednesday morning, and I had bounced out of bed, full of energy and plans. I dashed off to Rotary, thoroughly enjoying the camaraderie and the speaker. Most of the time our programs were serious, but today's featured a local magician who turned us into a room full of kids as we oohed and ahhed at his sleight of hand.

I was headed to the Taylor County Courthouse afterwards when my cell phone rang. I answered and, considering the caller, I pulled off the road to make sure I didn't lose the signal. It was Mrs. Harold Tredloe!

"Mrs. Cain?"

"Please, call me Donna," I said.

"Donna, this is Kathleen Tredloe, Harold's wife. I've thought long and hard about making this call, but I think it's for the best, and I hope you won't think I'm meddling. If Harold ever finds out I did this, he'll be furious. So, I'm going to ask for your total confidence and that means not mentioning it to his sisters as well. It's just too easy to let something slip."

"I understand, Mrs. Tredloe, and I promise it will go no further."

"Okay. But please return the favor and call me Kathleen."

"You got it!"

"Donna, I know Harold called you a while back. I could hear his end of the conversation even though he thought I was out of earshot. I know he sounded gruff and like he thought finding Joe wasn't a good idea. But here's what I want to tell you. Harold needs to know what happened to Joe. If Joe is still living, Harold needs desperately to re-establish a relationship, as hard as that may be. The situation with Joe eats at him every minute of every day although he would never admit that to anyone. Harold thinks he's a closed book and no one can see inside. I see. I don't want Harold to scare you off of looking for Joe. Believe me, that wouldn't be in Harold's best interests even though he may be too stubborn to ever admit it."

"Kathleen, when I hung up after the phone conversation with your husband, I was ecstatic. You see, Miriam and Chris had warned me that Harold would speak his mind and that he could be pretty stubborn sometimes."

That comment brought a snort of agreement from Kathleen.

"With that in mind, I figured if he didn't want me to look for Joe he would come right out and say so. He didn't. He grumbled, and he said he didn't know if it was a good idea, but he never said not to do it. I took that as a green light."

Kathleen Tredloe was silent for a few seconds and then chuckled and said, "You're absolutely right, but I'm amazed you understood what was going on. If Harold really didn't want you looking for Joe, he would have told you so in no uncertain terms."

"Kathleen, I want you to know how much I appreciate you calling me, and please understand that this conversation will never be mentioned to Chris or Miriam or anyone else. I realize that this is a delicate family situation that I've stepped into. I also know that without family help, I'll never find Joe. And, without Joe, we don't have a well."

"I think Miriam and Chris will give you all the help they can, and I know you're doing this for business reasons, not to patch a family back together again, if that's even possible. But, if you're successful, there's a chance we'll get Joe back. Just don't let Harold scare you."

"I promise you that won't happen. And really, Harold may never contact me again. Time will tell."

As I hung up the phone with Kathleen Tredloe, it really came home to me that I was the key to a family drama that could play out for better or worse. My motivation was to find Joe and get a signature on a piece of paper. Or, if deceased, to identify his heirs and get their signatures. Those heirs could well be his brother and sisters if he'd died with no wife or children. But something told me that Joe was very much alive. And, eventually, I hoped I could say "alive and well." But there was no mistaking that with each family meeting and phone call, I was becoming more and more emotionally invested in finding Joe for the family.

I continued my drive to the Taylor County Courthouse with my mind going back and forth between the problem with the booby-trapped drillsite and the call from Kathleen. But my attention focused on the drill tract issues as soon as I hit the center of town. Several Sheriff's Department cruisers were parked on the street including the Crown Vic that the chief deputy drove. Chief Warner was the guy most likely to know the score on the Croftons. He'd grown up in Taylor County and there just wasn't much he didn't know. His office was my first stop.

I stuck my head in the door. "Chief Warner, do you have a minute?"

"Yeah, whadda ya need?"

"I need to get a lease from a guy named Earl Crofton," I began.

Deputy Warner reacted very strongly to the mention of Earl Crofton. He sat up, tilted his head slightly to the right (body language seminars said that meant something but I couldn't remember what) and gave me a piercing look. At the same time, he yelled, "Ornick, get in here!"

I knew Deputy Ornick well enough to speak to or nod at as we passed each other in the courthouse halls, but I'd never really talked to him.

"What's up Chief?" he said coming into the room.

"This is . . ."

"Donna Cain, Deputy Ornick. I work for Dean Oil and Gas. I'm a leasing agent."

"Right. Sorry, I couldn't remember the name. Anyway, Ornick, she needs to get a lease from Earl Crofton. Go ahead Mrs. Cain. You were saying?"

"Well, as you probably know, his house is at the end of a long dirt road. It's isolated and I can't find a phone number. I'm really just checking to make sure I don't walk into a bad situation since I'll be going there by myself."

The chief and the deputy looked at each other weighing, I supposed, what they should and shouldn't tell me. I already knew there was a problem just by the chief's reaction. Deputy Ornick was the first to speak.

"I don't think you should go there, Mrs. Cain. How bad do you need that lease?" he asked.

"Well, that tract is only sixteen acres, but it's adjacent to the drillsite. On a horizontal drill, it might mean we'd lose one, even two legs if we didn't have it. It's pretty critical," I said.

Again, they looked at each other.

"Look, I can see I'm into something sensitive here, and I totally understand that there are things you probably can't share with me. But let me ask you this. If I send a letter asking Mr. Crofton to contact me, and, if he does, I arrange to meet him someplace public, like McDonald's, would that be safe?"

Chief Warner pointed to a chair in front of his desk, and asked me to have a seat.

"Give us five to ten minutes," he said, as he walked out of the room, Deputy Ornick in tow.

I sat and waited, wondering just what I'd walked into. True to his word, the chief and the deputy were back in under ten.

"Mrs. Cain, I just had a word with the prosecutor. I don't know you well, but I know he does since he's signed a few leases with you. He's mentioned you before and speaks highly of you. He just assured us we can trust you. For your own safety and the safety of your other company employees, and for our benefit as well, I want to bring you in on a few things. Ornick, push that door closed."

Deputy Ornick closed the door and sat down in the chair beside me. The chief continued.

"Mrs. Cain, we know your people were out there yesterday. At least I'm assuming they were Dean people now that you've told me there's a well planned there."

I nodded in agreement and the chief continued.

"The place is under surveillance, Mrs. Cain. We're watching Crofton's farm and that coal company tract as well. If there's illegal activity going on, we think it may be happening on that piece of land since the coal company doesn't really monitor it anymore. The drug task force is a part of this, our department is involved, and, eventually, there will most likely be federal charges brought. It's an investigation that can't be interrupted."

I was listening intently, thinking we were probably going to have to walk away from the whole project. And amazingly enough, the thought that my mind went to first was the fact that if we walked, I would have no need to find Joe and that would be a real shame. It was further proof that I was emotionally invested.

The chief took up the tale again. "Crofton is heavily armed. He was always a hunter, but we know some automatic weapons and some high-powered rifles have been purchased by some of his . . . 'associates,' we'll call them . . . and taken to his house. Your people could have been in real jeopardy if they had gone close to Crofton's tract. Luckily they went in from the other side and got scared away. That's an old logging road they were following when they ran into the nail strip."

Wow, these guys knew everything. The chief continued.

"We had a meeting this morning, Mrs. Cain, trying to figure out who it was that went on the property. You just walked in the door and told us. I need to talk to someone at Dean who is high up and who can call a halt to the company's activities there without telling everyone what's going on. We have to keep a lid on this for a while longer. I hope you understand and will cooperate with us. We'll get you your drillsite, but there's going to be a delay."

"I understand. You probably already know that tract is owned by Brake Mountain Coal. When our guys ran into so much trouble yesterday, they called the coal company and reported it. Brake was concerned, of course, and said they'd send out a security crew to take a look at the situation.

"Oh boy. We need to get that stopped, too," the chief said.

I gave the chief the name of the Dean CEO and the main number. He didn't waste any time picking up the phone, telling me to remain seated.

I'd only met Charles Dean a couple of times since the offices were about a hundred sixty miles to the south. I'd been impressed though. Charles Dean was friendly and down to earth. He'd worked in the oil and gas business from the bottom up, giving him a first-hand knowledge of all facets of the business.

"Mr. Dean, this is Chief Deputy Warner, Taylor County Sheriff's Department. How are you, sir?"

With the niceties out of the way, the chief asked for total confidence, explained that I was in the room, and why I had approached them. He then went on to lay out the situation, where they were time wise in their investigation, and why they needed the total cooperation of Dean Oil and Gas in order to keep our people out of harm's way and to make certain their investigation came to fruition in the manner they were hoping for. And, while it was clear it was a drug investigation since the drug task force was involved, he never got into details about what kind of drug activity was going on. But considering the reference to federal charges, I figured it was a lot more than marijuana.

From what I could tell just listening to one end of the conversation, Chief Deputy Warner had Charles Dean's attention. He'd made it very clear that Dean Oil and Gas would be putting their people at risk if they were to go out there. He also made it clear that this would be a temporary setback. From my observations, Dean had always been a very conscientious and caring company. They wouldn't put any employee at risk for a well.

They'd also talked about Brake Mountain Coal, and the chief wrote down the name and phone number of the person who had been contacted there.

The chief and Charles Dean concluded their conversation, and Chief Warner gave me a short report asking for my total confidence. Good grief, between this and Kathleen Tredloe's call, I was bursting with secrets!

Axel Was Up To No Good

Friday dawned with all the promise spring had to offer. Not a cloud in the sky, warm temperatures, light breeze.

I had just said good-bye to Sam and was making my way up the stairs when the phone rang. It was Miriam Baxter.

"Donna, sorry to call so early, but remember I mentioned having lunch this Saturday?"

"Yes," I replied, "I'm still good to go."

"Good! Let's meet at Roush's Diner at noon. Is that okay? There was excitement in her voice, and I wondered why.

"I'll be there. Just you, Chris, and I?" I asked.

"I think so. But you never know about Harold. I always tell him when we're going to meet, but, as you know, he's yet to show up."

"Well, maybe he'll surprise us." My tone of voice told her I didn't have high hopes.

We hung up and I had little time to think about the slim possibility of meeting Harold before the phone rang again. Busy day!

"Donna?"

"Yes, Tony?"

"Are you headed to the courthouse today?"

"As a matter of fact, I am. I have a couple of out-of-state wills that came in the mail yesterday, and I need to record them. Why?"

"I got some info back from the researcher looking up stuff on Axel Tredloe. I know this has nothing to do with getting this tract leased, but it's fun stuff. Axel was some piece of work, Donna."

"I'll be there about eleven fifteen, eleven thirty," I said. "How about we go to lunch?"

Tony said, "Sounds good," and we hung up. Should be an interesting day.

But my phone wasn't through ringing. About twenty minutes later, Aunt Betty called. She didn't even bother with the normal niceties, but launched right into, "Guess who I saw yesterday?"

"Don't know," I replied.

"Arnold."

"Who?" I said playfully, knowing full well who Arnold was.

"Professor Wilson!"

"Ohhhhh." I couldn't help but tease her. "I didn't know you were on a first-name basis."

She ignored my comment.

"I started a new class at Pitt. It's on Congress—the history, the structure, how bills move, etc. Very good lecturer."

Aunt Betty took classes for seniors at both Pitt and Carnegie Mellon. She was a busy woman!

"And Professor Wilson is in your class?"

"Yes, he is. And we talked at the break. He said he's working a possible lead for us. He said not to get too excited, and he wasn't ready to explain yet. It might lead to something and it might not. This whole thing is exciting!"

I laughed. If nothing else, my aunt was having fun with the search for Joe.

"You know, it is kind of exciting. I feel like a detective sometimes," I told her, and then filled her in on what was happening with the family and my upcoming lunch with Miriam and Chris, pointing out that there was a slight chance of Harold showing up.

"Did Professor Wilson give you any indication of a time frame?" I asked. "Did he say how long his lead might take to play out?"

"He didn't, but I really thought I saw some optimism in his eyes."

"Well," I said, "I've had the funny feeling from the beginning that the Good Professor knows more than he's saying."

Aunt Betty agreed and then said she was off to the library. She is truly a remarkable lady.

It was time for me to head to the Taylor County Courthouse and get the scoop on Axel. The drive over was pretty as I noticed more and more wildflowers in bloom, open fields now dancing with daisies, and a general sense of energy and happiness on the part of the birds, ducks, and geese I saw en route.

On arrival, I recorded my wills and descended to the record room to find Tony. As soon as he saw me he closed his book, re-shelved it, and grabbed his satchel so we could make our way to lunch. He was bursting to tell me what he'd found.

We ordered lunch at a quirky little local place just a block down the street. It wasn't fancy, but the food was delicious. Tony ordered a steak hoagie, and I went for what I think is the best fish taco I've ever had. As soon as we ordered, Tony started pulling papers out of his satchel.

"Donna, this guy Axel worked his way pretty far up the ladder under Lee Christmas. Remember, I told you Christmas was Sam Zemurray's head henchman. Zemurray was the Russian immigrant who started Cuyamel Fruit and then later took over and ran United Fruit. It's hard to believe, but Zemurray actually staged an invasion of Honduras and overthrew the government there."

"Tony, you're telling me a fruit company overthrew a government?"

"It happened, Donna. It's all documented. There was a former Honduran president in exile in New Orleans who had been really popular with the Honduran people. Zemurray promised to put him back in power, so this guy starts getting his friends on the ground in Honduras organized.

Meanwhile, Zemurray had a couple of old tubs—ships they used to move fruit—and, after they'd unloaded their banana cargo in New Orleans, they reloaded them with mercenaries and thugs for the return trip. They were mostly drunks and troublemakers that Axel and Lee Christmas had rounded up in New Orleans, so you can imagine what that trip was like. And, from the research, it looks like Axel and Christmas were both on board, with Christmas running the show and Axel second in command."

While Tony was telling me this, he was laying copies of old newspaper articles out on the table. They were from newspapers in New Orleans and an English language copy of a Honduran paper. I was quickly scanning through them as he talked, and they seem to have confirmed his story.

"Donna, when the ships pulled in to port in Honduras, the dockworkers thought it was just more empty boats ready to load up with bananas again. But all of a sudden a couple hundred men came up from the holds and poured onto the docks with guns. At the same time, a bunch of vehicles drove onto the docks, all driven by local guys still loyal to the old president. The guys from the boats jumped into the vehicles, and they headed to the palace and overtook it. The deposed president was in another smaller boat offshore, and, when the coast was clear, he came ashore and was welcomed by the people."

"Good heavens. It's hard to believe a government would be that poorly protected!"

"Well, from what I've read, the military and the police were a lot fonder of the old president who had been in exile. Some of them had helped depose him, but, under the heading of 'be careful what you wish for,' they found out the new president was worse than the previous one."

"So what did the fruit companies gain from this, Tony?"

"They got to keep their land. They'd taken a lot of land by force, and the president they deposed was going to nationalize it and put a heavy tax on fruit export to boot. The exiled president, in return for being put back in office, would give the companies a pass on both. They could keep the land they'd stolen and the fruit could be shipped out of the country tax-free. Of course, I'm sure the new president was getting his pockets lined as well."

"This is amazing. Tony, I think Miriam and Chris would love to see this. They know Axel was no angel, but they don't really know what he was up to. Could you make copies for me?" I asked.

"Those are your copies, Donna. I thought you'd want them. Any progress on finding your missing guy?" he asked.

I told him about my conversation that morning with Aunt Betty, including Professor Wilson's hint of a lead. I also told him about my upcoming Saturday lunch. There was so much happening so fast. But that was good.

Stop Scaring the Waitress

I'd just popped my head through the neck of one of my favorite, kind of nautical-style, blue and white striped shirts, when I noticed Sam watching me with a grin on his face.

"What?"

"You've changed clothes three times," he said. "That's not like you. You've met these women before, haven't you?"

"Of course, but there's a chance their brother might be there. It's Saturday and we've never had a Saturday meeting before. He might be free."

"Huh, so is he really good looking or something?" Sam was teasing now.

"I have no idea what he looks like. I do know he's married and grumpy so, no, I'm not interested. I just need to look right. Not like a pushover but not like a feminist either. I figure this guy thinks women have a place and ought to stay in it."

Now Sam looked confused. "But you usually give those kinds of guys a lot of pushback!"

"Too much at stake here," I said. I'll play any silly game I need to play to get Harold Tredloe's cooperation. I'm not out to change him. I eventually want his signature on a lease, but in the short term, I just don't want him to get in the way of finding Joe. Or, blow things up if we do find him."

"Well, good luck. I'm headed to the shop."

I looked in the mirror and decided that I looked just fine. I really didn't think Harold would show up anyway.

It was eleven thirty and I headed for Roush's Diner, an old Fairmont landmark. It was comfortably worn, spotlessly clean, and it had friendly servers and wonderful food. You couldn't ask for much more.

I got there a little early, and Chris and Miriam were already seated in a big booth in a corner, the kind with one big curved and cushioned seat. Roush's decor was mostly red, black, and white with a little silver thrown in. A high shelf surrounded the room and was filled with the first Mrs. Roush's antique pitcher collection. She'd passed some years back, but her son and daughter-in-law kept her collectibles dusted and in place. The family had never been big on renovating and redecorating, but the clientele didn't want the place to change anyway.

Chris caught sight of me first. "Donna," she said, a big smile on her face, "scoot in."

I scooted, saying hello to both of them. There was a catalog-sized, yellow manila envelope sitting on the table between them, and I could tell they were kind of excited.

I had my mouth open to ask what was in the envelope when the waitress, a painfully skinny and unusually tall redhead, asked what I wanted to drink.

"Unsweetened iced tea," I told her, and Chris and Miriam told her they'd have the same.

"Be right back for your orders!" My goodness, she had such a high, tinkly voice it almost sounded like bells.

"Look at the menu and decide, Donna, we're dying to tell you what we found," Chris said.

"Well, I hope she comes back quickly because I'm dying to find out."

Our bell tower of a waitress returned in a snap setting down three iced teas. Donna and Chris ordered salads, and I went for the Reuben.

"So what's in the envelope?" I asked as the waitress retreated.

Miriam opened it and pulled out a letter and some other paperwork along with a photo. The first thing she handed me was the letter.

"Read this, Donna. It's from Joe to Aunt Maud."

She handed me an 8 ½" x 11" sheet of lined notebook paper folded like a letter. I carefully unfolded it and began to read.

> *Dear Aunt Maud,*
>
> *I'm enclosing the signed general power of attorney and medical power of attorney. I kept copies.*
>
> *I want you to know how much I appreciate this. You're making the next few weeks infinitely easier for me.*
>
> *I have neighbors whom I trust who are checking on my apartment from time to time. I don't know what could go wrong but I feel better having someone look in. They have your number if there are any issues.*
>
> *I made a reservation for you at the Marriott for the nights of the third, fourth, and fifth. It's close to where I'll be and very nice.*
>
> *You warned me my head might start playing games with me, and it has. However, I'm still solidly in "go" mode.*
>
> *I'll call you on the 2nd. Make sure you get your car checked out and drive safely. I worry about you coming all this way by yourself.*
>
> > *Love, Joe*

Reading Joe's words was both emotional and frustrating. "This is Joe, and" I said to the sisters, "something he wrote about what he was doing. And yet, it gives us so little information. You didn't give me this in an envelope. Was there one?"

Both sisters shook their heads no.

"So we have no idea where he was when he wrote this. We don't know where Aunt Maud was going on the third, fourth, and fifth, and we don't even know what month, or year for that matter, those days were on. The letter isn't dated."

"But there are some things to think about in there, Donna," Miriam pointed out. "At Joe's age, why did he need a medical power of attorney? Was he ill? Was he embarking on a trip to some dangerous part of the world? His absence was supposedly temporary, because he mentions 'the next few weeks.' And, he had someone watching his apartment so he obviously expected to be back."

"The thing that worries me most," Chris said, "is that comment about Aunt Maud warning him that his head might start playing games with him. And he said it had. What was that all about?"

"So what else is in the envelope?" I asked. I was really hoping there was something that would shed more light on the missing details in the letter.

The next thing they showed me was a snapshot of Joe. It was a full body shot of him standing in front of an overlook somewhere, the kind where you pull off the road, look out over the mountains beyond and the valley floor below. It looked like spring with the trees in the foreground not completely leafed out yet.

Joe's hair was long, about shoulder length, and, once again, he was wearing nondescript clothing. Jeans, a tee shirt, sneakers. He was slim and appeared to be in good shape. Not buff but healthy. The wind must have been blowing because it showed a smiling Joe with his hair streaming back from his face. He looked like an easygoing, nice guy. Approachable!

"Chris and I think that shot shows him maybe ten or so years after he left." Miriam had taken the picture from me and was looking at it intently.

"We've both examined it with a magnifying glass," Chris said. "We can see the maturity in his face; it's not the same Joe we last saw. We thought the printing on his tee shirt might tell us something, but it just seems to be a Celtic symbol of some sort." Her tone sounded dejected as she said, "The picture really didn't give us much."

I disagreed because I thought it told us something very important. "I don't know," I said. "The picture says Joe was alive and well a good many years after he left. And the letter tells you that too. I'm feeling a sense of relief just knowing that much. And I wouldn't be too concerned about the medical power of attorney. I think you might have nailed it when you mentioned traveling somewhere that has its perils. It would be normal to have second thoughts about that. Maybe Aunt Maud just wanted to see him off."

Miriam and Chris both looked at me, the emotion showing. "We sat at my kitchen table and cried when we found these," Miriam commented. "Well, we laughed and cried, I should say. You're right, Donna, there was a sense of relief knowing he was alive. We think that picture was taken quite a few years after Joe left. It's not solid evidence that he's still alive, but it does tell us that he didn't meet a bad end as a young kid out on his own. The letter does concern us though. A health issue just seems to be the logical explanation."

I agreed with that theory but didn't express it.

"Here," said Chris, handing me a piece of paper. "This is a copy of the letter and the picture that we made for you. And here is probably the most important thing we found." She handed me a copy of the Maud Morgan Trimbly Inter Vivos Trust. And that's when lunch arrived.

Lunch looked delicious, but that came as a surprise to none of us. It always is at Roush's Diner. What did come as a surprise was the man who walked up behind the waitress just as she asked if she could get us anything else.

"Yes!" he barked. The poor girl had no idea he was there, and she literally jumped straight in the air, letting out a little bell-like yelp. "Get me a Coke. Good and cold."

"Oh. You scared me. Sorry! Coming right up." She skittered off, and I wondered if she had the nerve to return.

Nobody had to tell me who this was. The infamous Harold was finally making his entrance with a distinct lack of good manners. No hellos, no how are yous, no good to see you girls. Harold just entered barking orders.

Miriam and Chris were both looking at him with disdain.

"Harold, you could ask nicely. Waitresses aren't lackeys, you know," Chris said, clearly embarrassed by her brother's behavior.

"I don't know what a lackey is, Chris. But I do know what a waitress is and I'm thirsty." With that, he turned to me and said, "You must be Donna Cain."

"I am," I replied, with as much cool as I could muster. "It's nice to finally meet you."

That got no response. Well, there goes any enjoyment I might have had with my heavenly smelling Reuben!

"Scoot in, Harold," Miriam said, as she maneuvered her body, her plate, and her glass to the left. Chris and I automatically made the same adjustments. But, apparently, Harold wasn't a scooter. He turned around and grabbed a chair from the next table without even asking the three people already seated there if that was okay. Granted it was empty, but you usually say something like "Will you be needing this?" Not Harold. Make it another round of disdainful looks, this time from three strangers as well as the three of us.

Harold sat down on the outside of the booth, putting him closer to me than I liked and totally in the way of the waitress and anyone else going by. Chris had slipped the trust, which I desperately wanted to see, back into the envelope.

The waitress set a very large glass of Coke in front of him and skittered off again. I doubted she'd be back to check on us.

"So, I figure you girls have had time to find Joe, if he can be found. Whadda ya got?"

My mouth was full, and Chris was drinking her tea through a straw and looking at Harold like he was the most boorish thing she'd ever seen. Miriam, however, was going through a transition that you could clearly read on her face. She was moving from "Oh damn, Harold's here" to "Hold on buddy!" I hadn't really seen the assertive side of Miriam, but I knew I was about to. Her eyes were boring holes in her brother, and he saw it coming. It was all I could do not to smile.

"Harold Tredloe," she began. "This is a process and it's one we're making progress on. If you're here to try and stop it, just get a to-go cup for your Coke and head right out that door. I'll pay your tab!"

I thought she might say more but she didn't. She just remained in a lock-eyed stare down with her big brother and didn't flinch. I kept chewing and Chris kept drinking.

Harold was left blowing in the wind. He either had to come back strong or soften his approach. You could see the wheels turning. He was looking at Miriam, with some surprise, though not as much as I expected. It was clear that they'd been through this drill before. Finally he turned his attention to me. Round One to Miriam!

"Mrs. Cain, maybe you'll give me some idea of where we stand. My sisters have never been cooperative."

Miriam didn't miss a beat. "You don't mean cooperative Harold, you mean submissive. And, while we used to play that role, we stopped a long time ago. So, we'll be happy to bring you up to speed on what we're doing. In fact, we'd be happy to have your help."

"I don't know anything, Miriam. What would I know?"

I desperately wanted to say, "Well, for starters, Harold, you know why he left. You were there. You may be the reason!" But that would clearly have been out of line on my part. Instead, I took another bite of Reuben.

And, much to Chris's and Miriam's credit, they didn't express that thought either, although I knew they had to be thinking it. Instead, Miriam brought poor Harold in from the cold making a clear effort to include him.

"Harold, we went through Maud's papers. After she died and we cleaned out her apartment, I'd put her papers in a plastic storage tub up in the garage rafters and kind of forgot about them. Chris and I pulled them down, and we've been working our way through the pile. Take a look at this letter. It's from Joe to Maud and it's pretty vague. It's not dated and there was no envelope with it so we don't have a return address to give us a clue where Joe was or when he wrote it. Maybe you'll have some ideas we haven't thought of."

We sat quietly while Harold read the letter. And we all saw the same thing. A man trying desperately to keep any signs of emotion off of his face but not entirely succeeding. He was reading the words of his only brother, whom he hadn't seen or heard from for over twenty years. That's when I realized that Harold's gruff and overbearing manner was probably due to fear. It was a show of strength, misguided as it was, in the face of his taking the first step to really find out what was going on. Our search for Joe could get very emotional and that scared Harold.

Harold read the letter twice and then flung it to the middle of the table and said, "I don't get it!"

"Well, Harold, neither do we," Chris said, with a sigh. "The fact that he gave her a medical power of attorney is concerning, but it doesn't necessarily mean he was sick. We're thinking he might have been going somewhere that was dangerous. Maybe a mission trip or something."

"Well, what was Maud doing mixed up with Joe anyway? That woman never could mind her own business."

Harold's comment made me remember his remark about Maud when he called me. I don't think he was overly fond of his mother's sister, maybe due to the fact that Maud was a very independent woman. I could easily imagine Maud and Harold butting heads.

"She was his aunt, Harold," Miriam replied. "That's obviously who Joe would turn to and she would have felt a responsibility to help him. She would have wanted to help him. They were always close and you know Aunt Maud. She was a social worker at heart, not just at work. But there's more. We were just about to show Donna this trust when you walked in. Aunt Maud established a trust, and Joe was the beneficiary."

With that, she pulled the trust from the envelope and handed it to me saying, "Donna, I think you're used to looking at things like this. Again, it's pretty vague, but maybe you can get more out of it than we did."

Finally, I had my hands on a document that might tell us something concrete. This was an inter vivos trust established about four years before Aunt Maud passed away. It was dated February 10, 2004. I was far more used to reading testamentary trusts that were established in someone's will and didn't go into effect until after the person died. But I'd read a few inter vivos trusts that, for one reason or another, had been recorded. Most weren't.

As I read through the pages, I realized that the terms on this one were a bit odd. Money from the sale of certain stocks was put into the trust (the amount was not revealed), and the interest was to be paid to Joe in quarterly payments over a two-year period with the first payment being September 30, 2004, and then continuing through June 30, 2006. A bank was designated as the trustee and had the authority (at Maud's direction) to withdraw from the principal at any time for Joe's benefit, or to stop or redirect the payments. At the end of the two-year period, the trustee, again at Maud's direction, would have the authority to maintain the status quo or redefine what would happen with the money. At Maud's death it would become a testamentary trust subject to the instructions in her will. The trust was to terminate ten years after her death with all principal being paid to the beneficiary, Joseph Morgan Tredloe.

"Tell Harold what it says," Miriam said.

I was surprised Harold had sat quietly while I read the thing. But, as Miriam requested, I explained it for Harold's benefit and, to my surprise, he didn't say anything. I could, however, see the wheels turning in his head. Finally, he got another dig in at Maud.

"She took that husband she had for a real ride. That divorce court judge should be shot. It would be one thing if Maud had earned her money, but it all belonged to that poor bastard who made the mistake of marrying her. She ended up loaded, and then she gives it away."

Again, the sisters ignored him, and I followed their lead.

Chris spoke first. "Do you think he had a medical issue that they knew was maybe going to be a long recovery? Maybe a two-year recovery?"

"Chris and I have thought about that initial two-year payout," Miriam said, "and we've come up with a medical reason that might prevent Joe from working, which seems most likely, or maybe it was for education. A master's degree can be done in two years, and Maud would definitely have supported that. Or, it could have been an extended trip somewhere. If he was doing some kind of mission work, she would have been all over that too. And that would explain both the need for money and the powers of attorney."

Harold was looking doubtful. "Maybe he was just screwing around, and she was giving him two years to get his act together! And if he didn't, no money from Auntie Maud!"

Well, there was Harold with another totally unhelpful comment. And again, Miriam and Chris chose to totally ignore him. This time it worked.

Harold took a deep breath and said, "Look. Maybe I haven't been too supportive of this effort. I just don't think it will go anywhere. But, I know what you girls want to hear from me. You want to hear that I'll help, or at least not get in the way. Well, not getting in the way is probably the best I can do. I would help, if I could, but I just don't have anything to contribute. And, Miriam, I'll take you up on paying my tab. Gotta go!"

And with that, Harold got up and headed for the door. The sisters and I sat there in silence, each of us knowing that Harold Tredloe had just taken a big step. Even I, an outsider, could recognize that!

Telling On Great-Uncle Axel

Harold's exit left us—happy. He'd made a commitment not to get in the way and we each knew that, in his own odd way, he was on board. Certainly not out in front leading the charge, but not running the other way either.

We all finished our lunch with some unimportant small talk and then got back to business.

"So where do we go from here?" Chris asked.

I realized that I hadn't told them about Tony's upcoming search in Pittsburgh and that was important.

"Here's something I forgot to throw in the mix," I said. "Our head abstractor for Taylor County has worked the Allegheny County Courthouse in Pittsburgh. He's heading up next Friday to get Maud's will and to do a real estate search as well. I thought Joe owning real estate was a long shot, but, with the trust money from Maud, Joe may have been able to buy a house or condo. I'll also have him look for use of the power of attorney alluded to in the letter. If Maud used it for anything in Allegheny County it should have been recorded."

"Will the will tell us more than the trust?" Miriam asked.

"It might. It's the final instructions, so you never know. And there's something else I haven't told you, although it really has no bearing whatsoever on finding Joe."

We were all ready for another subject. Thinking and planning and plotting on how to find Joe was emotionally exhausting, even for me. Add a visit from Harold and we needed a break.

Chris and Miriam both looked eager to hear what I had and at the same time said, "So what haven't you told us?"

"It's about Axel," I told them. And with that, I proceeded to tell them what Tony had found out and showed them copies of the article he'd given me.

The story left both women shaking their heads and expressing thanks that it was a long time ago. I gave them the names of a couple of books on the Banana Wars that Tony had suggested, and we paid our tab, headed out the door, and said our good-byes.

New information always has to settle with me, and I do my best settling while asleep. The letter and the trust were significant developments, and I knew my subconscious would be diligently at work overnight. At least, that's what I thought happened while I slept since I often awoke with totally new revelations. I've always wished I could tap into that area of my brain at will, but I've never figured out how.

It had been a long lunch but a productive one, and I headed home mid-afternoon mulling over the letter and trust. But my thoughts soon turned to a pleasant evening, as Sam and I were going to Josh and Lindsay's for a Saturday evening bonfire in their yard. They'd had them before, and we were usually the first to arrive and the first to leave. We always had a good time, but they and their decades-younger friends kept far later hours than Sam and I.

So That's What the Letter Meant

I t was Sunday morning, and Sam and I were up later than usual. He'd gotten up around five thirty to let the dogs out and feed them, and then came back to bed. We didn't crawl out again until after nine.

"Why did we stay out until after midnight last night? We never do that!" I said, with coffee cup in hand waiting for the brew to finish. The night before had been a beautiful one with perfect temperatures and a full moon. We sat around the bonfire in Josh and Lindsay's yard far longer than we usually do.

"I don't know. I guess we were having a good time, but I sure feel it this morning," Sam said. He was moving as slow as I was, and we both had lots of yard and garden work we wanted to do.

I cooked my usual scrambled eggs and toast, and Sam had oatmeal with honey and fresh strawberries. As I cooked, a conversation from the night before came back to me. It was something Josh said that really stuck with me. Sam had been on the other side of the fire talking to Lindsay and her friends so I was sure he hadn't heard it.

"Sam, sometimes I'm really proud of how Josh communicates. He has a real knack for getting to the heart of an issue."

"Like what?" Sam asked.

"Well, last night he was talking to Brian and Kevin and me, and he said that people will sometimes say to him something like 'Hey Buddy, when is it okay for me to shoot somebody?' Josh says that what they want him to tell them is that it's okay to shoot someone if they break into their house to steal something. And you know what he tells them? He says, 'You protect life with a gun, not property.' If they still don't get it, he goes on to explain the consequences, both financial and possibly criminal, of shooting someone who isn't threatening your life. But it's such a simple way to put it. You protect life with a gun, not property. I like it."

"I like it too, but you have an awful lot of armed people running around these days just itching for a reason to pull the trigger."

"I totally agree."

My eggs were ready so I ate and read the Sunday paper while Sam caught up on Facebook. But little by little, Joe's letter to Maud and Aunt Maud's trust seeped into my head and took center stage. And, true to form, my thoughts on what I'd read had become more cohesive and organized overnight.

I moved quickly through my standard Sunday morning routine, cleaning up the breakfast dishes, watering the plants, and changing both beds. Those things always came first, and, after that, it might be work or play, depending on how many chores needed to be done and just how pressing they were.

This particular Sunday, my main goal (besides the yard work) was to reread the copies of the letter and the trust that Miriam and Chris had given me. I needed to really concentrate and absorb the finer points. For some reason I'd come to the conclusion that Joe had not been planning a trip. It had seemed a perfectly logical option at our Saturday lunch, but now I wasn't buying it and I didn't know why.

I went to my office, got the copies from the file I'd put them in, and began to read the letter. I read it slowly once through and couldn't see why I'd gone negative on a trip. And then it hit me.

There was no sense of excitement, which a trip almost always instills in the traveler, even if it's a challenging trip. And, if the trust was funding whatever was being alluded to in the letter, then by the time Joe wrote this he was a grown man, probably in his early thirties. He thanked his aunt in advance for "driving all this way." Would Aunt Maud, at her age, travel a long distance just to see him off on a trip? That made sense if he'd been a kid, but he hadn't been.

I read the letter again and focused on Joe's line that said, "You warned me my head might start playing games with me, and it has. However, I'm still solidly in 'go' mode." That made me think that Aunt Maud, true to her social worker self, was there for moral support for Joe for whatever reason. But what?

And then along came revelation number two, an angle that Miriam, Chris, and I had not thought of. Maybe Joe was going into a rehab facility. People often traveled long distances for good programs, so that made sense. Being gone a period of several weeks certainly fit. And Aunt Maud wanting to be there when he was admitted was logical too.

And, as to the trust paying Joe for a two-year period, maybe Aunt Maud was funding schooling of some sort when Joe was released so he wouldn't have the pressure of working and going to school at the same time. Not having that pressure would make him less likely to relapse. The pieces of the puzzle all fit together very nicely.

The more I thought about it, the more I knew I was right. After all, Joe had left home at a young age with no further contact with his immediate family. That had to be a major stress and some kind of substance abuse wouldn't be unusual.

However, figuring this out really didn't help much. Substance abuse rehab centers would keep patient lists confidential. And besides that, we didn't even know what state Joe was in when he wrote that letter, so knowing what center to approach for information was out of the realm of possibilities anyway. But at least we had a viable answer to what the letter was alluding to.

Miriam, Chris, and I had exchanged email addresses so I sent them both a quick message saying I had an idea about what Joe might have been talking about when he wrote the letter. I suggested that we talk on Monday not really wanting to interrupt their weekend.

With a feeling of satisfaction, I headed for the yard and a sadly neglected flower bed. Sam was already at work in the garden. We both went at it hard until the sun got the better of us, and then it was time for a three o'clock baseball game, the Pittsburgh Pirates taking on the Milwaukee Brewers. Workday done!

A Mysterious Cousin

Monday morning at eight sharp, Miriam Baxter dialed my number.

"Donna, we didn't want to bother you on the weekend. What did you come up with?"

"Well, consider this scenario." I told her what I'd come up with and how I thought everything fit, even the money in the trust being extended over a two-year period.

When I finished, Miriam responded with slow and measured words, the manner you speak in when you're still processing the information.

"Donna, I don't think Chris and I even considered that possibility because we come from a family of pretty much teetotalers. It's hard to get Tredloes to take a pain pill when they really need it. But you're right. Joe could certainly have been abusing something because of his situation, or because he fell in with a bad bunch of friends. And Aunt Maud would have been constantly pushing him to get help. I have no doubt she would have been there when he was admitted, no matter where it was, if nothing else then to make sure he went in. I really can't find any holes in your theory."

"Miriam, I really think we have the answer, but, unfortunately, I don't think it will lead us anywhere. We don't know what state the rehab center was in, and, even if we did, even if we could identify the rehab center, they would never tell us he was there, let alone give us his home address or any other information they might have. It's nice to figure it out, but it doesn't really do us any good."

"You're probably right, but you never know when a piece of information will unlock another piece of the puzzle down the road."

"That's true," I agreed. "It's one more thing we know. Or at least we're pretty sure we know. I will say that if the money from the trust was for education or training of some sort for after Joe got out, those records would be more accessible."

"Sure. Names of graduates are pretty easy to come by. But again, we don't know where the school or training center might have been. I think we still have to focus on Pittsburgh for that unless the trail leads us elsewhere. And Donna?"

"Yes?"

"I'm glad you figured this out, but it adds a new worry to the list. People who need rehab have to struggle all their lives, even if they do manage to stay clean. And most don't. I guess I'm glad, on the one hand, that we have an answer that makes sense, but on the other hand, I wish it wasn't the case."

"I know, Miriam. But some people do stay clean and go on to lead happy and productive lives. I guess we just have to hope for that."

Miriam and I wrapped up our conversation, and Miriam said she was going to text Chris and tell her to call during her break. She wanted to bounce the whole thing off of her.

We both hung up with a plan and a sense of purpose and, I hoped, on Miriam's part, not too much more to worry about.

I went right to work making a list of the things I wanted Tony to check for in Allegheny County. First up was Maud's will. That was at the top of the list. And then the real estate records, especially after 2004 when the trust was established. And he needed to look for the paperwork showing power of attorney that Joe granted to Aunt Maud on the off chance it had been recorded.

The toughest part was going to be checking for school records. There were so many institutions, and there were more things we didn't know than we did. We didn't know if Joe went to school, and, if he did, we didn't know what kind. It could have been a one-year training program, or a four-year degree or an advanced degree program. And, for that matter, we didn't know if the school was even in Allegheny County.

I picked up the phone and called Tony.

"Hey, Tony. Are you in the courthouse?"

"No, Donna. I'm at home today putting title packages together. What's up?"

"Are you still planning on heading to Pittsburgh on Friday to check records for me?"

"Yes, and I've been thinking about the things I should check and where. Donna, the Pittsburgh metro area includes more than Allegheny County. There are five counties that surround Allegheny and the metro really spills out into all of them, so that's a total of six. He could have been in any one of them."

"Oh my, I hadn't really thought about that. Tony, let's start with Allegheny. That's where Maud lived, and it makes sense that Joe would want to be near her. Then if we come up empty-handed, we can do the others. But Tony, we have new information. Joe's sisters went through Maud's papers and found out she established a trust well before she died. Joe was the beneficiary and money was going to him as early as September 2004. We don't think Aunt Maud was giving him money to buy property, but we're not at all sure so it bears checking."

Having explained that, I went on to tell Tony about the letter, the POA, and more about the trust. I also told him my rehab theory. He agreed that it made sense.

"Donna, I'll check for everything once I'm there, but I'm going to do some advanced Internet searches before I go. I pay for a couple of services for when I'm doing heirships and have to find people. I have some access to criminal records and some pretty sophisticated ways to tap into social media."

"Good heavens, Tony. It never occurred to me to do a simple Facebook search. How easy is that!"

"I already did it, Donna. Nothing turned up. Tredloe is a very uncommon name, which is a good thing when you're looking for someone. But some people use aliases on these sites, and that would sure make sense for Joe if he's trying to fly under the radar. Anyway, I'm leaving Thursday afternoon, and I'll be ready to hit the courthouse early Friday. Email me a list of everything you want me to check so I don't accidentally forget something. I'm going to keep thinking too. I might come up with some other ideas."

Tony and I said good-bye, and I sat there thinking that most of the time I feel better doing things myself. But in this case, I was glad to have Tony doing the research rather than me. First of all, he knew the Allegheny County Courthouse a lot better than I did. And secondly, he was just very, very good at his job. And, I could tell from his voice, that he'd bought into this search too. It was getting personal and neither one of us would be happy until we found Joe.

I hadn't been off the phone more than a couple of minutes when it rang again. The caller ID said "Arnold Wilson."

"Hello, Professor Wilson."

"Good morning, Mrs. Cain. Has your aunt told you we're in the same class at Pitt?"

"She has, and it sounds interesting. We should probably all know more about how Congress really works."

"Well, I think we're learning how it's supposed to work. I'm afraid there may be a gap between what we're being taught and what's really happening. Especially these days."

I laughed, totally seeing his point.

"Mrs. Cain, I was able to make contact with a cousin of Joe's on the Morgan side. Her name is Jill Morgan, and she lives in Ohio. I remembered her from Maud's funeral but couldn't remember where she lived. A few days ago, it occurred to me that she had given me her phone number and address when Maud was living. She had come for a visit and Maud included me in their dinner plans. Maud was frail at that point, and her niece recognized that she might not be with us long. Miss Morgan wanted me to know how to get ahold of her if something happened to Maud. Thank goodness, it was still in an old address book I had."

"Wonderful. Does she know anything?"

"I don't really know. I called her and explained the situation. She was kind of quiet for a moment and then said to let her think things over. She said she didn't really think she had any helpful information but she didn't want to totally dismiss it. I didn't think I'd hear back from her, but I did. And rather quickly. She called me the next evening to say she would like to meet with you. She said she wanted to know more."

"That's kind of curious, don't you think?" I said. "I mean she either knows something or she doesn't."

"It does seem odd. But maybe she does know something and just doesn't want to tip her hand until she knows if she can trust you. That thought crossed my mind anyway. Or, she may just be nosy and not know a thing. It's hard to say."

"Well, either way, the answer to the question of whether or

not I will meet with her is a resounding yes. Did she say where and when?"

"She said that Washington, Pennsylvania, would be a good middle ground, but she didn't say when. She wanted me to find out if you're agreeable to that and call her back."

"Professor Wilson, I'm agreeable to just about anything that will help us find Joe."

"And Mrs. Cain, there's one more thing and it's very important. She had one stipulation and that is that you not tell any of Joe's siblings about this meeting. She was adamant about that!"

"That's fine. I've learned to step lightly when it comes to family issues. I won't breathe a word."

Professor Wilson promised to call me as soon as he knew a date and time, and we hung up. I was elated. If Jill Morgan knew absolutely nothing, why would she want to meet? That didn't make sense so I was placing my money on the fact that she had some information. And no matter how little it might be, it was more than we knew now. My hopes were definitely rising.

Earl's in the Clink

It was a sunny and bright Thursday morning, and I was going through my typical morning ritual with no warning signs to tell me anything was amiss. Sam went to work, and I downloaded an older title the office had sent the day before and then headed to the Taylor County Courthouse to rerun it. We suspected there was something not right.

As I pulled up to the courthouse I noticed more than the usual number of sheriff deputies' vehicles. There were also two WV State Police vehicles, one marked "canine," and two US marshals' SUVs. It did catch my interest, but I just figured circuit court was in session with a big criminal trial. I knew that if a police agency was involved in the investigation and arrest, they usually have to appear at trial. Hence, all the vehicles. I was wrong.

I walked in the door and collided with the chief deputy. He was on his knees on the floor, his cell phone up to his ear with his left hand, and his right arm halfway up the dispensing area of the snack machine. I was guessing he'd put his money in and not got what he had paid for.

I was apologizing for the collision when he said, "Mrs. Cain, good timing. Head on in to my office. I have to finish this call."

Looked like my plans were changing. Now I was thinking all those cars might not be for circuit court. Maybe we had a little drill-site drama going on here. Why else would he want to talk to me?

I headed to Chief Deputy Warner's office through the hall door, which was open, and had a seat, just like I was told. There was another door between his office and the reception area. It was standing open as well. That office housed the receptionist, a couple of extra desks where the deputies sometimes did paperwork, the copy machine, the coffee machine, and all the other office-type accoutrements that make an area the place where everyone congregates. And congregating they were. I was catching snatches of conversation like, "I've been up since seven yesterday morning . . ." and "Can you believe all the booby traps?" I was all ears, but Chief Warner came in before I could get a feel for what was happening.

"Good thing you asked us before you went to see Earl Crofton!" he said, while closing both doors and trying to open some cheese crackers that he'd somehow snagged. I never saw anyone put money in those machines, so I was figuring they were on the stale side.

"This isn't to go anywhere," he continued, "but I need to ask you something. You have the title to Crofton's place, right?"

"Not with me, but yes."

"How long would it take to go get it?"

"A couple of hours to get home and back, but what do you need to know? It might be faster getting the answers out of the record room."

"I have a feeling that farm's been used for some things I don't want to divulge right now—and, for a long time back. We need to know the owners over the last thirty years or so. Crofton hasn't been there more than a couple of years. Now, I know I could get somebody in the clerk's office to do that for me, but I don't want to start any speculation. Rumors are flying the way it is. Can I trust you to get that info and not say anything?"

I was baffled and intrigued and a little concerned, but I said yes without hesitation, telling the chief that I could get the information in the record room in a half hour or less. I'd even bring him copies of the deeds. He was pleased, and I set off to complete the task.

My concern stemmed from the fact that I was on company time doing the chief's bidding. However, I also realized that any help I gave him might speed up the investigation and get us back in business on that land sooner rather than later. I had no idea how long the two properties would be held up in court or even if they would be. Heck, I didn't even know what had happened overnight, but I was betting something had.

That question didn't linger long. The minute I walked in the County Clerk's office, the deputy clerks filled me in on what they knew, which was a lot more than I did.

"There was a big arrest last night, police everywhere," LeeAnn said. "We think it's that Earl Crofton guy, and someone said your company was putting a well near there."

"We plan on it," I replied. "Why do you think he was arrested?"

"That whole area was crawling with police and federal agents and US marshals," Sandy added. "My brother lives on the main road just before you turn in to the road the Crofton place is on, and he said whatever it was, it was big. He said they took more than one person out in a van. The lights were on in the back, and he thought there were three of them handcuffed to something, and one looked like Earl."

I wanted to know everything they could tell me, which wasn't much beyond what they had already said. Apparently, Earl had been nabbed along with a couple of cohorts. I figured I could bank on that much being true, but why? What was the charge? Or had he been charged? I headed down the steps to get the deeds the chief wanted, my head reeling with possibilities.

The chief was right; Earl Crofton had bought the tract about twenty-six months earlier. Prior to that it was owned by a Helena Vanscoy for just over eight years, and before her it was owned by two men with the last name of Gagne. Definitely not a local name. William and Ramone Gagne had held title to the property for thirty-one years. I vaguely remembered all these names from my review of the title on Crofton's property. But something else was afoot in my head, and I couldn't quite get a handle on what it was.

I copied all the deeds and headed back to the Sheriff's Department. They were on the chief's desk in twenty-six minutes flat. He was on the phone again but mouthed "thanks" and gave me a thumbs up.

I left there and headed straight to the Assessor's office next door. I pulled Crofton's tract up on the computer, hit the aerial tab to see an actual photograph, and zoomed out so I could look at the adjacent tracts. The coal company tract, our projected drill-site, was to the north and extended down a tad on the west side wrapping around part of Crofton's land. To the south, and also coming up on the west side of Crofton to meet the coal company tract, was the two hundred forty-seven acres, the old Hagen place, that the Tredloe heirs now owned the oil and gas on.

When you look at aerials, you can see houses, fields, creeks, ponds, roads, and rights-of-way; whatever you can see from the air you see on the computer screen. And, superimposed over the photographs are the lines showing the borders of each tract, so you can tell where the tract boundaries are. My focus zeroed in on the northernmost tract of the two hundred forty-seven acres that Barrett Tredloe had bought and sold in seven pieces.

The northern parcel was adjacent to Crofton's tract. I noticed that it was all woods with no structures, no rights-of-way, and no access roads visible on the aerial photograph. In fact, that was the case with all of the seven tracts that had originally been part of the Hagen farm. However, in that northernmost part next to Crofton's property, I could see one small, but continual, break in the trees. And that break led right to the Crofton place. It wasn't big enough to be a driveway or road, but it did indicate something— most likely, an ATV trail.

When we review title, and the oil and gas isn't running with the surface, as landmen we don't pay a lot of attention to the surface owners. I'd seen the names on the Crofton tract but had no reason to really remember them. But I had the feeling that I'd seen at least some of them somewhere else, and I had. The computer showed the current surface owner on the wooded tract adjacent to Crofton as Helena Vanscoy, the woman Earl Crofton had bought the sixteen acres from.

That was curious, and my mind started working a mile a minute. I quickly clicked on the other six tracts making up the Hagen farm, and every single one said Helena Vanscoy. Even though Barrett Tredloe had sold each tract to a different person, they were now all owned by Helena Vanscoy. I checked the assessments and, sure enough, they were all going to a Louisiana address.

I headed back to the record room and started pulling the deeds on the tract adjacent to Crofton. This was title I had at home, but I wanted the answer now. Just as I thought, the adjacent forty-one acres, the northernmost tract of the old Hagen farm, followed the same owners back as Earl's tract. This was getting more interesting by the minute. I went as far as the Gagne brothers and was about to take my information to Chief Warner when it struck me that maybe some kind of nefarious use of the property went all the way back to that initial sale from Barrett Tredloe.

I remembered Tony saying that when Barrett Tredloe sold the seven parcels that made up the two hundred forty-seven acres, those tracts had gone to people in Louisiana. That sparked another thought. I hit the browser on my cell phone, went to Google and typed in "Gagne name origin." It said "French." It was a French name, and one site noted that it was a common name in Louisiana.

I was happy Tony was working at home. If he'd been in the record room, he would have wondered what I was up to, and I wouldn't have been able to tell him per the chief's orders. Since he was heading to Pittsburgh in the afternoon, he'd stayed at home in the morning checking some online Allegheny County sources for anything on Joe. If he found something, it might give him a head start and make his time in the courthouse on Friday more productive.

Next I searched for the deed to William and Ramone Gagne. But the Grantee Index for *G* showed no property transfers to William and Ramone. If they didn't get the property by deed, then someone probably died and left it to them. I headed for the fiduciary records, hoping that person's name was Gagne. In Taylor County there was one, and only one, Gagne in the will book index. As the will made clear, Charles Gagne was the father of William and Ramone, and his will had been recorded as an out-of-state will in Taylor County. It had been probated in St. Bernard Parish where Charles had lived. I went back to the Internet, and it showed St. Bernard Parish was located just east of New Orleans.

Charles Gagne's will was signed and dated in 1958, but the senior Gagne didn't die until January of 1971. The 41.8-acre tract of land, the northernmost surface parcel in the two hundred forty-seven acres, was willed to William and Ramone with the stipulation that there be no timbering, no rights-of-way, and no structures. That was odd.

So I went back to the Grantee Index, letter *G*, to see if Charles got it by deed, and he had. In 1931, Charles Gagne was deeded the land by Jacque Prudhomme. I didn't have to look that one up to know it was both French and a common Louisiana name. It was also ringing a bell; sure enough, Prudhomme had bought the land from Barrett Tredloe in 1916 with the oil and gas clearly reserved to Barrett.

When Barrett Tredloe sold to Prudhomme, he had put no stipulations on the use of the property. But, when I checked the deed from Prudhomme to Charles Gagne, I saw Prudhomme had stipulated no timbering, no structures, and no rights-of-way, just like Charles Gagne did in his will. Something was going on here. Going back to 1916, the owners of the property wanted to make sure it stayed wooded and unoccupied. But wait a minute. I hadn't really read the deed I'd copied from William and Ramone to Helena Vanscoy. It was in my file and, sure enough, it had the same restrictions.

In West Virginia, the obvious reason to keep a tract wooded was for hunting. But surely they'd want to build a hunting cabin, especially if they were traveling all the way from Louisiana. The restrictions placed on the land didn't make a lot of sense.

I knew I should go straight to the chief with this find, but I wanted some time to think about it. And, besides that, I really needed to get started on the title I'd come to do some problem solving on in the first place. This proved to be easy when I found a missed deed and the whole thing suddenly made sense. It took about forty-five minutes to finish the job, and I was headed home.

I walked in the door around two, and the first thing I did was check the title on the other six tracts that made up the Hagen farm.

Barrett hadn't sold any of them to Jacque Prudhomme. However, within two years, each of the owners he had sold to had then transferred their title to Prudhomme. Obviously, that was the plan in the first place. After it got into Prudhomme's hands, the surface followed the exact same path that the northernmost tract did; Prudhomme to Charles Gagne, Charles to William and Ramone, and then, from them to Helena Vanscoy. Roads, rights-of-way, and structures were prohibited in all of the deeds.

I spent the rest of my day with all this information churning through my brain. I ended up with lots of theories but no real evidence. As a consequence, I alternated between feeling guilty about not going back to the chief with what I'd found, and then thinking that it would turn out to be nothing and I'd be embarrassed. Finally, Sam came home.

He walked around the garden, kicked the soccer ball for the lab, and eventually made his way to the house. He walked in the door looking sweaty and tired and said, "It's way too hot and muggy to cook much. I bought a good loaf of crusty bread and two steaks, so why don't you make a big salad, I'll grill the steak, and we'll call it a day!" I thought it was a fine plan.

My brother was at a county-recycling board meeting and was going to grab something to eat on the way home, so I agreed wholeheartedly with the menu. A dinner without a potato is not on my brother's list of acceptable meals. We often eat rice while he eats potatoes, and everyone is happy.

"Sam, I've got to talk something out with you," I said, while pulling lettuce, mini-peppers, olives, and grape tomatoes from the fridge."

"What's wrong?"

"Nothing's wrong, but I think I might have stumbled onto something."

With strict orders that it was totally confidential, I told him about the task the chief had assigned me and the information I'd found for him. I filled him in on what the clerks had told me about Earl Crofton and two others being taken out in handcuffs. I then explained the ownership history on the tracts, the restrictions on the land, and the fact that the beginning of all this, whatever "this" was, may have gone as far back as the conveyances out of Barrett Tredloe. And in my mind, that really meant it went back to Axel.

"Sam, I have a feeling Barrett Tredloe was a pawn in all this. He may have been totally unaware of what was really going on or just refused to see it. Here's the theory I think most likely: I think the buying and selling of the Hagen property was a money laundering scheme for Axel. He had money he stole or got from illegal sources, and he needed to park it for a while in something that would hold its worth. Land's usually good for that. And, he had to do it in Barrett's name because if he went to jail for whatever was going on, the courts could take the land."

Sam was nodding his head, indicating he was with me so far and it made sense.

"And then the tracts were sold to people in Louisiana. Was this how Axel got his money back? Or, did he owe all these people money, and that's how he paid them? But whatever happened, why did they let Barrett keep the oil and gas? They were from Louisiana and that's oil and gas country, so they knew what the minerals could be worth. It just doesn't make sense!"

"Well, Donna, here's a thought. Did you ever consider that Barrett's getting the oil and gas might have been a way to buy his silence? Maybe he got it in return for looking the other way. Or maybe that was the deal with Axel from the beginning. Maybe Axel told him, 'If you buy this property and agree to sell it when I tell you to, you can keep the oil and gas.' I mean, even though it was Axel's money, it took time and effort on Barrett's part to do all the buying and selling. He should have gotten something. Maybe Axel had to sweeten the pot to get him to do it. After all, Barrett had to know the money wasn't clean."

"That does make sense, Sam. You know, Miriam and Chris see Barrett as an honest man, but they also say he was very protective of Axel. He had to know Axel wasn't always walking the straight and narrow."

"But, Donna, you haven't told me what happened out there last night. Why were Crofton and the other guys arrested?"

"I don't know and the chief isn't saying. He told me to keep quiet, but he didn't really tell me anything concrete to keep quiet about. He wanted to know the ownership on the Crofton tract for the last thirty years or so, and I got that for him in short order. But then, on a hunch, I took a closer look at the surface deeds on the Tredloe oil and gas acreage, which is the two-hundred-forty-seven-acre Hagen farm that Barrett bought and sold in parcels."

Sam looked puzzled. "What made you do that?" he asked.

I explained that I'd brought it up on the Assessor's computer system and then switched on the aerial photo option.

"Sam, that northernmost tract, a little over forty-one acres, has no access. You can't see a driveway or even a tractor road coming in from the main road through the other tracts. But you can see a slight break in the trees indicating some kind of path going to Barrett's original homeplace, the sixteen acres Crofton is now living on. That seemed odd, and that's why I checked it out. That, and the fact that the Gagne and Prudhomme names seemed familiar from someplace else, and they were. I would have seen them on the title of the two hundred forty-seven acres, but I wouldn't have paid much attention because they didn't own the oil and gas. They were just surface owners."

"And the deeds going back were in lockstep with Crofton's tract until you got to Crofton?"

"I was just looking at the northernmost tract of the Hagen farm at first, but yes, Helena Vanscoy owned that and the Crofton tract until she sold to Crofton. But that's not all. The entire Hagen farm, all seven tracts, was eventually owned by Helena Vanscoy, and it all has the same restrictions in the deeds. No development or structures of any kind. It's wooded land with no pastures, no nothing. Do you think I should go to the chief with this?"

"Donna, I absolutely do. It bears investigating. If it's nothing, it's nothing. The police are used to running down leads that go nowhere. They do that all the time."

And then I remembered Tony's connection to his friend's wife in the library system in Louisiana. She'd have access to all kinds of research sources including newspaper articles, which might tell us quite a lot. I had a feeling Prudhomme and the Gagnes weren't the most savory of fellows, and their names just might have been in the local rags more than once.

"What are you thinking?" Sam asked, after watching me with a glazed-over look on my face.

"I'm thinking I have to bring Tony into this. He has a friend in Louisiana whose wife is a researcher in the state library system. If we feed the names to her—Prudhomme, the Gagnes, and Helena Vanscoy—we might at least find out what they were up to. If there's no evidence that they were criminals or shady, then I'm probably wrong."

Sam agreed that it was a good idea, so I picked up the phone and called Tony. It was about seven thirty Thursday evening, and he'd just finished dinner at his brother's house in Greentree, a southern suburb of Pittsburgh. I could hear kid's voices in the background.

I didn't tell Tony everything, just that I had a hunch that might prove interesting, and I wondered if his friend would be willing to run Jacque Prudhomme, the three Gagne names, and Helena Vanscoy through her databases. Tony teased me about being so mysterious but said he'd email her right away. We chit-chatted for a while about his plans for the next day's search and then hung up.

The Professor Gets Caught

I slept fitfully that night. I was in the midst of one of those early morning dreams where you're half asleep and half awake. My last solid dream image was of me on the deck of a pirate ship with a swarthy, Hollywood version of a pirate. Even while waking I was grasping that image, trying to hold it in my mind's eye and I was smiling. Good grief, it was Johnny Depp! He could make me smile any day. However, the more awake I got the more I realized the dream probably began on a decrepit banana boat with that bone-headed Axel running the show. Glad I dressed it up a bit.

Wakefulness also brought the realization that I had to dump all this stuff about the ownership history of the land in the chief's lap and get on with all the other things I got paid to do. Finding Joe was tops on my list, but I had many other tasks that needed attention as well.

It was Friday, the day Tony was searching the Allegheny County records and the day I was to meet with William and Jenna Parker on an oil and gas lease on their one-and-a-half-acre lot. Mr. Parker was a geologist working for the oil and gas company that supplied gas to homes, businesses, and industry in the area. I was indebted to him because he'd helped me with four of his neighbors who had been very difficult to deal with. They had listened to him, though. I had already talked to two of them, and they seemed much more inclined to at least look at the lease documents and then meet with me.

I had prepared the Parkers' documents after our first conversation and mailed them, so they'd have a chance to review. My meeting was at eleven, and it was really to discuss the terms and see if we could come to an agreement. I printed a second copy for me, made some phone calls, and was ready to go.

I was almost to the Parkers' house when my cell rang, and it was Tony.

"Donna, I have Maud's will, and there is something here of interest. She doesn't really shed any more light on the trust or the purpose of the trust except to direct that all of her remaining assets go into it. However, her executor is Professor Wilson and, after her death, the will directs that he would become her trustee, rather than the bank."

"Tony, that means Professor Wilson does know about Joe. You're not the trustee of a trust and not know anything about the beneficiary!"

"My thoughts exactly, Donna."

I was quiet for a moment, mulling this latest revelation over. I could feel things coming together, but I was too distracted at the moment to get all the pieces in place.

"Tony, I know the will won't tell you how much money was already in the trust, but does her appraisal and settlement show how much more money went in after she died?"

"Yep. It was just over one point two million."

"Good grief! Miriam and Chris said their aunt did very well in the divorce and then invested wisely. She must have, because I can't imagine she ever accumulated that much as a social worker."

"I agree, Donna. It looks like Maud was one shrewd lady."

"Tony, the part about Professor Wilson being the current trustee is very revealing, and I need to think it through some more. But I'm headed to an appointment and have to run. If you turn up anything else, call me."

"Will do. I may hear from Lenai soon too. I fed her the names last night."

Lenai was his buddy's wife who was the research librarian. I thanked Tony for his help and hung up. I was willing to bet Professor Wilson knew exactly where Joe was, so why this mysterious meeting with Joe's Ohio cousin? Of course, it hadn't been scheduled yet, so maybe it was just a diversion. I was confused.

My meeting with the Parkers went well. There were a few changes they wanted, but they were very reasonable and I felt I could get an approval from the company on all of them. I told them I'd be back with them as soon as I knew, and headed out the door. I hoped the distraction I was feeling wasn't apparent to them.

Back in the car, I got a grasp on the information my brain had been searching for. It was Miriam's disclosure to me that Aunt Maud had sent twenty-five thousand dollars to her, Chris, and Harold well before her death. There was a reason for that: Aunt Maud did not want them at the reading of her will, but she didn't want to leave them out either. Before she died, she gave them china and crystal and family quilts in addition to the money. Those are all things very commonly bequeathed to people in a will, but Aunt Maud didn't do it that way. She was protecting Joe's privacy, and Professor Wilson was in on the whole thing hook, line, and sinker.

But again, why? Why did Aunt Maud not try and build a bridge between Joe and his family, at least between Miriam and Chris and Joe? Who knows what Harold had done. Maybe he didn't deserve to know where his brother was, but what had Miriam and Chris done to deserve losing Joe.

No doubt about it. We were getting closer. And then, the phone rang again. It was Tony.

"Donna, those names you gave me. Bad dudes, Donna. Really bad dudes!"

"Do you mean Prudhomme and the three Gagnes?"

"Yes. Nothing came up on Helena Vanscoy other than society page mentions, according to Lenai. I'm forwarding you an email with attachments as we speak. Lenai downloaded copies of the newspaper articles. But you're not at home, are you?"

"No, I'm headed into Taylor County to record a will. But, I can stop at the library, forward the email from me to the library, and get printouts. I don't want to wait until I get home. So, it's interesting stuff?"

"Oh yeah. I'm not sure what mystery you're trying to solve, but these guys made for interesting reading!"

Tony's email popped through within seconds, and curiosity changed my plans. Instead of going to the courthouse first, I made a beeline for the Taylor County Library, a small but very nice facility. They have a good family genealogy section that I sometimes use to untangle local families I have to bring forward from a hundred years ago or more. And, to cap it all off, the people who work there are wonderfully helpful and nice.

I checked the email and saw there were four attachments for a total of twelve pages. I asked the librarian working the desk if I could forward the message to the library and get the printouts. She gave me the email address, and we were in business. It took six minutes and a dollar twenty for me to have all twelve pages in hand.

Seven of the pages contained newspaper articles, and the other five were excerpts from various histories or other works on Louisiana characters most noted for graft, corruption, and crime.

I found a comfortable seat and started reading, beginning with the articles.

Jacque Prudhomme was a well-to-do importer and businessman who had owned quite a few warehouse facilities on the docks, as well as the cranes and other equipment needed to unload ships. I knew that docks worldwide had always had the reputation of being a seedy, underbelly kind of environment, and it didn't sound like Prudhomme had done much to improve the image. He'd been charged twice with importing stolen antiquities and rare minerals, specifically Mayan statuary and Guatemalan jade.

On my two trips to Guatemala we had visited Mayan ruins where our guides had explained that over the ages, some of the most valuable statuary had been stolen and sent out of the country. And, on both trips, our last two days had been spent in Antigua, a beautiful old city that was once the colonial Spanish capital of Central America and is now Guatemala's most popular tourist city.

Both times we stayed in a centuries-old hotel that had once been a convent. It was a rambling one-story building made from now-decaying brick and stucco, both of which were part of the charm. There was an open courtyard in the center filled with tropical plants and birds, and that was surrounded by a veranda on all four sides. The veranda provided a very charming dining area, and the food was excellent.

Just outside the hotel entrance was an upscale jewelry store with guards stationed at the door. Armed guards are common in Antigua. I remember walking to a small, urban minimall on my first trip. We were going down a very nice, tree-lined street when Harris, my fellow Rotarian who was on the WVU Dental School faculty and led the trips, pointed up ahead to where seven or eight guys were standing on the walk outside a good restaurant. "Those are personal guards," Harris told us. "Whoever they're guarding is in the restaurant." Sure enough, as we got closer, while you didn't see their weapons, you could clearly see that their clothing was hiding weapons. Lots of humps and bumps and bulges. Different world.

But, the two guards outside the jewelry store were there primarily to guard the jade that the store specialized in. I had gone inside on my first trip and learned that jade comes in colors other than green, but that green is the most valuable and prized. And it was very expensive. That was about all I remembered, not being a jewelry or gem buff.

The article I was reading said that Jacque Prudhomme was charged twice with the importation and sale of illegal goods, and twice he beat the rap. It painted Prudhomme as a man who was well-connected and able to pay his way out of any predicament. The next article was a translation of a story in a 1928 Guatemala City newspaper about the theft and export of Guatemalan jade. The Guatemalan officials quoted in the article fingered Prudhomme as the mastermind, the guy directing and paying for one of the biggest jade smuggling operations in the country. And, it made it very clear that it was the unscrupulous thugs in the banana trade who were on the frontlines plundering the nation's antiquities and jade at Prudhomme's bidding.

I tried to put it all together. We had Axel in the banana trade in Central America; Prudhomme owned unloading facilities and warehouses on the docks in New Orleans where the bananas and contraband were received; then Prudhomme ended up with land in Taylor County, West Virginia, all of which had once been owned by Axel's brother, Barrett. My original theory had been that Axel owed money to all the people Barrett had sold the seven tracts of land to and, when Axel couldn't pay up, he told Barrett to deed them the land in lieu of money. Now I was thinking maybe that wasn't the reason. I kept on reading.

Next up was a newspaper article on Charles Gagne, father of William and Ramone. It was dated 1952 and was just a short blurb on his trial and conviction for money laundering and tax evasion. There wasn't much detail, which told me that he probably wasn't that big of a fish. The next article noted that Gagne had been released from prison after serving thirty-one months of a four-year sentence. He'd apparently been a model prisoner so the parole board sent him home. The money laundering and tax evasion charges fit in nicely with crimes that would have to be committed if you were bringing stolen property into the country. I figured Charles Gagne and Jacque Prudhomme were in cahoots, and Prudhomme was calling the shots.

But then came Charles Gagne's sons, William and Ramone. Several short blurbs from New Orleans newspapers showed them charged with petty crimes including theft, consorting with prostitutes, and public drunkenness. While the articles on Prudhomme and Charles Gagne led me to believe they were into more sophisticated crimes, the information on William and Ramone painted them as garden-variety ne'er-do-wells. They were two-bit criminals who never made the headlines but lived in the small print in the second section, bottom of page ten. And then, only if space allowed.

My imagination was running wild. I had something, but I didn't know what. I gathered my documents and headed for the chief.

Maybe I Do Know Something

Before leaving the house that morning, I had put together a simple timeline for the chief. It had two columns with the first showing the ownership of the sixteen-acre Tredloe homeplace, now Crofton's. Beside it, I detailed the ownership of the northern tract of the two hundred forty-seven acres. I knew that looking at it side by side made it more clear and impactful. Below, I noted that the other six tracts had been sold to Prudhomme as well, and from there on, they followed the exact same ownership path.

On my way to the courthouse and the chief's office, I tried to remember what he knew and what he didn't know. Wow! There was a lot the chief didn't know, beginning clear back with Axel. He had lived a long time ago, so there was no reason the chief would have known anything at all about Axel's antics in Central America and New Orleans. I'd only provided him part of the title on the Crofton tract, and I hadn't given him anything about the ownership of the tract adjacent to it. He had no idea that it ran in step with Crofton's tract. But did any of this mean anything? I kept swinging between being sure I had something concrete and thinking it was all smoke. I decided if the chief was available, I'd talk to him. If he wasn't, I might just hold up and dig a little deeper.

Less than five minutes later I was walking down the hall towards his office. The outer office was empty, so I peeked through the chief's door and there he sat, brow furrowed, two feet on the desk, leaning back in his chair with his arms crossed.

"Mrs. Cain, whadda ya got?"

Well good grief, was he expecting me to have something? I guess it was the papers in my hand.

"I'm not sure, but I've come across some information that I find interesting, and I thought you should know about it. Maybe it means something, maybe it doesn't."

I laid the paper in front of him with the two columns showing the timeline of ownership on the Crofton sixteen-acre tract and on the northern tract of the two hundred forty-seven acres. Exactly the same ownership until Helena Vanscoy sold the sixteen acres to Crofton. I then noted that the ownership on the other six tracts on the Hagen farm went in lockstep with the northern tract.

I could see the wheels start to turn in the chief's head. He put both feet on the floor and pretty much came to attention.

"So how big is this other tract? And all those other ones, too?" he asked.

"A little over forty-one acres in the northern tract. All seven tracts together come to two hundred forty-seven acres," I replied. The chief was definitely interested.

"Where is it in relation to the Crofton place?"

"It borders it on the south and southwestern side. And Chief, it's all heavily wooded and there's nothing on it. Deeds and wills going back to Jacque Prudhomme have restricted any development on the property! And I think there's more you should know."

The chief was barking orders on the radio now, calling in his lead investigator. He wasn't far away, but, while we waited, the chief alternated between thanking me for coming in and impressing on me just how important it was that I not talk to anyone about what I knew. I heartily agreed because I really didn't know what I knew. All I had was a set of facts that bore no conclusion, at least to me. I was getting the feeling, though, that it was making some sense to the chief!

Detective Bob Bauer joined us and the doors were closed. The chief handed him the sheet showing the lines of ownership and then suggested that I start at the beginning, so I did. I could see from the looks on their faces that they didn't expect the beginning to be quite so far back.

I explained Axel Tredloe's involvement in the Banana Wars in Guatemala and Honduras. I told them about Barrett buying the seven tracts in the old Hagen place with Axel's money and about how he sold it all to people in Louisiana. I explained how Prudhomme bought the northernmost tract but all the people who bought the six other tracts sold to Prudhomme within a couple of years. And, I told them about the restrictions on timbering and rights-of-way and structures, which were included in the deeds and wills associated with the land. I then handed them the articles and information I had just received from Tony, dividing them up between them.

To say they read with interest would be an understatement. They would periodically look at each other in a meaningful way. I saw light bulbs going off and questioning looks as they tried to make sense of things.

They were trading the articles back and forth. Detective Bauer finished first and then shuffled through all of the papers again, finally looking at me and saying, "But what about Helena Vanscoy? You left her out?"

"I didn't leave her out," I said. "The researcher just didn't come up with anything meaningful on her in Louisiana. There were some society page mentions but I guess not much more."

I hadn't explained how I'd gotten the information on Prud-homme and the Gagnes, so I told them about Tony's friend Lenai, carefully adding that I hadn't told Tony why I wanted the information.

"So, Mrs. Cain, you think this bunch was smuggling stolen jade and art or statues or whatever up here?" the chief said.

"I have no idea, Chief. It's just that Tony and I—Tony is our head abstractor who did this title—have been saying all along that there's a story as to why this land was bought and sold like this. Not the Tredloe homeplace that Crofton lives on, but the two-hundred-forty-seven-acre Hagen place that Barrett Tredloe bought with Axel's money and then sold, but reserved the oil and gas. New Orleans was apparently home base for people in the Banana Wars like Axel. These tracts were all sold to people in Louisiana, so we figured Axel owed them money he couldn't pay so he paid them off with land. But the fact that all of the land ended up with Jacque Prudhomme—it just seems fishy. What did this guy from Louisiana want with all of this land that he bound up with restrictions so nothing could be done on it?"

Detective Bauer was looking at me oddly. "And tell me why you know all this?" he asked.

I explained that to do the oil and gas title, we start with the surface title and go clear back to the eighteen hundreds. We then come forward again following the oil and gas if it's reserved in any of the deeds along the way.

"Bottom line, Detective Bauer, none of what I'm telling you has a thing to do with the oil and gas ownership. The only reason Tony and I paid attention was because the current heirs I'm working with told me some stories that had come down about Axel. The stories were interesting and I told Tony. Tony happened to know about the Banana Wars and got curious, so he asked his friend's wife, Lenai, to run Axel Tredloe's name through her data-bases. Like I said earlier, she's a researcher in the Louisiana library system. She found some information and it pointed to Axel being quite involved in the banana trade as well as all kinds of illegal activities that apparently went hand in hand with it. To us, it was just a good story. But maybe it's more."

The chief was quiet as a mouse, but I could see his mind going a mile a minute. Detective Bauer was thinking hard as well, so I just kept quiet. Finally, the chief started talking again.

"Bauer, we need to see an aerial of this land!"

"I looked at it in the Assessor's office the other day," I told him. "It's densely wooded, no rights-of-way, no structures, no roads. But, on the northern part, you can see a slight break in the trees indicating some kind of path or narrow trail from the Crofton property."

They both looked at me like I had two heads.

"How did you get your hands on an aerial?" the chief blurted.

"Right next door in the Assessor's office, Chief. They have them for the whole county. You can just pull them up on the computer and print them if you want a copy. Well, for five bucks."

I was always amazed at how little one office in a courthouse sometimes knew about another.

But the chief dispelled that thought, saying, "I knew that. Forgot!"

He headed to the outer office, got five dollars from petty cash and sent me next door to get a copy.

I was back in no time, and I could tell he and Detective Bauer had talked about what to do with me. I still didn't know much, but I knew something was up and they were trying to keep the lid on it, whatever it was.

I handed the chief the aerial photo. I'd zoomed out so you could clearly see the northern tract, Crofton's sixteen acres, and another five hundred feet or so surrounding it on all sides. Any access, or lack thereof, was clearly visible.

"Chief, those photos were taken in 2010, so they're a couple of years old. I guess some things could have changed," I told him.

"I doubt it, Mrs. Cain, I doubt it. From everything we saw out there, the Crofton place was surrounded by woods and not much else. Look, it was a heads-up move on your part to realize that what you knew might be important. Hell, you even started digging out the facts. The word on the street is that it was a big drug bust. The media is beating on us for the details, but we don't think we have the whole picture yet. We think there was some drug activity, but it may just have been a diversion in case we did come in. All that booby trapping on the coal company tract made it look like a drug operation. That's what people do to keep you out of their meth labs and marijuana fields. But we didn't find much of that going on."

The chief asked again that I keep it all under my hat saying, "We honestly don't know what we've gotten ahold of here. And with what you've told us, we probably need to call in some experts. But we want you to know that we do appreciate your help."

"I'll stay quiet, I promise you that. But you do have to understand that I'm being paid to get these tracts under lease and in a position to develop the oil and gas. With all that's happening, I just hope that's going to be possible."

"We could have it tied up for a while, but I promise you that I'll do all I can to free it up as fast as we can for your purposes. We know whose nickel paid for all this work and we won't forget it. Can we call you if we have questions about the ownership?"

"Not a problem," I said.

Chief Warner and Detective Bauer both gave me their cards, and I gave them mine.

"And about Helena Vanscoy," Detective Bauer said, "anything on her would be helpful."

I told him I'd do some online searching. Women were always harder to research than men because of potential name changes with marriages and divorces, but I figured something would come up.

When I left the chief's office he was poring over the aerial and Detective Bauer was going through the articles again. As usual, my curiosity was working overtime. Just what had I stumbled on?

After the meeting in the chief's office, I recorded the out-of-state will I'd recently received from a county in Florida. It was part of the chain of another tract I was trying to lease, and I'd been waiting weeks to get it. Some courthouses fill your requests quickly and some take their good old time about it. As soon as I was done, I headed for home. It was just after four when I got in my car and the phone rang. It was my third call of the day from Tony.

"Donna, I've looked at real estate records and haven't found Joe's name anywhere. And there's no recorded power of attorney. I haven't done the schools yet, but I think I can do that from home. I have a feeling you can access alumni lists online."

"Yeah, I would think so, Tony, but I'm not even sure you should try. Now that we know Professor Wilson is the trustee on the trust, I think he's the guy we have to work on. It's been a busy day, and I haven't had time to think about it much, but that seems like our key."

"I agree Donna, but I figure Joe's calling the shots. Think about it. If Joe was dead and Professor Wilson knew the family was actively looking for him, well, that they were on board for you looking for him, don't you think he'd tell you?"

"Yes. I do. Good point, Tony. If Joe was deceased what reason would the Professor have to keep it a secret?"

"So, Donna, maybe Professor Wilson isn't the one in charge. He might not be talking because Joe doesn't want him to talk."

"You could very well be right, Tony, but what about the whole proposed meeting with the cousin? I'm not sure now how that fits in."

"Well, here's another line of thought. It's possible that Wilson doesn't know Joe. Think about it. The person appointed as trustee on a trust is someone that the person setting up the trust has confidence in. In this case, we can assume that Aunt Maud trusted Professor Wilson so she made him trustee. But really, he and Joe may not have known each other at all. I mean, it's possible the payouts from the trust are going directly into a bank account that Joe has access to. Maybe Professor Wilson has sent information through the bank that you're looking for him. Maybe the cousin is someone Joe knows well. If he wants someone to check you out and get a better sense of what you're up to, he'd probably choose someone he's close to. But Donna, I'm just saying it's possible. I don't think it's the likely scenario."

"I'm sure glad you're a part of this, Tony. I'm not sure my mind would have gone down that road but I agree, it is a possibility."

"And think about this, Donna. If the family wanted to find Joe, they might use the promise of money to tempt him. For all he knows, this whole lease thing could be one giant story to get him to come forward. You could be someone the family hired to find Joe and you're just using the lease story as bait! You know Joe probably doesn't need the money, but he wouldn't realize that you know that."

"Oh Tony, surely he doesn't think that!"

But then the realization that we all see things from our own point of view kicked in and I knew Tony could be right. From Joe's point of view this could be one big hoax!

"Well, Tony, for now let's put all our eggs in Professor Wilson's basket. Call off the search until we give this some time and see what happens. I just really, really hope that Joe comes around if he's the guy calling the shots. I'm going to call Miriam Baxter and let her know the deal with Professor Wilson. Can you scan me a copy of the will when you get home?"

"Sure, but it'll be Sunday. I'm heading to a Pirates–Padres game with my cousin and his wife tomorrow afternoon and then, out on the town."

I told Tony to enjoy himself and decided to wait until I got home to call Miriam Baxter. But after thinking about it a little more, I decided to wait until Saturday. I really needed to sort out what I should tell her and what I shouldn't. Finding Joe was very personal to her and Chris. If they knew that Professor Wilson was the trustee on a trust that benefitted Joe, they might just pick up the phone and call him. He had a landline and the number was probably available. I really couldn't not tell them about the Good Professor's involvement, though, because Miriam and Chris knew Tony was in Pittsburgh getting the will. They would want to know what it said, and they would eventually read it and know I'd held out on them. I needed to think about this one.

Food and Wine Always Help

I pulled into the drive at home and, before I could get out of my car, Sam pulled in beside me. The hound was baying, as he always does when we get home, and the lab was madly dashing around the yard in search of his soccer ball.

"You look tired," Sam said, while kicking the ball just dropped at his feet.

"I shouldn't be, but I am. I think it's mental fatigue. I've got a lot of new information today, and my brain is working overtime trying to sort it all out."

Sam was looking like he had something up his sleeve.

"Well, I think you should fill me in over a glass of wine and a good dinner that I didn't cook."

Since I knew he didn't mean a good dinner that I cooked, I quickly said yes to the invitation to go out. I needed some downtime.

Sam and I both took quick showers, put on clean clothes, told my brother to order take-out from the local watering hole (they really did have good food), and headed into Morgantown still trying to figure out which restaurant we wanted to go to.

We ended up at a locally owned establishment downtown that we were both fond of. It was the first place I'd ever had shrimp and grits. Heck, it was the first place I'd ever had grits period; they just weren't big in north central West Virginia. We ordered wine and a fruit and cheese plate, telling the waiter we'd hold off on our dinner order until the appetizer arrived. After the wine was served, I started telling Sam about the events of the day. He asked a few questions as I went, but for the most part, he just listened.

I finally finished, and Sam sat for a minute, mulling the whole thing over. Finally he said, "Donna, you realize you've walked into the middle of what may be a major crime investigation. In fact, it sounds like this isn't just a recent crime. It may be an ongoing crime stretching back almost a century."

"You know, I guess it's possible. The fact that people from Louisiana have held on to this property for so long has to mean something. And when you add in that they have criminal backgrounds—well, at least Prudhomme and the three Gagnes, we don't really know about Helena Vanscoy—something's up. I mean, the two Gagne brothers who were always being charged with petty crimes. You have to think they would have sold the property and taken the money if the land wasn't of some practical use to them."

"What have you told the office?" Sam asked.

"Nothing. Joanne was on vacation this week. It's funny. I've been so busy I haven't really thought about her being gone, but I think she'll ask for some updates next week. Of course, she knows there's an investigation and it may take a while, so I don't think there will be any pressure to cough up this information. I shouldn't even be telling you, but I have to hash it out with someone!"

"You know I won't talk."

"I know, and I appreciate it."

Just then the fruit and cheese plate came. It was a beautifully laid out arrangement of smoked Gouda, a mild Camembert, and a really tasty white cheddar arranged with red grapes, thin cantaloupe and honeydew wedges, and slices of a very tart apple that tasted great with the cheddar. I ordered my favorite shrimp and grits, and Sam went for the New York strip.

"Donna, on the subject of Joe, you do know you're going to find him, don't you?"

"Sam, I think Tony's right that it all depends on what Joe wants to do."

"I realize that, but chances are that after all these years, Joe would like to have his family back as well. Unless he's just a drug-crazed guy who's lost all purpose in life, I think it's very likely that he'll come forward. Given the information about Professor Wilson being the trustee, I think Joe knows full well what's going on, and he's probably thinking more about how to do this than whether or not he's going to do it."

"I hope you're right. We really need him. But I still think Joe was going into rehab when he wrote that letter to Aunt Maud. And, if that's the case, he could have serious drug issues and not be a sane and thinking individual. And really, if he did come forward under those circumstances, I know Miriam and Chris would be relieved to at least know something about him, but they would be crushed that his life had taken that path."

"So what's your next step?" Sam asked me.

"I don't know yet. As usual, I'll just sleep on it tonight, and maybe I'll wake up with a plan. At least, I hope so."

The waiter came back shortly with two delicious dinners. We got refills on our wine and enjoyed a very relaxing Friday evening.

The Professor Produces

I f only we could clutch that moment between sleep and wakefulness. My brain was pleasantly afloat on a sea of dreams while I was being serenaded from the real world by birds singing in the early morning half-light. I tried to hold on to my dream state, but to no avail. Miss Blue, our big black, long-haired cat was speeding me along the road to reality by pushing the top of her head into my hand urging my fingers to scratch, rub, or pet. Okay, I'm awake!

I yawned, stretched, kept Miss Blue happy, and probably dozed off a couple of times before getting up to fill her food bowl. It was six forty-five, and I knew Sam had already been up at five thirty or so, fed the dogs, and gone back to bed. I was brushing my teeth when Friday's events made their way into my head.

The night before, when Sam and I got home from dinner, we both looked at the phone and saw there were two messages. I punched the button and we listened to message number one, which was Miriam wanting to know if I knew whether or not Tony had found anything. I felt bad that I hadn't called her. Of course, she was anxious, but I still wasn't sure what to tell her.

The second message was Professor Wilson saying he had a date and time that Joe's cousin could meet me in Washington, Pennsylvania. It was like there was a script, and he'd popped up right on cue. It was probably only a few seconds that I stood there after the message ended, but Sam noticed.

"What's wrong?"

"This is getting very real," I told him. "At this point, I don't know if I'm nervous that I might find Joe or nervous that I won't. Either way, there are consequences, and I'm not really in control of them."

I was surprised at how Professor Wilson's call was affecting me. I sensed I was getting very close, and I knew I was too emotionally attached to the outcome. I needed to disengage and approach it solely from a business perspective. Finding Joe was my job, pure and simple.

"You'll be fine, Donna. Either way, you've given it your best shot. Your intentions are honorable, and remember, you could end up making a lot of people very happy."

"Or very sad. It could go either way, Sam. But there's no turning back now, and I honestly do want to see it through."

My words from the night before popped back in my head as I went down the stairs. It was getting very real and I was apprehensive. I shook it off, got the coffee started, and went outside to feed the ducks and the birds, both of which were congregating and rather noisily at that.

By the time I got back in the house, I could hear Sam stirring. I got his favorite cup from the cupboard along with mine. Back in the day, there had been quite a few pottery and glass factories in northern West Virginia. We had the right kind of silica sand and an abundance of cheap natural gas. I'd grown up eating breakfast, lunch, and dinner on restaurant ware. My mother had chosen a reddish, flowered pattern called Dayton produced by Carr China in Grafton. After Dad passed away, Mom gave me all the Carr she had. She was more than ready for something new.

Restaurant ware is very heavy and, as the name would imply,

it was produced for use in restaurants and diners. It was cheap, durable, and hard to break. The set Mom gave me was short on plates (okay, you could break it if you tried hard enough), and I had wanted to find a few replacements. I probably looked for four or five years in junk and antique shops until I finally ran across three Dayton pattern plates in Elkins. They were in an antique store, stashed in a stack of odd plates in the bottom of an old china cupboard. Nothing special, I thought. The owners probably forgot they had them, considering where they were, and I figured I'd get them all for five bucks or so. And then I turned one over, saw a price sticker, and exclaimed, "Forty dollars a plate!" A friend who was with me said, "You're not going to pay that, are you?" My reply had been, "I'll pay whatever it takes to get them out of here."

My mother had passed away a few years before and my second thought was, "Mom would kill me if I paid that!" So I didn't. The lady in charge gave them to me for thirty-seven fifty each if I paid cash. I did. Oh my! Little did I know how collectible our good old everyday dishes had become.

Since then Sam and I have been looking for Dayton and other Carr pieces, as well as restaurant ware by McNichol, which was in Clarksburg, West Virginia, where I grew up. My favorite morning coffee cup is a white McNichol cup with a thin, green line around the top.

So this Saturday morning, I filled it to the brim, made my breakfast, and contemplated just what to tell Miriam. Sam sauntered in, looking not quite awake, said good morning, filled his cup, and powered up his laptop. He didn't like to eat right away. I was taking my last bite of eggs and toast when the phone rang.

As parents of a cop, when the phone rings either early or late, your adrenaline surges. I grabbed the phone and looked at the caller ID. Miriam Baxter. Huh, I still hadn't figured out what to tell her.

"Good morning, Miriam."

"Donna, I'm sorry to call this early. You were up, weren't you?"

"Absolutely. Not a problem. I apologize for not calling last night, but Sam and I went to dinner and it was kind of late when we got back."

"So did Tony find anything?" Miriam's voice was filled with both hope and anxiety. I really felt bad for not calling the night before.

"Miriam, he did. Aunt Maud's will names Professor Wilson as the trustee when she's gone, and apparently Joe is still the beneficiary."

"So that means Wilson knows where Joe is!" Miriam had the same reaction Tony and I had had.

"Tony and I said the same thing at first. But then we thought about it. Miriam, the money could be going to a bank account that Joe has access to. But yes, we agree that Professor Wilson probably knows Joe's whereabouts. The Professor told Aunt Betty that he was working on something that might be a lead. I hope you and Chris will trust me to keep working on Professor Wilson little by little. Tony pointed out that if he knows where Joe is and has told Joe that we're looking for him, then Joe is probably the one calling the shots. If that's the case, then pressuring Professor Wilson won't be the answer. I think we're going to have to make it as comfortable as possible for Joe to come forward."

Miriam was silent for a moment before she spoke.

"So, Donna, you think there's a chance Joe will come forward?"

"I do, Miriam. I think if Professor Wilson knows where Joe is and he didn't want us to find him, or if Joe didn't want to be found, he would have just shut us down. But he's talking to us. He's leaving the door open. But I think we have to go very easy."

I knew what I was saying sounded very flimsy to Miriam. She knew nothing about the meeting with the cousin, and that's what made it so much more hopeful for me.

"Donna, you're afraid Chris or I will pick up the phone and call Arnold Wilson, and I promise you we won't."

"Wow, can you read my mind, or what? If I were in your shoes, I would be inclined to do that. But yeah, I don't think that would be good. I think we're walking on eggshells here, and we're just going to have to be patient."

Miriam agreed with my assessment, so we said our good-byes with a promise of updates from me when I knew more. Sam looked up from Facebook saying, "Nice job. You handled that without telling any fibs at all."

"Yeah, but Sam, what about those pesky sins of omission? I think I may have committed a few of those. Now, I wonder how early I can call the Professor."

"It's eight fifteen. Most seniors get up pretty early. I'd go for it," Sam said.

I decided to clean up the breakfast dishes and give him at least until eight thirty. I made it until eight twenty-nine.

Professor Wilson picked up the phone on the second ring. Good, he had been up.

"Mrs. Cain. Glad you caught me. I'll be heading out the door in about ten minutes for the farmer's market. Same one your aunt goes to. In fact, I may see her there. She said in class yesterday that she was going."

If nothing else came out of this, Professor Wilson and Aunt Betty had certainly hit it off, and that was a good thing. They had a lot in common.

"Aunt Betty loves that farmer's market," I said, "and it's a beautiful day to be outside. Professor Wilson, I'm excited to hear you have a meeting set up."

"Mrs. Cain, could you make Tuesday afternoon around four o'clock at the Eat'n Park in Washington, P-A?"

"Absolutely!"

"She says it's on the Route 19 exit off Interstate 79."

"I know exactly where it is. What's Joe's cousin's name?"

"It's Jill. Jill Morgan."

"You said before that she lives in Ohio. I hope she doesn't have too long a drive."

"I don't think so. As I understand it, she lives just a few miles west of Wheeling. Not that far. Now Mrs. Cain, please understand that I don't know how much, if anything, this woman knows. She really hasn't told me much, kind of a quiet person, but I have to assume that she either has a connection to Joe or, for some reason, she thinks she can find him. I have made it clear that finding him is your purpose."

"I understand, Professor Wilson. And, as we discussed before, this meeting will be totally confidential."

"Good, she's really adamant about that."

"Professor Wilson, I really appreciate this. Joe's sisters have found a couple of clues as to Joe's life after he left home, but the clues have been very vague, nothing that would lead us to him. So I'm really hoping his cousin will be the key to finding him. Thanks again for your help."

"Well, I haven't done much, and it may turn out to be no help at all. But I hope it will be. Good luck with the meeting, Mrs. Cain. I do need to depart for the market."

We said good-bye, and I told Sam the Professor's side of the conversation. As we were talking, I realized something. "Sam, if you were Professor Wilson, wouldn't you have said something to me like, 'Mrs. Cain, please let me know how the meeting goes.'?"

"Yeah, I think I would have. He didn't say anything like that?"

"No. No, he didn't. I think that means he knows he'll get a report back from Jill Morgan."

"Or from Joe after he talks to Jill," Sam said.

"That may be more like it. I think Tony hit the nail on the head when he said Joe might be sending his cousin in to size me up and see if the offer of lease money is legitimate. But I can't say that's not exactly what I'd do as well. We're offering thousands of dollars to lease oil and gas that Joe and his siblings didn't even know they owned. At least his siblings are here and they know what's going on around them with the gas boom. It may sound very fishy to Joe. I'd be leery if I were him."

"I'd be surprised if Joe is totally focused on the oil and gas and money angle. It doesn't sound like he needs it anyway. This is an opportunity to reunite with the family," Sam pointed out. "That's a pretty big deal, Donna."

"I agree. But, Sam, we may just be building up a fantasy scenario here. There is a chance that neither Professor Wilson nor Jill have any idea where Joe is."

"If you had to place a bet, is that where you'd put your money?" Sam knew just how to challenge me.

"No, that isn't where I'd put my money. I do think the Good Professor knows Joe and knows exactly where he is."

"Why didn't you tell him you knew he was the trustee on the trust?"

"I don't think that Professor Wilson knowing that I know will change anything for the better. As long as he's making moves to help us, I'm just going to roll with it. If we hit a wall, I'll talk to him about it. For now, I just think I need to put the whole thing out of my mind until Tuesday and see what the meeting brings."

Sam agreed and left for the usual Saturday half day at the shop. I was headed for the shower when Josh pulled in, so I walked outside to greet him.

"Hey, Josh."

"Mom, can't you stay out of trouble?"

Hmmm, what was this about? "I'm not in trouble, Josh. What are you talking about?"

"Last night Taylor County picked up a guy we'd put an alert out on. I had him on a parking lot security video at a convenience store trying to choke a woman through the window of her car. It was late at night and the store was closed, but someone saw what was going on from the road and yelled at the guy to stop. He ran, but I identified him from the video because I've arrested him for domestic violence before. They picked him up in Taylor County in a stolen car and called us, so I went down."

"Good. I'm glad you caught him. But how's that get me in trouble?" I was playing dumb until I figured out what Josh knew.

"Well, Mom, Detective Bauer was there. Nice guy! When I introduced myself, he said, 'Cain, huh? You're in Mon County. Any relation to Donna Cain?'"

I was trying to look puzzled and perplexed. Wasn't working.

"Mom, from what he told me, they've got a major investigation on their hands and some of the information you gave them has been key. Actually, I'm kind of proud of you!"

"Well thank you, Josh."

"It was pretty heads-up for you to realize that what you knew might be of value."

Wow, it's amazing how good it feels for your son to tell you he's proud of you. It's usually the other way around.

"Josh, from the very beginning Tony and I have been saying that something was up with the way the Hagen farm was bought and sold. And then the more I found out about the coal company tract being booby-trapped and then the arrests came along on the old Tredloe farm . . . it just all looked very suspicious. But they really haven't told me much. I don't know who, other than Earl Crofton, was arrested, and I don't know why."

"Well, apparently Crofton was hiding a couple of other guys who were wanted out of state on some pretty serious charges. Bauer didn't say what. It sounds like Crofton was small potatoes, but he was an accessory since he was hiding the guys so they've got enough to hold him for a while. With what you told them, they think there's a lot more to the story, but they don't have it all figured out yet. They also told me they brought the Feds in on it."

"Good grief. I'm really glad I didn't try to go see Earl Crofton."

"Yeah, Mom, me too. I keep telling you to get your conceal permit. You almost came face to face with those murdering lunatics responsible for the corpse you found, and now there's this mess. It's scary out there."

"I'll think about it, Josh. I'll seriously think about it."

What to Tell Joanne

Monday morning rolled around way too fast. I was just sitting down at my computer with my last cup of coffee when Joanne called. She'd been on vacation the week before, so I was expecting a call, just not this early.

"So, any news on the drillsite or the Crofton tract? And how's the search for Joe going?"

Good grief. She wasn't wasting any time!

"Well, yes, there is something happening, Joanne. The sheriff has put a gag order on me, but, yes, there is something going on." I was really scrambling.

"A gag order. He seriously put a gag order on you!"

"Well, not exactly. He just asked me to keep quiet. The problem is, I'm not sure what I'm keeping quiet about, but I do feel an obligation to tell you. None of this has hit the papers, so please don't let it get out of the building. Last Thursday there were arrests at the Crofton place. Crofton was taken in along with two other people, but I'm not sure who they were or what the charges are."

"Don't you think it was drugs, the way the land next to him was booby-trapped? That makes sense."

"It does make sense, but the chief thinks there may be more to it. Joanne, I walked into the courthouse on Friday, not knowing anything was going on, and the first person I saw was Chief Warner. He called me into his office and asked if I had the title to the Crofton place. I told him I didn't have it with me and asked him specifically what he wanted. He said he needed to know who had owned the place for the last thirty years or so. That was easy, and I had the information back to him pretty quick. But, on a hunch, I looked at the surface owners on the two hundred forty-seven acres that the Tredloe heirs owned the oil and gas on; remember, it was bought and sold in seven separate tracts. Well, now I think at least the northern part of that land may be involved, and whatever is going on there may go back to Axel Tredloe and his cohorts in the early part of the nineteen hundreds."

Joanne was quiet for a few seconds. Finally she asked, "So did you tell the chief that?"

"Yes, I did. Joanne, I don't know what it all means, but I think you've heard me say more than once that there was something going on way back when with the old Hagen farm."

"I do remember you saying that. Donna, what do you think it was?"

"I don't really know, but the trail seems to lead back to Louisiana and to people who, according to newspaper reports at the time, weren't very savory characters. I don't think the chief knows what's really going on yet, but I do know they've called in the Feds."

"So this could take a while, but until you find Joe, we're kind of at a standstill anyway. Any progress on that?"

"Maybe. Tony got a copy of Maud's will. Her inter vivos trust became a testamentary trust in the will, and she changed the trustee from the bank to Professor Wilson with the bank becoming the successor trustee in the event of Professor Wilson's death or inability to serve. And, it appears that Joe is still the beneficiary. We both think the Professor knows very good and well where Joe is, but I don't think it's time yet to press him on the issue. He's set up a meeting with a cousin of Joe's who lives in Ohio. I meet with her this Tuesday at four o'clock in Washington, P-A. Professor Wilson says he doesn't know if she knows anything or not, but she has agreed to meet with me."

"Don't you find it odd that he would set up the meeting with the cousin if he knows where Joe is?"

"Yes, I do. But, as Tony pointed out, she may know Joe far better than Professor Wilson does. He was Maud's friend, and she obviously trusted him. But it doesn't mean that Professor Wilson and Joe knew each other well. Maybe, not at all, but I doubt that. If the cousin and Joe are close, Joe may want her to check me out and get more information about what's going on. It's just really hard to say. However, one of the conditions of meeting with her is not telling any of Joe's siblings about it. I've agreed to that."

"Wow, you're leading kind of an exciting life these days. In the last few months, you've found a dead body, you've gotten in the middle of a criminal investigation, and you're on the hunt for a missing person. It's not nearly as much fun here in the office."

"I can't say it's not interesting, and I'll admit I'm having fun with it. Well, everything but the dead body. But please make sure anyone you tell about the whole Crofton thing knows not to say anything. I wasn't supposed to talk, but I feel an obligation to keep the company informed. And besides, I think the chief's main concern was that the story not get out locally until they could get a little further along in the investigation. As soon as I know more, I'll let you know. And I did remind the chief that we really need to get moving on the drillsite. From what I know now, that may be the property least involved, so let's keep our fingers crossed."

Joanne and I hung up, and I breathed a sigh of relief. I didn't quite tell her everything, but everything I told her was true. I did have an obligation to the company. They were paying me. And besides that, the chief couldn't keep the lid on things forever.

The rest of my day was spent getting leases in the mail to out-of-state oil and gas owners and trying to find the living heirs of three brothers all of whom died prior to 1972, two in Ohio and one in Arizona. The three brothers had all been raised in Taylor County and had inherited the oil and gas from their father. I ended up finding and talking to two sons of one of the brothers, and they were looking for addresses and phone numbers for their cousins.

Tony called around midday saying he had gotten home late on Sunday and had totally forgotten to email me a copy of Maud's will. He'd then headed out early in the morning to the courthouse, forgetting again. He gave me his solemn promise that I would have it when he got home. I saw it on my email about 8:00 p.m. but decided not to download it until the next day. I knew if I read it, my mind would be hard at work into the wee hours of the morning processing the details.

This Wasn't in the Playbook

Tuesday morning dawned bright and beautiful with not a cloud in the sky. When I came downstairs, Sam was plugging in the waffle iron, and I could smell Italian sausage frying in a pan. That's a smell that's hard to ignore! We get it from a little Italian grocery in Rivesville where it's still made on-site. I rarely eat waffles in the morning because I like mine slathered in syrup and, unfortunately, that much sugar doesn't always sit well with me early in the day. But I just couldn't resist fresh, home-made sausage and waffles from scratch.

"Could you make me some too?" I asked.

"Coming right up!" What a husband.

"Sam, you remember I'm meeting Joe's cousin in Washington at four o'clock today, don't you?"

"I remember. I sure hope she knows something and isn't just playing games. Donna, have you considered that Joe could be in prison?"

"Yes, I have. It's certainly possible and, after we figured out that he was probably in rehab, which rarely seems to work, the idea that he might be in prison kind of gained a little weight with me. I hope that's not the case, but it would explain Professor Wilson's reluctance to tell us what he knows, or at least what I think he knows. But hopefully by this evening I'll have more clues to this puzzle or maybe even the answer."

Sam handed me a plate, and I lathered my waffle with butter

and syrup and dug in. Oh my! A little syrup on the sausage was pretty heavenly as well. I was in line for a light lunch today, a very light lunch.

As with all days on which something you're excited about is scheduled to happen, the minutes were ticking by ever so slowly. I read Aunt Maud's will from beginning to end. Tony had given me a good summation, and there were really no surprises there. I spent the rest of the morning processing signed documents to send to the office. At ten forty-five the phone rang and it was Miriam Baxter.

"Donna, anything new?"

I assured her there wasn't, as of yet, and then she got on with the real reason for the call.

"Donna, Sunday we had a family picnic, and Chris and I could see that Harold had something he wanted to say to us. He kept trying to get us aside, but there were about twenty-five people there, so it was kind of hectic. Anyway, towards the end, Chris and I walked down to a little creek to see if he would follow and he did. Poor Harold, when it comes to expressing his feelings he's a total basket case. I think you've picked up on that."

"Oh yeah. All bluster and bravado!" I said.

"Exactly. Well, Harold asked us, and with a lot of sincerity, if we'd found anything on Joe. And, he said he had thought a lot about things, and he was willing to help if we needed him. You could have knocked Chris and me over with a feather. In fact, we got kind of teary. That sent Harold scuttling off muttering something about 'damn women.' But we got him later. When he and Kathleen were leaving, Chris and I both hugged him as he was about to get in the car, and we said thank you. Kathleen was smiling from ear to ear. She knew what was going on and was proud of Harold. We were all proud of Harold. I don't know what brought about the change, but there you are!"

"Wow. Miriam, that's good news. It's one less battle to fight if we do find Joe, and maybe he can help. Do you think Harold would tell you what happened the night Joe left?"

"I don't know if he would tell us, and I don't know if it would help. I guess it's kind of like your position with Professor Wilson. If you've got them going in the right direction, you don't want to apply too much pressure and have them go the other way. If Harold's coming around, and is really sincere about helping, I think he'll speak up if he knows something that might get us closer."

"I agree. Whatever happened the night Joe left is unlikely to help us in the search anyway. But that is progress with Harold and that's good."

Miriam and I hung up, and I continued processing documents. Finally, lunchtime rolled around, and I kept it to some grapes and a few crackers with goat cheese to compensate for my big breakfast. After lunch, I started getting ready. The meeting was at four and the location was really only an hour away. However, construction was always a possibility or accidents or whatever. I decided to leave at two thirty. By two there was nothing left to do, and I just had to get moving, so I got in the car and headed north. I was anxious, excited, dubious, and hopeful all at the same time. My mind kept going through possible scenarios, most of them pretty fanciful: things like Joe joining us at a signal from Jill, Joe calling me on the way home after Jill had a chance to call him and report the meeting, or even Joe sitting in a booth with Jill when I arrived. Okay back to reality.

The trip up was almost exactly one hour—no construction, no accidents. I piddled around in a strip mall very close to the restaurant and at twenty of four spotted a pair of deeply discounted, casual, black flats I just had to have. I hurried through the purchase and walked into the Eat'n Park exactly at four.

"Just one?" the hostess asked.

"Actually two. But I don't know the person I'm meeting. It's a woman, though. She may already be here."

"I seated a woman just a few minutes ago, and she said she was waiting for another lady. You can go see if that's her. She's just around that corner."

"Thanks!" Why was I so nervous? I needed to get a handle on my feelings or I was going to blow this. I rounded the corner to see a pretty woman with shoulder length, light brown hair seated in the booth. She smiled, and my nerves went away. She was just one of those very approachable people and, for some reason, that was not what I was expecting.

"Jill?"

"Yes, you're Donna?"

"I am. Have you been here long?"

"No, just a few minutes."

We chatted a while, mundane things like our trip to the restaurant, my new shoes, the weather, etc. We were hitting it off and relaxing into an easy banter. But, of course, that wasn't why either of us was there. She approached the real subject first.

"Donna, I hope you'll respect my position in regards to Joe. I think it's only fair to tell you that I'm not going to reveal what I do or don't know, at least not now. And I guess it's fair to say, maybe never. Joe left home for a reason, and I have to respect that."

Okay, so she held all the cards, but that statement alone made me absolutely sure she was a solid link to Joe.

"I understand. I know I'm deep into a huge family . . . issue, I guess you'd say. And I will assure you that no one in the family knows I'm meeting you. I'm not certain they even know you."

Just then a waitress approached. It was too early for dinner so we both ordered drinks and pie. Well, it wasn't too early to spoil dinner! I had iced tea and coconut cream and Jill went for black coffee and apple. When the waitress left, Jill continued.

"You know, I don't know if Joe's brother and sisters would remember me. I think we only met once at a family reunion, and that was years ago. Joe and I were about the same age, seven or eight, and his sisters and his brother were a good bit older. But Joe and I really hit it off. I can remember catching craw crabs with him in a little creek at the park where the picnic was and chasing his sisters around with them."

She laughed and so did I. I could see Miriam and Chris running and screaming like most girls were prone to do in those situations. But I noticed that Jill's speech had gone from free and easy, before we got into Joe, to much slower and deliberate. She was thinking very carefully about what she said.

She continued, "There's one thing that's very important to me. Well, important to Joe, I should say. But, well, I guess I'm asking what they think now. The family has never looked for . . . for Joe before, at least I don't think they have, and now, you're the one doing the looking because you need something signed. Professor Wilson explained that much to me. I guess what I'm asking is, does the family care one way or the other if Joe is found or not?"

Thank God I was on firm ground on this one.

"Jill, Miriam and Chris would be ecstatic if I found Joe. And, we all feel that big, bad Harold has come around as well. Miriam called me this morning to tell me how much Harold has softened."

Jill was looking at me very intently, and I thought I saw her eyes moistening just before she looked down. She remained silent, her reaction proving just how close she and Joe were. I continued.

"In the beginning, when I ran into the problem of Joe being gone, I told Miriam and Chris that I wouldn't go forward with the search without their help. And then Harold called me one day. He was gruff, and he said he wasn't on board, but he didn't tell me not to look for Joe. With guys like Harold, I consider that an okay to proceed."

"What did Harold tell you about Joe leaving?"

"Nothing. Nothing at all, and he's never told Miriam or Chris what happened the night Joe left either. But Miriam and Chris have told me a lot about Joe, especially in that last year at home. I know their mother died, and I know Joe was probably more . . . well, a much gentler kind of male than his father or brother. I know there was tension between the three of them."

Jill smiled a knowing smile at what I'd said. I was guessing she'd heard the stories from Joe more than once—stories about Joe being happier in the kitchen than the garage, about his father and brother not reacting well to that. Just then the waitress brought our order, and we were quiet through the first couple of bites.

"This is good coconut cream. How's yours?" I asked.

"Very good. I should have gotten ice cream but a girl's gotta watch her figure, right?"

We both laughed. She could have eaten a gallon of ice cream and still have been thin.

Jill took a big breath, paused a second or two, then said, "I think you're saying they thought Joe was gay."

"They thought he might be, and they've said as much. But they really don't know. And, Jill, I thought it odd too that they didn't mount a big search for Joe through the years, but they said they were angry. They told me that they had never been negative towards Joe about what his father and brother perceived as more, well . . . maybe, female behavior. They said they'd never said a word to him about any of that. Joe was a much loved brother to both of them. And so they were both very angry that Joe never contacted them and told them what happened. They could see him not contacting his father or Harold. Who knows what they did or said the night he left. Maybe him not coming back or calling was justified when it came to Mr. Tredloe and Harold, but not the girls. They just felt they never deserved that from Joe."

Jill was getting emotional. It was taking everything she had not to shed tears. I didn't know whether to let up or keep going. I kept going.

"Jill, I think for a long time they simply expected every phone call to be Joe. Or they expected him to walk in the door. But it never happened. And then so much time passed, they didn't know where to start, even though they always suspected Joe had turned to his aunt Maud in Pittsburgh, but she would never confirm that. But Jill, Miriam and Chris, and I think Harold as well, would give anything to have their brother back."

Jill was staring at me and not saying a word. I simply looked back, my mind trying to process what I was telling her that was so profound. I didn't think I'd said anything that she and Joe couldn't have imagined as a possible scenario.

As we looked at each other, I realized that a revelation was making its way into my brain. It arrived as a fully formed fact—a lightning bolt that made me look at Jill with far more scrutiny than was polite. I had been delivered an irrefutable fact without any evidence to back it up. But I knew what I knew; I just didn't know yet, why I knew it.

Thank goodness they'd given us extra napkins because my tears were instantaneous and it would take every last napkin on the table to sop them up. I held one to my cheeks and covered my mouth with my palms in an attempt to get myself under control. I was smiling and crying, and then a bigger smile as it really sunk in, and then even more tears. This was so totally unprofessional!

Jill sat frozen, staring at me with incomprehension. And then she began to understand what was happening. Her face went through a kaleidoscope of emotions starting with a look like a cornered animal, transitioning to anger, and finally arriving at something that looked like reluctant submission, or maybe even relief.

Meanwhile, the waitress had approached to refill our drinks but had backed away after witnessing the emotional mayhem in our booth. Jill spoke first, her voice very quiet and hesitant.

"You know."

"Yes."

"How?"

Complete sentences were a little tough at the moment, and she was asking me a question I didn't know the answer to. But I had to say something.

"I'm not sure. I haven't figured it out yet," I answered, still hiding behind my napkins and my hands.

"Why are you crying?" she asked.

"I'm not sure about that either," I blubbered. "And I'm so sorry. It's very unprofessional of me. But I think maybe it's simply relief that you're not dead."

"You thought I was dead?" she asked, sounding a little shocked.

"Well, it was certainly a possibility your sisters and I had considered!"

Jill smiled, a very small, very pensive smile, finally saying, "I never thought about that. Maybe we should finish our pie."

I agreed. Eating can be calming, and we both needed that.

Finally Jill looked up, more under control, having had time to think about the situation, and said, "Some people never figure out that I used to be a man. And if they do, it's usually not this quick. I didn't think you'd see it in one meeting."

"I didn't see it. I still don't, actually. You're a very pretty woman and your voice is . . . well, it doesn't sound male. I think it was your emotional response to what I was saying. It was strong; too strong, really, for anyone but Joe. And, if we had a recording of this conversation, I think we'd hear a pause, a little extra time for you to think every time you said 'Joe.' You had to be very conscious of not saying 'me.' You did slip and say it once. I guess I was picking up on that without really processing it right away."

She smiled faintly, nodding her head and shrugging her shoulders in the realization that she had given me clues.

"And Jill, I'm really sorry I got so emotional, but this was a total surprise. A good surprise! You have to understand that since I started this search, I've had all kinds of scenarios in mind about what or where Joe would be when we found him, or if we even would find him. 'Dead' was definitely one of the potential outcomes, prison was another, on the streets, maybe. None of us knew. But this ending, this wasn't on our list at all."

I was finally smiling without the accompaniment of tears.

"But I can guarantee you this," I continued. "Your sisters and I didn't sit around thinking we would find a healthy, functioning human being who looks like they're doing okay in the world. I guess we were assuming the worst."

And now, it was Jill's turn to cry. And laugh. We both laughed. Lord knows why. Just a relief of nervous tension maybe.

She got herself more under control and said, "I thought I could be totally cool and pull this off. But there's one thing I hadn't bargained for. I responded with emotion because you were speaking with emotion. You knew more than I expected you to know. You answered some questions I've needed answered for a long, long time. I didn't see that coming. I thought you'd be more detached, that this would be more business for you and less personal. My sisters have confided in you, and it shows. You spoke with passion about finding Joe, and I just wasn't ready for that."

I waved the waitress over for more tea and coffee. She approached with caution, and I jokingly told her we were both menopausal, although Jill was a bit young for that. She chuckled, took more napkins out of her pocket, and assured us she'd keep us well stocked.

"Jill, this should just be business for me, but I don't really have the ability to detach myself from the emotional aspect. Your sisters have confided in me. They've been honest about their feelings, and I've watched them struggle with their emotions. There's no way I can remain immune to that. I hope you can understand."

"I do. If I were in your shoes, I would probably have done the same thing. But, Donna, since I didn't expect our meeting to go in this direction," Jill said, shaking her head from side to side, "I have to tell you, I'm totally unprepared. I'm not sure what you knowing this means. I haven't wrapped my brain around it."

Oh boy, I hadn't thought about the implications of me knowing either, but I knew what my answer had to be.

"Jill, this goes nowhere unless you want it to. I've made Miriam, Chris, and Harold all aware that if I find you I have to abide by your wishes. I have a document that needs signed, and getting it signed by you is my job. My company doesn't pay me to reunite families. Would I be happy if that happened as a result of my efforts? You know the answer to that, but it's totally your call."

Jill was deep in thought, still trying, I was sure, to sort out her own emotions and desires. And then, the big clue suddenly dawned on me.

"Wait, there was another clue! It was a picture, a picture of you that your sisters found in Aunt Maud's stuff. You're standing on an overlook somewhere with your hair blowing back in the wind. And you are that picture: I'm now looking at the female twin of the Joe in that photo. I knew there was something else, and I couldn't put my finger on it."

Jill thought about the picture, but said she couldn't remember when or where it was taken, but thought it must have been a trip somewhere in Pennsylvania with friends. We both fell silent again. I was thinking just how tough this was going to be. Leaving as a brother and coming back as a sister would be astronomically complicated. But that was only if Jill chose to come back. Still her party, still her decision.

She finally spoke. "Do you think they'd be happy to have me back as Joni rather than Joe?"

"You said Joni!" I said.

"Joni is really my name. I wanted a variation on Joe just to make the transition easier. But I do have a cousin, Jill Morgan, who lives in Ohio. And I am very close to her. She's the little girl I played with at the family reunions. That was a true story. Jill knows I was borrowing her identity for this meeting. And, just in case you didn't keep it a secret from the family, she was prepared to field any phone calls if they tracked her down."

"So you legally changed your name to Joni Morgan?"

"Yes. So, what do you think? Let's put Miriam and Chris in one group and Harold in another. I know you say Harold's come around, but Harold doesn't know about this."

She gave me a knowing look, and I had to agree that "this" wouldn't go down well with Harold!

"Would Miriam and Chris welcome me back?"

"Jill—Joni, I've gotten to know them pretty well. As I said, they've shared a lot with me, including some tears. Honestly, it would be a shock. But yes, I think Miriam and Chris would welcome you. They'd have to adjust, but I'm sure the people in your life who knew you before and after had to do that as well."

"They did. Some found it easier than others."

"Well, I guess all I can tell you is that your sisters wanted to go forward knowing you might be a drug addict, in prison, dead, or any other number of endings that've gone through their heads. I don't think they ever expected an older version of the brother they once knew to come back to them with nothing unchanged. They didn't think being estranged from the family for over twenty years meant everything was okay. And Joni, you seem pretty okay to me although I know none of this could have been easy for you."

She smiled, and we just sat for a few minutes drinking coffee and tea, and thinking.

"Donna, I need a little time. I came here to take a small step, to get a feel for what Miriam and Chris were thinking. And Harold too, I guess. But instead, I'm way further down the road than I intended to be. I never considered the fact that you might figure it out. Would you be willing to give me your phone number? Tentatively, I'd like to meet you here next week if that works for you. But I'll call you and confirm. I hope you won't think it rude if I don't give you my number. I'm just not ready yet."

I reached into my purse and got my card. It had my home number, my cell, and my email.

"Joni, that's fine. And please understand that this goes nowhere. Don't worry a minute about that."

I had Allie to Thank

I started home around five forty-five, right in the crunch of the evening commute traffic. I headed south on I-79 as Joni headed north. I was drained. I'd like to say I was productively thinking about a plan, but I wasn't. Although the thought did occur to me that, plan as I might, the ball was totally in Joni's court.

Joni and I had not talked at all about the documents I needed signed. She didn't ask me to explain them, and she didn't ask me how much money she stood to make. Sam had been right when he said that the money might not be the top priority with Joe.

Wow, this was going to be hard. In my mind Joe was one person, and Joni was another. If I thought about Joni, I thought in female pronouns. If I thought about Joe, the pronouns were all male. My tears at the table were from relief that Joe was still with us, safe and sound. But he wasn't; Joni was. And I was beginning to realize that, while I was okay with it on one level, even happy really, on another level, I was sad to lose Joe. I'd never met him, but I knew a lot about him and, from his sisters' point of view, he'd been a wonderful guy. I would never meet that Joe. And if I was feeling this way, how would his sisters feel? It almost seemed appropriate to mourn his loss.

Maybe thinking of Joni and Joe as separate people was natural. Maybe if I talked to people who'd been close to someone who switched genders, they would tell me it's a process that you go through, that you eventually get the two beings synthesized into one in your mind, and that you start getting the pronouns right without thinking.

I turned on the radio and finished the drive home just letting my mind wander. The fact that Joe was found had not really sunk in. And then, suddenly, my mind wandered to Allie. How did I not think of Allie when I was sitting in front of Joni? Without Allie, my realization that I was looking at Joe—the former Joe—might have brought with it an entirely different reaction on my part. Possibly a negative reaction and, certainly, a far less informed one.

A few years ago, I had to locate and contact just over a hundred thirty people, all of whom owned a small fraction of the oil and gas under two-hundred-plus acres in western Harrison County. Some were local, but most were scattered all over the country, and not one of them knew they owned any oil and gas.

One day I called Allen Roger Tyndale in a little town east of Columbus, Ohio. I went through my spiel about how he owned this, what he owned, and what we needed to do. He listened patiently and then said, "Well, I guess I should tell you that I've changed my name."

"You mean you legally changed it?" I said.

"Yes."

"I've never dealt with a name change before, other than married names, of course, but I believe you have to file papers in your local courthouse?"

"Everything's on file," he told me.

"Okay, I'll order the documents, but for now, tell me your new name, and I'll get it on my spreadsheet."

And he did tell me. "Allie Tyndale," he said.

I heard Allie but then thought he must have said Allen.

"Allen Tyndale," I said back to him.

"No. A-l-l-i-e . . . Allie. Allie Tyndale."

"I'm sorry," I said, "I misheard you."

Allie was used to the misunderstandings. She was also incredibly patient and proceeded, for the next hour or so, to educate me in detail. It was a very eye-opening conversation.

She told me about the confusion and frustrations people in this situation face, about not understanding why your feelings and desires don't conform to the body you were born with. She told me about how some people never figure out the issue and that, way too often, the result is suicide.

From that point on, I'd paid more attention, than I would have otherwise, when I saw or heard something about transgender issues. Allie had certainly opened my eyes. There's nothing like getting the story firsthand from someone who's lived it.

I don't think my reaction to Joni had been at all negative, and I had Allie to thank for that. She had given me some real insights into the whole transgender issue, and it had made me more aware, more attentive, when I heard something about it on the radio or saw an article in a magazine. Bottom line, thanks to Allie, I probably had a little more awareness than the average person.

And that last thought led my mind to Harold. Oh my, Harold. Harold would never understand this.

Sam was at his Tuesday night soccer game when I got home. I'm usually still awake by the time he comes back, and tonight I was sure I would be. There was so much running through my mind, I knew I wouldn't sleep well.

I greeted the dogs, said hello to two of three cats—the orange, stripy tom apparently out on the prowl—and cleaned up the kitchen. A styrofoam container told me my brother had gotten a to-go order from the local watering hole and I could see Sam had eaten the leftover rice and veggies from the previous evening. I knew which was which because my brother won't even consider tasting rice. They both thought they'd cleaned things up, and I did appreciate the effort.

The mail was on the island, and I had two signed leases back from out-of-state owners, both people I really needed to get on board. That was good. Landmen are judged by the amount of ink they get. One of them was significant acreage.

I hadn't eaten dinner, but I wasn't all that hungry, having consumed a generous piece of calorie-laden pie, so I grabbed some grapes and almonds, a glass of tea, and settled in on the couch watching a *Seinfeld* rerun that I'd seen countless times before. My eyes were on the screen, but my mind was definitely on Joni and Joe. No luck yet in separating the two even though, on a rational level, I knew perfectly well they were one and the same.

The rest of the evening was spent in mindless piddling, walking from room to room, putting a shirt away here, throwing a couple of old magazines in the recyclables, and gathering up the shoes that collect downstairs and putting them where they belong upstairs. They were all the kinds of things you can do without thinking, but at least I was being somewhat productive.

I finally realized I'd never get to sleep if I couldn't settle my brain down, so I prepared the bathroom for a relaxing soak in Dr. Teal's Pure Epsom Salt Soaking Solution with Lavender. Not only does this wondrous concoction help you sleep, I find it also gently dispels the aches and pains that seem to have become the norm over the last year or two.

I got a vanilla scented candle and placed it on a high shelf out of feline reach, started the bath, dumping in a generous portion of salts, got several towels, and pushed a small stool over by the tub so my ChapStick and towels would be in easy reach.

Just as I was stepping into the heavenly smelling water, our youngest cat, Minnie, entered the room talking up a storm. She's the most vocal cat we've ever had and has a repertoire of sounds that go far beyond the usual meow. In fact, we often hear her coming down the hall muttering what you would swear is a sentence. And, like now, those sentences often end on a high note, making you certain she has just asked a question.

I explained to her that I was going to soak in the tub to relax and, hopefully, quiet my overactive brain. She thought it was a swell idea, at least I think that's what she said, as she jumped up on my stool and peered over the side of the tub. I watched as my ChapStick rolled out of reach towards the toilet. Darn! If I didn't retrieve it, I knew it would bug me and the whole idea was to relax! I stood up and made the couple of steps on wet feet that put me in reach. I got back in the tub and secured the ChapStick in the soap dish out of Minnie's reach.

Minnie watched with a quizzical look on her face as I descended into the water making it rise in the tub. She cocked her head at an angle considering the little waves that went past, finally dipping her paw in and flinging the water in all directions. That was followed by multiple walks back and forth across the top of the tub, reaching down to test the water with her paw and happily shaking it off against my protests. But, as usual with felines, she quickly grew bored, jumped down, and sauntered out of the bathroom, tail in air.

Now for some relaxation!

Out Like a Light

I t was five thirty in the morning when my alarm went off. Wednesday being Rotary day, I had to roll out extra early. I was in a deep sleep and definitely having a hard time getting in gear. That was odd. Usually, my mental alarm goes off, and I wake up shortly before the clock starts emitting its annoying beeps programmed to increase in volume if I don't hit the button.

I'd slept in the back bedroom thinking the less noise the better and, just after turning the alarm off, I heard Sam coming down the hall.

"Are you okay, Donna? You were snoring away when I came home last night. You're usually awake."

"Sam, I don't snore. And yes, I'm okay. I can't believe I slept like that." I still wasn't fully awake.

"I figured you'd wait up to let me know how the dinner went with Joe's cousin."

"Oh my, Sam. It hadn't come back in my head until you said that. Tell you what, let me get my shower, you get the coffee made, and I'll tell you what happened before I leave. There's a lot to tell, so it will just have to be the CliffsNotes version for now."

"Well, I guess you're going to keep me hanging, so hurry up," Sam said, as he left the room.

As I made my way to the bathroom, I made a mental note to get more of Dr. Teal's soaking concoction. If it could make me sleep that well when I was that keyed up, I wanted a wheelbarrow full.

I tried to move quickly but wasn't all that successful. By the time I got downstairs, I only had about five minutes to spare. Sam handed me a cup of coffee and stood looking at me expectantly.

"Did she tell you anything?" he asked.

"Sam, this can't go anywhere. You can't tell anyone what I'm going to tell you!"

"So it's really bad, isn't it?"

"No, Sam, it's not bad. It's complicated, it might be shocking to some, but it's not bad."

I started smiling, actually getting teary-eyed again.

"What?" he asked, with anticipation.

"Sam, I met with a woman and that woman was Joe. It wasn't Joe's cousin, Jill. It was the former Joe, now a woman."

I could see Sam's mind going a mile a minute.

"You mean he's a transvestite?"

"No, Sam. He's not just dressing like a woman. He is a woman. At least—well—that's my take on it."

I realized that I didn't know how Joe had gotten from male to female, and I certainly hadn't asked. But as I thought about it, I realized that no one could do that good a transition with just makeup and clothes.

"And he told you all this? He told you he used to be Joe?"

"She. She, Sam. Those pronouns are tough. I'm having a hard time too. But no, she didn't tell me. I figured it out, and it wasn't from how she looked. She's really pretty. Sam, I have to run or I'll be late. We'll talk a lot more this evening. Sorry."

I gave Sam a quick hug and kiss and headed out the door. I left him in a state of confusion and looking like an abandoned child at the airport.

I'd just gone through the buffet line and sat down at Rotary with my breakfast when Harris came over and took the seat beside me.

"So," he said, "any luck in finding your missing person?"

The question caught me totally unprepared and my look must have told him I knew something.

"You found him?" he asked.

"Well, I guess my face tells you I may have, but the situation is a little tricky and I can't talk about it. Let's just say I promised not to talk about it until things unravel a bit. I'm sorry."

"No, that's okay. If you need to keep it quiet, you need to keep it quiet. I bet eventually I'll hear an interesting story though."

"You have no idea, Harris. No idea."

Our speaker was a physicist from West Virginia University talking about dark matter. Professors were always dicey as speakers. Yes, they knew their stuff; however, we weren't interested in dry lectures at seven o'clock in the morning. Give us the info, but entertain us too. Every once in a while, we'd get someone hell-bent on feeding us the latest data on a subject via a PowerPoint presentation, and we'd all start going back to sleep. But this guy knew how to make a very complicated subject fun and interesting. He told us stories, he used humor, he somehow made it matter to our lives here on earth and, in return, he got a very attentive audience. I bet his classes were always in demand.

When I left Rotary I was headed straight to Taylor County. We were in the curative phase on many of the tracts that we'd leased. "Curative" means crossing all the legal t's and dotting the i's. The attorneys will tell you all the little legalities in the title and assessments that aren't quite perfect. They point out old leases that were never released, tax assessments that need corrected, things like that.

Getting a tax assessment corrected was my main agenda for the day. When you're putting in multimillion-dollar wells, you want to make certain that nothing is lost in a tax sale. That means getting the correct assessments on the books, and it's not always an easy task. So, I was headed to the Assessor's office with certified title in hand in an effort to prove the correct ownership on one of our tracts and get it taxed properly.

As I approached the Assessor's office, just down the hall, standing in the doorway of the Sheriff's office, was Chief Warner.

"Mrs. Cain. I was thinking about calling you. Got a minute?"

He'd turned and was walking into his office before he even finished the question, assuming I would follow. I did.

"What's up, Chief?"

"Did you find anything on Helena Vanscoy?"

"I hate to admit it, but I haven't really looked. I've been super busy."

"I think I told you we have some federal assistance on this," he said, sitting down and pointing to the chair across from him. "They have pretty easy access to just about everything, so finding her was no big deal for them. She's dead and has been since 1998. Don't know why the taxes are still going to her!"

"Well, Chief, it's not all that unusual for someone to be dead and their name remain on the tax tickets for years. We run across that all the time. The Tax office doesn't really care whose name they're under as long as someone is paying the taxes. Did you look to see if her taxes were being sent to a new address after her death? And, did someone check to see if she had a will wherever it was she died?" I asked.

"I don't think anyone checked the taxes, but I would imagine the will was looked for. I haven't heard anything, though. Actually, I'm surprised they called me with this much info. Can you check the address on the taxes? That's a good idea."

"The answer to the address question is right next door. Where did she die?" I asked.

"Tennessee. Nashville. According to the Feds, Helena was a first cousin of the two Gagne brothers who owned the property before her. Their dad and her dad were brothers. The boys weren't too bright, but Helena was a Vanderbilt-educated socialite who we think had a lot going for her with the exception of honesty. She was investigated a couple of times for tax evasion but never convicted. The Feds are trying to track down the case files, but I haven't heard back yet. I don't know what they suspected her of, but they often go after people for tax evasion when there are other crimes involved. It's usually easier to prove. And get this, in college she majored in art and art restoration, so it kind of fits right in to what her family may have been up to."

I was deep in thought trying to put everything in perspective.

"You're right, Chief. It all fits together. The evidence in those newspaper articles pointed to Prudhomme and the Gagnes stealing artifacts in Central America and bringing them to the United States. Sounds like Helena Vanscoy could have been educated specifically to assist in that venture. And maybe, just maybe, she was the real brains of the operation."

"Maybe. Don't know anything yet. But as always, Mrs. Cain, this is all mum. I'm telling you this because you've helped us quite a bit, and I never know when you might know something you haven't told us because you didn't think it was important. I find that most of the time, it's some little detail that blows a case wide open. Can you check that address thing?"

I told him I'd be right back and headed next door. I realized I had never looked at the tax ticket to see where Helena Vanscoy lived. That was an oversight on my part.

I said hello to the clerks on my way to the back of the office where they kept the landbooks. I pulled the 1998 book to get the address. If she died in 1998, the address wouldn't change until 1999. I was surprised to see it was a Louisiana address, not Tennessee. It was, however, in Helena Vanscoy's name. I pulled the most current book, and it was exactly the same. That told me that most likely someone in Louisiana had been in control of things before Helena Vanscoy died.

Nevertheless, there had to be a legitimate new owner after Helena's death, either by will or intestate descent if there was no will. The address in the book was 243 Bouchard St., Gretna, Louisiana.

I pulled up MapQuest on my phone to see how far Gretna was from New Orleans. The answer was five point five miles, an estimated ten-minute drive on the Pontchartrain Expressway. The little map showed Gretna on the west side of the Mississippi. It indicated a bridge, which I guessed would be a very long one since it was so close to the Gulf of Mexico.

I then entered the address in my Google search and looked for the Zillow listing. Zillow usually offers an aerial of the property as well as all the specs on the house. The aerial showed a residential street with big trees, and what appeared to be older, multistory homes. From above, you couldn't tell much about the house, but I could see it had a reasonably large yard. Comparing it to neighboring properties, my guess was the house sat on two lots. There was a back alley and a large building in the back that appeared to open onto the alley. Judging from the size, it was probably a three- or four-car garage.

Zillow listed the house as off the market, two stories with four bedrooms, two and a half baths, twenty-eight hundred square feet and an approximate value of one hundred eighty-five thousand. Under "last sold," there was no data. That usually means the house has not recently changed hands.

I took all of my discoveries back to the chief including the info on the house. I even brought it up on my phone so he could see. It got a resounding "Huh!" but, other than that, no comment.

The chief and I concluded our business, and I went back to the Assessor's office to present the certified title on one of many other tracts I was working on in an effort to get the assessments corrected. The online info on Gretna had said it was in Jefferson Parish, so before sitting down with the assessor, I made a mental note to check to see if the Jefferson Parish property tax records were online. More and more were these days, and I really wanted to see who owned 243 Bouchard St.

Just as I was entering the office, my cell rang. I backed out into the hall and answered without looking to see who it was.

"I had a doctor's appointment this morning and had to wait forever," Joanne said.

Egads! Joanne. I hadn't thought at all about what to tell her. Where had my head been!

"So, Donna, did the cousin tell you anything?"

Nothing was coming out of my mouth because nothing was coming out of my brain!

"What's wrong?" Joanne asked.

"Joanne, nothing's wrong. In fact, quite a lot is right. I was sworn to secrecy, but I can tell you that Jill is a solid connection to Joe. Jill knows Joe . . . well . . . very well. I'm sure of that. But, I believe we've opened the lid on a very complicated situation."

"Can't you just get him to sign the lease and be done with it?"

I could see that my reluctance to tell all was frustrating Joanne, and I totally understood why. Joanne saw things as black and white. She didn't give a lot of credence to the gray areas in between.

"At this point, no, I can't just get him to sign. I don't know if we'll ever get Joe to come forward. Look, I need some time to build a little trust. Believe me, I'm working on this but unfortunately, I don't hold the cards."

Now it was her turn to be silent for a few seconds.

"I guess you're saying Jill and Joe hold the cards, and you have to wait to see what they do, is that it?"

"That's it!"

Poor Joanne. She continued, still sounding frustrated. "So, let me make sure I understand the position we're in. The property we need is under investigation, one of the main lessors is playing a cat and mouse game, and our ground people are afraid to walk on the drillsite for fear of being injured by booby traps."

I couldn't disagree, so I simply said, "That's a pretty good summation, Joanne."

"I'm glad this isn't the only well unit we're working on, because I don't know if we'll ever get to the end of this one. But Donna, this unit is pretty important to us. We've already paid for a lot of leases and, if we don't get them into production, that's money down the drain."

"I know. Don't lose hope, though, because what I can tell you is that progress is being made on all fronts."

"I sure hope so because I have to report something up the chain and, quite honestly, Donna, this is starting to sound more like a plot for a book than a drilling project. I'll tell them something, I guess."

"Joanne, I wish I could help more. I do think it will go one way or the other soon, though, and I'll be able to talk. To you, anyway. And I assure you, I'm doing everything I can."

"Well, I didn't think you weren't. It's just frustrating."

Joanne and I said our good-byes, and I, once again, headed into the Assessor's office.

Renee de la Corte

I was home way before Sam, my meeting with the assessor having gone very well. I always have to show her the part of the certified title pertaining to assessments and then lay out the supporting evidence. All of the county assessors are well aware that the oil and gas assessments have a lot of mistakes in them, but they aren't willing to make changes without solid evidence, and I don't blame them.

I arrived home to find a couple of phone messages that needed quick callbacks, and my phone continued to ring throughout the afternoon. That was good because I was getting responses from people I needed to talk to.

It was close to four before I had a few minutes to check Jefferson Parish, Louisiana, where the city of Gretna was located. I did a search for property tax records, and, as usual, several paid sites came up and then the official Jefferson Parish Tax Assessor's page featuring a beautiful picture of the bridge crossing the Mississippi on the Pontchartrain Expressway. It was actually a very sophisticated site giving you several ways to search, one being by address. Whoopee!

I typed in 243 Bouchard Street and up came the info. It was owned by Renee de la Corte, and the taxes were current. It also described the parcel by size and identified the city lot. That's really about all the information you're going to get on an Assessor's site.

The information was clear, but it did leave me wondering whether I had a man or a woman, given the strong French influences in Louisiana. I was thinking Renee with two *e*'s was the female spelling and Rene with one *e* was the male spelling, but I really wasn't sure so, as usual, I did a search.

Renee is the French form of Renata and is a female name when it has two *e*'s. When I searched Rene with one *e*, I found that it could be male but was usually female as well. Okay, so my Renee was a female. But who was she? Back to the search engines.

Running Renee de la Corte in Gretna, Louisiana, got me a White Pages listing with no phone number, offers of paid information from Spokeo and Intelius, and an obituary listing for none other than Helena Vanscoy. Bingo! It wouldn't have come up if Renee's name wasn't in the obituary somewhere.

In my business, obituaries are absolute gold. I most often use them when I'm searching for family members. They tell you who everyone is in relation to the deceased and, quite often, give you the city and state they're from. I had to think the Feds had already found this obit, but it was new to me.

It took seconds to download and print. It was Helena Vanscoy's obituary, and Renee de la Corte was her daughter. No husband was listed, but I didn't know if de la Corte was a married name or her maiden name. Helena could have been a de la Corte before she was a Vanscoy. It didn't really matter though. Renee was Helena's daughter, and that was valuable information.

I had been hoping to find a Facebook or other online page for Renee, but nothing had popped up. The obituary said Helena had died at age ninety-one, so Renee was probably well over fifty and not into social media.

I hit the back arrow to see if there were any sites worth looking at other than the obituary listing and struck pay dirt again. There was a business-listing site that showed Renee de la Corte as the director of an LLC called Southern Arts and Investments.

Hmmm . . . that fit very nicely with her mother's degree and, what appeared to be, the illicit business many of the other family members had been involved in.

My next step was to bring up the Louisiana Secretary of State site and hit the Business Search tab. All states have them, and I use them rather frequently in my job. Renee de la Corte was listed as president of Southern Arts and Investments, Michelle Lyon was vice-president, Arthur Lyon was treasurer, and Patricia Gagne was secretary. I grabbed the obituary to check, pretty sure that it had identified Michelle Lyon as another of Helena Vanscoy's daughters and I was right. Arthur Lyon was listed as her husband. Patricia Gagne wasn't in the obit, but I had to think she was a cousin. Interesting!

I decided to let the information simmer in my brain and see what emerged. In the meantime, I heard a truck crunching gravel in the driveway. The dogs were barking joyfully, as opposed to their aggressive barks saying a stranger was nearby, so it had to be Sam and he was a good half hour earlier than normal!

I was still downloading information and making some notes when Sam came through the back door, climbed the steps, and stuck his head in my office door.

"Did you come home early to cut the grass?" I asked.

"No, I came home early to hear more about your meeting with Joe."

"Joni!" I told him laughing.

"But wait, you said Jill this morning, didn't you?"

Poor Sam. "Give me a few minutes," I told him, "and let's sit on the porch. I'll tell you everything, I promise."

I wrapped up what I was doing, got some iced tea, and headed for the porch. Sam had already made himself comfortable and was checking Facebook. He put his tablet down and looked at me.

"Sam, not only do I have all this about Joe, now Joni, to tell you, but I think I've discovered a lot more on the whole Crofton–Gagne issue too. But I'll tell you about Joni first."

I relayed the whole meeting with Joni to Sam in as much detail as I could remember. He listened intently and, at times, I could see the wheels in his head turning.

When I was done, he looked at me kind of funny and said, "So now you know where he was when he wrote that letter to his aunt Maud."

He caught me off guard and, just as I said, "No I don't," I suddenly did.

"Sam, he wasn't in rehab—he was going through some kind of procedure or therapy or whatever, and that makes everything fit. That's why he said he was having second thoughts and, of course, Aunt Maud would be there for moral support. I can't believe I didn't think of that right away."

Sam was just grinning, happy he'd provided such an important detail.

"So, Donna, how do you think Joe, now Joni, will handle this? What's she going to do?"

"I honestly don't know. The fact that I figured it out totally threw her off track. I don't think, at that point anyway, she really knew what she was going to do. And Sam, you were right. This is about the family, it's not about money. She never asked how much she would get for leasing. In fact, she never asked anything about it. Aunt Maud left her in a pretty comfortable financial situation."

"Does she work?" Sam asked.

"I don't know. I didn't ask."

"Is she tall for a woman? Were her hands larger than normal or her feet?"

Sam was asking all of the obvious questions, the things you

would look for if you thought the woman in front of you might have once been a man. I hadn't looked for any of those things, and I was trying hard to remember.

"Sam, she was tall. But you and I both watch women's basketball, and we've grown accustomed to female six footers, so she really didn't seem unusually tall to me. Joni was five nine, maybe five ten. And I don't remember really looking at her hands or feet. Even if I had, it may not have registered if they seemed large."

"So, what happens now, Donna?"

"She said she would call me. She apologized for not giving me her phone number, but said she just wasn't ready, and I understand that."

"Do you think she will call?"

I hesitated, trying to determine if I was just putting an optimistic spin on things or if I was being realistic.

"I do think she'll call. It may take a little time, and that's not going to be easy for me. But her reaction to what I was telling her about her family, what I was saying about how much I thought Miriam and Chris wanted me to find Joe, that hit hard. She got very emotional. Sam, as hard as it might be to go back to your siblings after twenty years and drop this kind of a bombshell on them, as hard as that would be, it's infinitely better than living your whole life wondering if they would have accepted you and you never made the move to find out. If it were me, I would rather make the move and be rejected than live my life never knowing."

We were both quiet for a few moments as we mulled over the implications of the whole thing in our heads. And then Sam asked the ever reoccurring question.

"What about Harold?"

I started laughing because it was like an old forty-five going round and round in the same groove. "What about Harold?"

"What about Harold?"

"I don't know. Harold is always the final question on every-body's mind. He's the fly in the ointment, the wild card. I think I'm coming to the conclusion that Joni should focus on Miriam and Chris, and let Harold do whatever it is that Harold will do!"

"Well, from what you've told me about how Miriam and Chris handle him, it doesn't sound like he'll be in control of them."

"I totally agree. At one time that might have been the case, but not now. Let's start dinner, and I'll tell you what I've found out about Helena Vanscoy and company."

Sam looked confused and said, "Who?"

Boy, I had a lot to bring him up to speed on.

Shortly after Sam left on Thursday morning, Josh showed up. It was just after nine, an odd time for him to be stopping by. I headed down the stairs just as he came through the back door.

"Hey, Mom. Got any cereal? I had a ten o'clock court appear-ance scheduled and didn't wake up until nine. All I had time to do was put on my clothes and jump in the car, and then they called and said the judge is running late so they pushed the hear-ing back an hour. Now I have time for breakfast and, since you're on the way, and my mother, I thought you might feed me."

I pulled some Frosted Mini-Wheats out of the cabinet, and he got the milk and bowl.

"So Mom? You and the Taylor County chief making any progress?" he asked with a grin.

"Actually, we are, Josh."

I proceeded to tell him the information I'd found on Renee de la Corte and brought him up to speed on the Prudhomme and Gagne shady dealings as well as Helena Vanscoy's art background.

Little by little he stopped grinning and showed some interest. By the time I was done, his comment was, "I think something went on there."

"Josh, that land has been owned by people with Louisiana roots for close to a century now. Why? It doesn't appear that any of them ever lived there. It's not what you'd call investment property. There is just no obvious tie. But I think they kept it for a reason, and I think it was a nefarious reason."

"What do you think it was?"

"My best guess would be that they hid stolen property there. The Banana Wars took place primarily in Guatemala and Honduras. The companies employed thugs and ne'er-do-wells who stole and plundered jade and cultural treasures when they weren't working their day jobs, which, come to think of it, was stealing and plundering arable land for the companies. New Orleans was the point of entry for the banana boats, so I imagine that's where most of the stolen goods came into the country. And, of course, we can't forget that the tie to the land started with Axel Tredloe's money."

"Tell me again who he was?"

"He would be the great-great-uncle of the generation of Tredloes I'm trying to lease. He was their great-grandfather's brother, and our research shows he was involved in the Banana Wars."

"You're connecting the dots pretty well, Mom."

"Josh, I don't know much about stolen art or antiquities, but I would imagine you'd have to lay low with them for a while after you stole them. I mean, I think the authorities and legitimate dealers and collectors would be on the lookout for them."

"Boy, Mom, that's not an area I know much about. My criminals are all busy stealing generators and TVs and guns so they can hock them and buy drugs. There could be a Van Gogh on the wall, and they wouldn't have a clue. But then, neither would I, so who's to talk."

Josh and I both laughed.

"I'd probably miss it too, Josh. But anyway, that's the only theory I've come up with. The chief says the Feds are doing the investigation in Louisiana now, and I don't think they're very good about keeping him informed. He commented that he was surprised they'd told him as much as they had. To tell you the truth, I don't even know why the Feds are involved."

"Well, interstate trafficking would be enough to trigger their involvement. And you're right about the information flow. They typically want to know everything you've got, but they're not very good about feeding information back down the line."

"Well, Josh, I'll keep you posted. I'm heading to see the chief today with the new info I got on Renee de la Corte."

"So Mom, not to change the subject, but have you found your missing guy?"

"I think I'm getting close. I'm talking to a couple of people who certainly know him, but I don't think he's ready to come forward just yet. And, who knows, it may never happen."

Josh had finished his cereal, said good-bye, and headed out the door. I really hated not coming clean with him on Joni, but I felt it was a secret I really needed to keep. And, to tell the truth, I wasn't sure what Josh's reaction would be.

I gathered up a couple of titles I needed to talk to Tony about and was getting ready to leave when Joanne called.

"Are you headed to Taylor County anytime today?" she asked.

"I was just going out the door when you called. What do you need?"

"One of the field guys left a right-of-way agreement for a

waterline with Lester Bolings on Jacobs Run. He called this morning and said he'd signed it. Can you pick it up and overnight it to the Charleston office? He's the last one we needed to sign, and I want to get it processed so we can give the contractor the go-ahead to lay the line."

Joanne told me where Mr. Bolings lived, and I said I'd do it on my way to the courthouse. Little did I know what she'd just dropped in my lap.

Down in the Hole

Jacobs Run Road was cut into the sides of the two hills that flanked a narrow valley. The road would cling to one side of the hill and then you'd descend just a bit crossing a bridge over the actual Jacobs Run and continue on the other side of the hill until it crossed back again, then repeat the whole process. Occasionally the valley widened out and the bottomland would either be fenced for pasture or used for hay. So as not to waste what little flatland there was, and to stay out of the flood plain, the houses were situated on the sides of the hills.

On the side of the south-facing hill is where I found Lester Bolings's house a mile or so in. I caught sight of Mr. Bolings waiting for me on the front porch. Joanne had called to tell him I was coming.

I pulled into a narrow, gravel drive and said hello as I got out of the car. Mr. Bolings waved and grinned. He was sitting in one of two matching rockers and, as I stepped onto the porch, he pointed at the other one indicating I should sit. I suspected that I was in his wife's chair and, over the course of the conversation, he told me all about her. She'd died a couple of years before, leaving a husband who was obviously in pretty good health.

We eventually got around to talking gas wells.

"I hear you're putting a well in down near where they hauled all those people out the other night."

"Yes sir, we're trying. That might hold us up a little, though."

"You know, I grew up on that road. There was only two houses on it back then: the old Tredloe place, where they arrested those guys, and the house I grew up in. It's gone though. Burned to the ground in sixty-five."

"Mr. Bolings, did you ever know any of the people from Louisiana who owned the Tredloe farm and the old Hagen place?"

"Well, I'll tell ya, they were fairly unknowable people. That thing about Southerners being friendly you sure couldn't prove by them. Kept to themselves when they were there, and that wasn't real often. And besides, my daddy always told me to stay away from 'em. Said he didn't know what they were up to, but it wasn't anything good!"

"Did he ever say what he thought they might be up to?"

"I don't think he really knew. They used to go in there in an old panel truck, kind of like the small delivery trucks grocery stores used to use. Might be there a couple of days, and then they were gone. And then, oh somewhere I'd say in 1945, maybe '46, we started hearing noises a good way down in the woods. It went on for about a month. Banging and sawing, and that panel truck was going in and out more than normal. Heck, that's the only time I ever remember them fellas staying that long."

"Did you ever go down there to see what they were doing?"

"Course I did. I would have been fourteen or fifteen, and you know how boys that age are. A buddy and I snuck down there one day. Old Willie Watson. He's dead now. We was hearing noise and we could tell where it was coming from, but we kept getting closer and closer and didn't see no people anywhere. But then Willie spotted the tops of some two-by-fours sticking out of the ground a couple of inches. We moved in a little closer, and we could hear voices but still couldn't see a soul."

Mr. Bolings was a born storyteller, and he was really getting into this one.

"We crept in a little more and could actually hear what they was saying, although with those deep South accents, hearing wasn't always understanding, if you know what I mean. But when we got close enough we realized there was a big hole in the ground, and they were down in it. We got down on our hands and knees, and snuck up enough to see that the two-by-fours were anchoring plywood to the sides of the hole. We could see the top of a ladder coming up, too."

"So what do you think they'd dug the hole for?"

"Don't know, but we laid low behind some bushes and kept listening. We were both scared to death someone would come up the ladder, but they didn't. They was talking about having a couple of steel plates made to go across the roof of this thing and how they was going to get 'em in there and in place and then make sure it was waterproof. And then they started talking about the tunnel and the reinforcements for the tunnel roof."

"A tunnel? Did they say from where?"

"Nope. And we decided we'd best get out of there. We were trying to act brave to each other, but we were plenty scared. Whole thing was strange."

"Mr. Bolings, it sounds like they were building a bunker."

"That's what Willie and I figured, too, but we couldn't figure out why."

"They must have been hiding something. I mean the mid-forties would have been well before people were building bunkers because of the Cold War."

"I never did know what they dug that for," Mr. Bolings said, shaking his head from side to side. "And I didn't dare tell my dad and see what he thought 'cause he would've tarred my hide if he'd know'd I'd snuck down there."

"Do you think you could find that same spot now, Mr. Bolings?"

"I reckon I could. But you're going to have to let me in on what's going on 'cause I can see your mind going a mile a minute."

I wasn't going to get anything past this guy!

"I think that bunker, or whatever it is, might be very important to the investigation going on there. And Mr. Bolings, I really don't know much about the whole thing, but I do know the Feds are now involved, and I do have a theory of my own that a secret underground storage space would fit right into. I think they might have needed a place to hide some stolen property. And sticking it in a hole in the ground in West Virginia sounds like a pretty good plan to me."

"Well, I suppose that's as good a theory as any as to what they was doin' down there. And, now that I think about it, I'm sure I could find it. There was a small stand of honey locust that me and Willie walked through as we got close. You know what honey locust is, Mrs. Cain?"

"Yes I do, and I wouldn't want to run into one in the dark!"

Mr. Bolings chuckled. Honey locust is a tree that sports very substantial, very long clusters of thorns protruding out of its trunk. Some of them are eight to ten inches long. A mature honey locust trunk looks like some sort of medieval torture system, and I couldn't help but think that the tree had been used in evil ways through the ages. It wasn't a terribly common tree, but they were native to the area.

"That was over sixty years ago," Mr. Bolings said, "but I would think those trees would still be there or at least other trees they spawned. You want to have a look?"

Well, of course, I wanted to have a look. The logical, cautious side of me said go tell all of this to Chief Warner. The adventurous, throw-caution-to-the-wind side of me said go find the thing, or at least evidence of it, and then go tell Chief Warner. Side two won, but then a little good sense set it.

"Mr. Bolings, we can go in my Jeep. But here's the deal. I don't know if any areas are still marked off out there with police tape, but I think we have to agree we won't cross any lines if they're there. Okay?"

"Well, if we see police tape, maybe you could stay put and I could mosey on down and have a look. I'm just an old man wandering around his old stomping grounds. And I can play senile with the best of them!"

With that, he flashed me an ornery grin, and I decided having one of us on the right side of the law should suffice! I secured the signed right-of-way agreement in my satchel, threw it in the back seat, and waited as Mr. Bolings locked the door to the house and climbed in beside me. We were off.

After we made our way out of Jacobs Run Road, it was less than a mile to the little road out to the old Tredloe farm. We'd only gone a quarter mile or so when Mr. Bolings said, "There on the right. That's where the house stood."

I slowed as we approached the old homeplace where Mr. Bolings had grown up. There were a couple of spruce trees and evidence of daffodils, their early spring blooms now gone. The burned out house had been torn down, but a few old foundation stones embedded in the ground easily marked where the house had stood. And, up the hill, a bit behind it, was the old stone springhouse, something almost all rural West Virginia homes used to have.

As we pulled to the side of the road, Mr. Bolings took a long look at it and said, "Lot of good memories in that place. My dad was tough but fair, and my mother was a saint. She thought kids should pull their own around the house, but only to a point. She wanted us to have fun and she made sure we did. Ate well too."

He reminisced some more and then pointed to a deer trail through the woods on the lower side of the road. "Look at that. Same trail that was here when I was a boy. That's a mature woods and there's been no logging over the years. That means little underbrush to speak of and an easy walk for us."

"Mr. Bolings, are you up to a walk like this?" I hated to ask, but I knew he was past eighty.

"I walk in the woods or up the pasture behind the house every day the weather will allow. If you don't keep moving when you get old, Mrs. Cain, you end up not being able to move at all. Don't you worry about me."

And with that, we set off down the deer trail. I had a fleeting thought that I should be working and this might not be considered work but, then again, it might. The sooner this investigation was over, the sooner the drilling could commence.

We went about five hundred feet or so and Mr. Bolings stopped, shielded his eyes with his hands, and started looking at the trees. He pointed slightly left off the trail and started off again. I followed, scanning the trees up ahead for those pesky thorns. Finally, I spotted what I thought might be a honey locust.

"Mr. Bolings, I think I see a honey locust. I pointed and he said, "By nab, I think you're right!"

This was downright exciting. When we got to the honey locust, we stopped. It wasn't a big stand, but you could see some of the trees were very old. Three or four were on the ground in various stages of rot having succumbed to old age and wind, I suppose, but there were young ones, too, so it didn't look like the honey locust were going away at any time soon.

"Look at the fur hanging from some of those low lying thorns, Mr. Bolings."

We both moved in for a closer look.

"Good scratching places, I suspect. Most of that's deer fur, but I figure that's some bear hide hanging on that one," he said. "Too dark for deer."

We continued on and both grew more quiet even though we knew no one was around. Mr. Bolings was moving slower, and I could tell he was tapping into those long ago memories to get us in the right place.

We were walking slightly downhill to a small area that did have underbrush. There were some saplings but no mature trees. It was obvious there had been a longtime break in the canopy, allowing sunlight to filter down. Mr. Bolings and I both stopped at the edge of the brush.

"That's the place," he said. "That's where they dug that hole in the ground."

"You can tell it was cleared at one time, can't you?"

"It was. Look up. There's still a hole in the canopy. That shows this area was kept clear long after me and Willie was here. It would have bigger trees on it by now otherwise. And those bushes are sitting in a small depression—not much, couple of inches maybe. That'd be normal if a big hole had been dug there."

His words made sense, and we both just stood there looking at the brush-covered clearing and thinking. We were very quiet. The birds weren't saying much, and the wind wasn't blowing. It was a very peaceful forest. A nice place to be.

"Mr. Bolings, would you mind if I shared this with the Sheriff's Department?"

"You think it's worth sharing?"

"Yes, I think it might be just one more piece of the puzzle. And maybe an important piece. But they may want to talk to you. You're the guy that witnessed them digging that hole."

"That's okay. I'll talk to 'em. I've drunk all last year's 'shine anyway so they won't find anything illegal if they head for the house."

There was that grin again. I had no idea if he was kidding or not. I'd give it a fifty–fifty.

Mr. Bolings and I climbed up the gentle hill we'd come down, and I could tell he probably did do a lot of walking. He wasn't winded. We both got in the Jeep, and I dropped him off at his place with many thank-yous and a promise to be in touch if I found out anything new. But I had a feeling he'd be seeing a deputy before he saw me.

Caught in the Act

I made my way out of Jacobs Run for the second time and had just hit the main road when my cell rang. I answered without looking at the ID and was more than surprised to find myself talking to Joni Morgan.

"Joni, I'm way out in the woods, and I might lose you. Cell towers aren't too abundant out here, but I'll call back if I do. Hold on though, because I think there's a place to pull off at the top of this hill."

I pulled off onto a grass-covered track leading to a gated entrance to a farmer's pasture. I sure hoped they didn't come along.

"Okay, I'm sitting on a hill, and I have three bars. It's good to hear from you."

"Are you sure you can talk now, Mrs. Cain?"

"I'm sure, and we're on a first-name basis, remember?"

"I do. Donna, I'll get right to the point. I know you're working."

"It's okay. I have time. And remember, you're a person I'm supposed to be talking to for work."

"I'm sorry. I have to admit that I lose track of that aspect of it. I think you can understand that the family angle of this situation kind of overpowers the business side of it."

"And rightly so. I'd feel the same way."

"Well, Donna, I've given the whole thing a lot of thought. In fact, it's about all I've thought about since we talked. I've known for a long time that I was going to approach my family sooner or later. So it's not that I don't want to. I've wanted to forever. But it's a very scary proposition. I've seen some people like me try it and succeed. And I've seen others really suffer when they were rejected."

I could tell Joni had been thinking about what she would say to me, and it was pouring out fast. All I could do was listen, since any comments that came to mind seemed inane anyway.

"But, I know now the time has come. And, quite honestly Donna, I've been positioning myself for this for several years. There's a lot I didn't tell you last time we met, like where I live."

"Joni, once I knew you weren't your cousin from Ohio, I just took it for granted you lived in Pittsburgh."

"I live in Morgantown, Donna."

Good grief. Joni was living about a half an hour's drive from any of her three siblings!

"And I work for West Virginia University. I'm a diversity specialist. I teach a course for master's-level education students, I consult for some of the bigger departments on hiring and personnel matters, I lecture for one of the courses at the law school— just a variety of things. And, quite honestly, I help the university stay out of trouble. LGBTQ issues are certainly a large part of it, but I cover race, disabilities, and a lot more."

"Joni, how long have you been in Morgantown?"

"Four years. And last year, something magical happened. At least it was to me. And that's what I want to tell you about, but not on the phone. Can we meet again? And this time we can meet in Morgantown. But please, Donna, not a word of this to my family. If I'm going to do this it needs to be in a very controlled, very gentle way, if that's possible."

"Your family will never learn it from me, Joni. It's certainly not my place to break the news."

Joni and I tossed around a couple of places and finally decided on a small, very cozy, family-owned Italian restaurant, both of us agreeing that we really liked their house Cabernet. And who knows, a little wine might help the process along.

Since it was already Thursday and they weren't open on Monday, we made a date for the following Tuesday at six. I had told her I was more than willing to meet on Friday or over the weekend, but she said there was something she needed to do in preparation for our meeting and it might take her a few days.

We hung up with me running possibilities through my mind of what that "something" might be, but I couldn't even come up with any ideas. Good grief! Tuesday really seemed like a long way off.

I pulled back onto the road and headed into town to overnight the Lester Bolings waterline agreement to Joanne and to see if I could talk to the chief. It was certainly an action-packed day.

The post office was just down the street from the courthouse, so I parked midway between the two. I dashed into the post office and put the agreement in an overnight envelope, filled out an address label, paid the fee, and was back on the street heading to the courthouse in no time.

The chief's hall door wasn't open so I poked my head in the outer office and said hello to Elaine. Elaine was the administrative assistant for the department and, from my observations, was the glue that held the place together. I had to think she'd been there a while because she wielded some power over the newer deputies, and I think the chief depended on her to keep them informed and somewhat in-line. She glanced up and said, "The chief's at an evidence collection seminar. Be back tomorrow, though. Anything I can help you with?"

"No, no, I just had something to tell him. It'll wait."

Darn, the bunker was big news, and I was itching to tell the chief. Oh well. It had been there over sixty years already, so it wasn't like it was going to disappear before tomorrow. I was still disappointed.

I headed downstairs to find Tony and ask him some questions about the two titles I had in hand. Tony had two other abstractors on the job, and they were all working in the overcrowded record room. That wasn't Tony's cup of tea, and he looked relieved to have a reason to leave. In no time at all, we were out the door and headed to the coffee shop down the street.

"So, Donna, how's your search going?"

He'd asked me that question recently and knew I couldn't tell him any details, but he was dying to know and I didn't blame him.

"Tony, you know I can't say much—you'll understand when it all comes out. Well, if it all comes out, but, as of this morning, I'm pretty sure it will. I got a phone call that makes me much more hopeful that the issue will be resolved and Joe will be found."

"When you can talk, I want every little detail."

"I won't leave out a thing!"

We'd just walked into the coffee shop where we both ordered coffees while drooling over the pastries, which we managed to resist. The place was fairly empty so we took a table as far from the other two occupied tables as possible. When you talk about title, you're mentioning family names, and you never know who might be related to who. And besides that, I'd decided to tell Tony about the bunker, and I sure didn't want anyone else to hear that story.

Tony and I got settled and I started relating the details of my visit with Lester Bolings, explaining to Tony where Mr. Bolings had grown up, and telling him, in detail, about our little field trip to the site of the bunker. I needed to keep quiet about what the chief had told me, but the chief didn't know a thing about the bunker so I figured I could talk. Tony was all ears.

"Tony, that bunker would be a perfect place to hide stolen art, antiquities, or whatever else our suspects, through the ages, might have spirited out of Central America, or anyplace else, for that matter."

"Donna, you could easily be onto something. How big do you think the bunker is?"

"I hadn't really thought about it, Tony, but the slight depression in the ground that Mr. Bolings pointed out to me was pretty big. I guess the hole that was dug would be the outside dimensions and a little more. The walls would be thick I would think."

I thought about it more and told him the depression was probably about ten-by-twelve. If that was the case, Tony thought the interior would probably be at least nine-by-eleven.

"So, Donna, did Mr. Bolings have any idea where the entrance to the tunnel might be?"

"No, he didn't have a clue. But Tony, if there's a slight depression where the bunker is, wouldn't it be logical that there would be a depression that followed the tunnel?"

"Depends on how they dug it. If they dug from the top down, yes. If they simply burrowed through from the entrance and fortified the roof as they went, probably not."

"Digging from the top down would be hard enough, but I can't imagine how difficult it would be to dig it all underground. It would be backbreaking work and, I would think, dangerous."

"I agree, but people have been digging tunnels that way for thousands of years and still do. Think about drug smuggling, border crossings, jailbreaks, robberies. If it's a secret tunnel, that's how you dig it!"

"You're right, but I wouldn't want to be the one doing the digging!"

Tony was fascinated with the whole idea and, the more we talked, the more we knew we had to get a good look at the ground around the bunker to see if we could see any evidence of the tunnel or its opening. But I was dragging my feet knowing full well we shouldn't be out there, even though I was dying to have a second look.

"Donna, it's almost lunchtime. It's what, fifteen minutes to get there, if that?"

"About that."

"Okay, and we'll talk title on the way out and make the time count. What can it hurt?"

I reluctantly agreed and, since we wouldn't be eating lunch, Tony and I both ordered big gooey pastries, grabbed our coffees and extra napkins, jumped in my car, and headed to the bunker. We talked title for maybe five minutes and then gave up due to lack of focus. We were both too excited over what we might find.

I had just pulled off the road where the old Bolings house had stood, and Tony and I were getting out of the car when we heard gravel crunching and realized another car was approaching from the direction of the Tredloe farm. Damn!

We'd both jumped back in, and I'd just started the engine when the vehicle rolled around the turn about forty feet from us. It was a sheriff's cruiser with Deputy Ornick behind the wheel and Detective Bauer riding shotgun. They pulled up beside us and got out, as did we.

I quickly introduced Tony as our lead abstractor and the person who had done all of the history and research on the land. Hands were shaken, and then both Ornick and Bauer looked at me with expressions that said I needed to explain why we were there.

"You're probably wondering why Tony and I are here."

Slight nods in the affirmative.

"I just came from the chief's office. I was going to tell him what I'd discovered, but he wasn't there. Then I told Tony what I'd found, and we realized that we might be able to put together a lot more of the story if we just took another good look. Well, this would be Tony's first look, but . . ."

Detective Bauer put his hands up in front of him, palms out, in a clear indication that I should stop babbling, and said, "What story? Start with the story."

"Well, it all began this morning when I had to get a signature from Lester Bolings." I explained everything in detail and watched as their interest grew.

"So you're telling us there's a bunker down this path," Deputy Ornick said, pointing the way I'd indicated, "and you can show us where it is."

"Yes, it's not far. And Tony and I thought it would be helpful if we could find the tunnel."

"It would be helpful, Mrs. Cain, but neither of you should be out here on your own. Criminals own this land and in all probability, the three we arrested weren't the only three people involved."

Detective Bauer was lecturing us, but at the same time he was motioning us toward the path, which he and the deputy were already headed for. I was providing direction from the end of the line and, as we got further along, I pointed out the honey locust grove that made the depression in the ground easier to find. As we approached the bunker site, Ornick and Bauer both stopped a few feet back and indicated that we do the same. They made a complete visual inspection of the area before going any closer.

"Tell us again what Lester Bolings said he'd overheard," Bauer asked.

"He heard them talk about how to get the steel plates in here and in place for the roof of the bunker. And he also heard them talking about how they were going to reinforce the roof of the tunnel."

"And when?"

"Around 1945 or 1946," I answered.

Detective Bauer turned around and gave me a skeptical look. "That's well over fifty years ago, and Lester Bolings is in his eighties. That could be what he heard, but it might just as easily be his imagination talking."

But Deputy Ornick wasn't of the same opinion. "I don't think so, Bob. I know Lester pretty well. In fact, my whole family does. He and my uncle were good buddies, and Lester can remember things in detail that my uncle's long forgot. We've always been amazed at Lester's memory. He could probably tell you what the temperature was the day he overheard all that."

Tony had been silent the whole time, but I knew he was thinking. Tony was always thinking. And then he said, "If they used steel, or any metal, in the tunnel roof, you should be able to find it with a metal detector."

Detective Bauer was on his haunches brushing the leaves and other forest detritus from the side of the depression so he could see just how far down it went. But with Tony's suggestion, he got up, brushed his hands off, and said, "Excellent idea. But first, let's see if we can find any visual evidence of a tunnel, just like you two were preparing to do."

There was a bit of extra emphasis on that last part, but he was sort of smiling so we knew we were off the hook. After all, we had coughed up some pretty important information.

"Ornick, we don't have a metal detector at the office do we?" the detective asked.

"Not that I know of, but my dad loves to find stuff, and he actually has a pretty good one. I can borrow it. But if we want to take a look while we're here, I'm thinking the tunnel would go towards the house or the outbuildings."

It would be a long way to dig, but we all agreed that the direction made sense, so we fanned out about twenty feet apart all walking in the general direction of the farmhouse. I was more than happy they were letting us take part and was thinking hard about what I might see that would indicate a tunnel down below. I soon learned that it wasn't what I would see but what I would feel.

I was walking through some pretty deep leaf litter, uniformly soft and cushy, when all of a sudden my next footstep put me on something more solid. I took another step and felt the same solid base before my brain sounded the alarm. What on the forest floor felt like that?

"Hey guys, I think there's something solid under me here. It sure doesn't feel like just leaves and dirt!"

The other three headed my way as I was trying to find the edge of whatever I was feeling with my foot. I couldn't.

Ornick was wearing heavy-duty boots, and he started scraping away the leaves with his feet. After getting five or six inches of leaves, general rot, and whatever else out of the way, Detective Bauer finally reached down with his hands and pulled a piece of rotted, indoor–outdoor carpeting up, displacing the final bit of muck that was covering it.

It was hiding a steel slab about three-and-a-half feet square with a rusty, old metal handle attached in the middle. The slab was sitting about an inch down in a concrete enclosure. Ornick got a good grip on the handle and, after a few tugs, was able to pull the metal covering up and out of the concrete.

We all stood there peering into a hole that was about three feet square with a dilapidated metal ladder affixed to one side. The light penetrated enough that we could see the concrete walls went down maybe four feet, and then it looked like the dirt was held back by some kind of metal mesh. It certainly didn't look all that substantial or inviting, and the detective and deputy both agreed that they needed the right equipment to make a foray into the hole.

Deputy Ornick put the metal back in place and laid the carpeting over it. We all helped push leaves and litter back on with our feet but the finished product wasn't that good; it could easily be spotted as a recently disturbed spot, so we then went to work with our hands and, when it looked more like the forest floor around it, we spent some time walking on it to pack it down.

"The average person would never notice," Detective Bauer said, "but if anyone who knows this opening is here comes by, they'll know someone has uncovered it and get spooked."

Deputy Ornick gave it a few last stomps and said, "I think we need to get a camera out here in a tree."

"It wouldn't hurt to have a night-vision camera," Tony offered. "If I were trying to sneak in here, that's when I'd come."

The detective and the deputy both agreed that was a good idea, and then they spent a couple minutes impressing upon Tony and me that, while they appreciated our help, there was an element of danger to being out here.

Detective Bauer gave us a stern look and said, "No more investigating on your own, and that's an order!" Tony and I both nodded our heads in the affirmative.

"And, I think you both realize how important it is not to talk about this, right?" Tony and I answered "Yes, Sir" in unison and then felt silly. But we did understand, and we meant it. With that, we all made our way back to the cars and parted company.

Hoodwinked Again

Between speculating on what Joni needed a few days to do before we met, and wondering just what would turn up in the newly discovered bunker, my head was in turmoil and my concentration suffered. On Friday, I processed signed documents to send to the office. I'd done it many times before so it didn't require great concentration, but I found myself making mistakes and having to redo because I just had no focus.

Over the weekend, Sam accused me of being physically present but mentally elsewhere, and I couldn't really argue. I'd brought him up to speed on Joni's phone call, as well as finding the tunnel entrance, and he kept coming up with comments and questions on both.

Tony, however, was being vintage Tony and doing research. He sent me several articles on art and antiquities theft. I learned that it was a billion dollar, international black market that was hard to police due to wildly different, and sometimes conflicting, laws from country to country. He sent articles indicating that some police agencies didn't take it very seriously or simply didn't have the expertise to deal with it. And he also directed me to the National Stolen Art File, known as the NSAF, which was operated by the FBI. It looked impressive, but I certainly had nothing concrete to enter into the database and look for, even if it would allow me to, which I didn't think it would.

Monday finally dawned, and I knew I needed to spend the

day reviewing new title even though what I really wanted to do was call on the chief to see if they'd entered the tunnel and opened the bunker. But other than that, I didn't have a single reason to go to the courthouse. I fortified my willpower and remained in my home office both Monday and Tuesday. As Tuesday dawned, my attention turned to Joni and whatever revelation might unfold at our six o'clock dinner.

After a long day reading title, it was finally time to go, and I did my best to wipe my mind clean and just flow with whatever happened. My drive to the restaurant was spent trying to choose my entree from a menu I knew pretty well. Amani's had wonderful stuffed shells, but there was a Portobello and fettuccini dish that I absolutely loved, and their vegetarian lasagna was one of my favorites. I arrived undecided but quite hungry.

I spotted Joni the moment I walked in. She waved me over to a cozy table in the corner, a four top, beautifully set, and lit with a candle in an etched frosted bowl making it even more inviting. I'd always loved Amani's color scheme featuring soft creams, a silky mauve, and a smoky gray-green. It was just a very relaxing atmosphere. I looked around the room and noted that it was a typically slow Tuesday evening, with only four other tables occupied.

Joni stood up as I approached and made a slight movement toward shaking hands, but then she gave me a quick hug and sat back down. Now that I knew she'd started life as a male, I couldn't help but wonder if she didn't sometimes have trouble not doing those things men are commonly taught to do, like standing up when a woman first enters a room. The pitfalls seemed endless.

We sat down across from each other, and I said, "Joni, I'm really glad you called me. I wasn't sure you would."

She just smiled. "Well, there wasn't even the slightest chance I wouldn't call you. You're part of a path that's coming together,

Donna. I just had to get my bearings and think," she said laughing, "and think, and then think some more. But it didn't take me long to realize that I just need to move forward!"

Joni seemed very animated, and I assumed that was probably from nerves. It made me very eager to hear what she had to say. Something was coming.

"Donna, I need to get right down to why I wanted to meet. Last year, before fall semester classes started, I looked at my roster for the class I teach for master's-level education students, and one name popped off the page. Thea Baxter!"

"That's Miriam's daughter!"

"Yes it is. And Donna, even though I knew it was very unlikely this girl would ever figure out who I was, I was scared to death. Not because I didn't want to know her. I was excited beyond words about that. But, I didn't know if I could control my reaction to her and, believe me, it was tough to do. The first day of class when I called roll, I choked up saying her name. I turned my back to the class feigning a coughing spell. But I got control, turned back around, and called her name again. She said 'here,' and I had to do a little more coughing before I could go on."

"Joni, I can't imagine how you held it together."

"I wanted to grab her and hug her. She was a three-year-old when I left home. I remember holding her when she was a baby. I loved playing with her and even babysat her a few times. And now there she was in my classroom, the spitting image of Miriam. Same eyes, same hair, and Miriam's big, beautiful smile."

"That was last fall. Did you ever tell her?"

"No. She knows I was once a man. Transgender issues are a part of the class, so I make no secret of how I came to be who I am. My class is an elective, and the students who choose to take it typically want to know more about a variety of issues and how to deal with them in the classroom. We have to have some very serious and uncomfortable conversations in that class, and sometimes I use a little humor to lighten things up. Especially if someone says something really insensitive. Most of the time, they don't realize it. I've always tried to follow this rule: If someone means to be offensive towards me, then I'll take offense. If there was no offense intended, I weigh it differently and use it as a teaching moment. Not everyone knows the right words to say."

"It certainly gets complicated."

"It does. But Donna, Thea and I really hit it off. Of course, I worked hard to make that happen. But she liked the class so much she decided to do her thesis on junior high and high school students who are trans—all of the phases they go through from their own realization on, and how teachers can deal with the issues that get in the way of those kids getting a good education. It derails a lot of kids. And, honestly, I suggested the topic to her because, unfortunately, there hasn't been a lot of research and publication on it. But that's good for Thea, because fresh subject matter can be hard to find for a thesis."

"So you're her advisor?"

"No, no. I'm not, at least not technically. That's not a role I fill, but she's run it past her advisor who's totally onboard. Thea is entering her second year this fall, and that's when she'll do her thesis. She wants to get some planning done over the summer, though, and she's asked me to meet with her and help get her started."

"She's going to want to know more about your story, Joni. I mean, I can't imagine that she won't. You're research she can reach out and touch. Anecdotal, yes, but real—very, very real."

"I know, Donna. And I'm going to tell her my story. I think Thea is my best entry back into the family. She took my class, so she knows and understands far more about trans issues than the rest of the family. And we've become friends in a sense. There's a big age difference, but we talk about things that friends talk about. Thea should be okay with this."

"So when are you going to tell her?"

"This evening. She's joining us here. I asked her to meet me at six thirty."

With that surprise announcement, I'm fairly certain my jaw literally dropped. "Joni, I'm here! How's that going to work?"

"Donna, I was going to do it over the weekend. That's why I put off our dinner. I just never got up the nerve. I kept rehearsing how I would tell her. First one way, then another. Nothing seemed right."

I was just looking at Joni, my mind racing, looking for some logical reason I should be at this table for this announcement. Nothing was coming to mind and, apparently, Joni could see that.

The waitress arrived with two glasses of Cabernet. Since I'd told Joni how much I liked it, she'd taken the liberty of ordering for both of us. I took a much bigger drink than normal.

She just smiled and said, "Feel better?"

"Maybe after another glass or two, even though one's my limit."

"Donna, once my mind went to the possibility of having you here when I tell Thea, I just knew it was right. You've become my bridge, my emotional crutch. Well, you and, hopefully, Thea. You're an outsider, not family. Families can get awfully emotional, and they often say things they don't really mean when no one else is around. I need someone else around, and that someone is you. With you here, I can do it. I hope you're not upset by this. I know, I really caught you by surprise."

"Not upset. That's not the right word. Concerned, I guess. I have to look at it from a business perspective even though, as you well know, I've become emotionally involved as well. I guess I'm just thinking, professionally, should I be here?"

"From a professional perspective, I don't think you should, and that's why I didn't tell you in advance. I've pulled a fast one on you, and that gives you a story to tell the office if you ever have to. I need you here. And, I need Thea to trust you, and you to trust her, if we're going to pull the rest of the family in. Does that make sense?"

I had a couple more sips, big sips, of wine and realized that I had no intention of leaving. I felt honored that Joni wanted me to be present. I smiled and saw a look of relief in Joni's eyes that I wasn't heading for the exit. "I'm here, Joni. I won't leave."

Just then she looked up, smiled, and waved at someone approaching from behind me. Showtime!

When Thea got to the table, I could see she was confused by my presence since she thought the purpose of the meeting was to discuss plans for her thesis with Joni. I knew Thea's name from conversations with Miriam, but I'd never actually met her. She did look like a young Miriam, with curlier hair going a bit more towards red, an athletic-looking body (a runner would be my guess), and a warm easy smile. Just like Miriam, she was naturally pretty.

Joni introduced us, first names only, telling Thea that I was a friend she thought might add something to the conversation, and then we got into general chitchat, mostly about Thea's frustrating day trying to find a "new" used car. The waitress approached and took Thea's order for a Chardonnay, and then we all three perused the menu to be ready for her return.

"Donna, what's your favorite?" Joni asked.

I told her my top three choices and said I was leaning toward the mushroom-fettuccini dish. Thea had never been to Amani's but said she almost always ordered manicotti when eating in a good

Italian restaurant, and Joni said she was going for the vegetarian lasagna. The waitress returned with the Chardonnay, and we placed our orders. But the moment she walked away, an awkward silence descended upon us. I tried to fill the void.

"So Thea, I understand that you're doing your thesis on trans children in junior high and high school?"

"Yes. Joni suggested the topic, and when I saw how little research there actually was, I thought it was a great idea. And, with Joni's real life experiences . . ."

Thea stopped talking, and looked at Joni with alarm, realizing that she was just assuming I knew Joni was trans.

Joni was just putting her wine glass to her lips, but stopped and said, "She knows, Thea. It's okay."

We spent another ten minutes or so with Joni and Thea talking about avenues of research, good sources of information, etc. I hoped Thea wouldn't notice that I really didn't have much to add other than a few comments like "that makes sense" and "I think that would be my choice." I actually heard Joni chuckle at one point, knowing I was swimming in unknown waters.

The salads arrived and diverted our attention, followed closely by the main course, all three of which we deemed absolutely delicious. As we finished, we each ordered another glass of wine, and the waitress delivered those in short order.

"I'll have to run twenty extra miles this week to make up for this," Thea said.

Aha! I'd pegged that one right. The heavy Italian fare had left all three of us more than full, so we asked the waitress to please not even show us the dessert tray. If I see tiramisu, I eat tiramisu!

After the dishes had been cleared, Thea turned to Joni, her mouth open ready to say something, but she abruptly stopped.

Joni looked like she was about to jump off of a ten-story ledge. I was guessing it was time to make the leap so I sat still and waited.

Another deep breath and Joni said, "Thea . . ."

Thea sensed Joni's anxiety and said, "Joni, what's wrong?"

Joni's mouth opened and nothing came out. We all sat for a few seconds although it felt like five minutes. Thea was sitting beside Joni, so Joni had to turn to talk to her, and it was awkward.

"Thea," I said, "Joni has something to tell you and I think it would be far easier if you were sitting across from her. Take my seat, and I'll move over."

Thea looked a little perplexed but picked up her wine glass and moved to my place, directly across from Joni.

When Thea sat down, Joni reached across the table and took both of Thea's hands in hers. Thea really looked confused then, sensing this was way out of the typical teacher–student code of conduct and probably assuming really bad news was coming. I glanced around the restaurant and saw it had thinned out considerably. Thank goodness!

"Thea, did you ever think there was anything coincidental about my name?"

After a few seconds of thought, Thea said, "No, nothing I can think of."

"Thea," Joni was speaking so softly we struggled to hear, "the hands you're holding held you when you were a baby. Think about the name. Jo—ni Morgan."

We both watched Thea as she processed what Joni had just said. Words weren't needed. Thea's face went slowly from confusion to a realization that Joni had once been Joe, and then to true elation! Joni and I both knew step one was a success.

They both stood up hugging and crying and laughing and exclaiming. I sat there taking in every moment while dabbing my eyes with my napkin. The poor waitress approached with the check and then backed away, taking cover in the kitchen. We sure could stage drama in a restaurant! The people at the couple of tables that were left were sneaking furtive looks, wondering what the good news was and probably thinking there was a baby on the way, or someone got engaged.

When the commotion died down, the waitress appeared with the check, which Joni picked up and insisted on paying, telling me to not even think about leaving the tip. She then explained to Thea who I really was and the fact that my search for Joe had been responsible for moving Joni along faster than she might have done otherwise.

As we walked out, Joni and Thea decided to go to a nearby Starbucks and continue talking. I bowed out, with Joni promising to call me as soon as she made plans for the next step, whatever that might be. This time, I knew I would hear from her.

You Found What in the Bunker!

I headed home and was still up when Sam got home from soccer. I told him all about dinner with Joni and Thea. It left him shaking his head and smiling, pointing out that Joni's coming out to her family was probably on the fast track now.

"Donna, do you think the sisters will take it all in stride and be as happy as Thea was?"

"Right out of the gate? No! But, in short order, I think they will. I was thinking about that on the way home. Thea and Joni were already well acquainted, and Thea already knew Joni was trans. On top of that, Thea had taken Joni's class so she knew far more about it than the average person. Thea is at a much, much higher level of understanding than Miriam and Chris will be when they hear the news. But yes, I do think they'll get there."

I went to bed happy that the process was under way, but I also knew the hard part was yet to come.

The next morning, I had just walked through the court-house doors when Elaine spotted me as she headed down the hall toward the bathroom.

"Mrs. Cain! The chief said if I saw you in the courthouse to tell you to stop in. He's in a hearing, but he'll be back in an hour or so. Stop by, okay?"

"Sure, Elaine. I'll still be here."

As much as I wanted to talk to the chief to see if they went into the bunker, I was also nervous as to why he wanted to see

me. I had a feeling he was going to tell me, in no uncertain
terms, to stay away from the crime scene. There wasn't a chance
that Ornick and Bauer hadn't told him about finding Tony and
me there. But they all had to admit that we'd given them some
darned good information. That bunker had to figure in somehow!

I spent the next hour going back and forth between the record
room and the Assessor's office trying to figure out a mapping issue
on another tract. On my last trip between the two, I ran into
Chief Warner who was just getting back from his hearing.

"Mrs. Cain! Come see me. Please."

The please was an afterthought, and I was a little apprehensive
considering his tone of voice. But, as always, I obediently followed him into his office.

"Hear you and a coworker were doing a little investigating on
your own the other day!"

"Yes, but I did come to see you first. Elaine said you were at a
training."

"Mrs. Cain, don't do that again. And yes, before you remind
me, you did tell us something very valuable, and I bet you're
dying to know if we followed up on it."

"I have been wondering."

"Well, we had four deputies, three guys from the water
department, and a bunch of equipment out there the next day."

I must have looked confused because he quickly explained
that the water department guys are used to working underground
and have the knowledge and equipment to do it.

"So did you find anything?"

The chief leaned back in his chair and smiled. "We did,
Mrs. Cain, we did! I'm surprised you haven't already heard the
scuttlebutt. We found a body. A really old, leathery, wrinkled,

witchlike-looking body that gave everybody out there that saw it nightmares! It wasn't a pretty sight."

I was more than taken aback.

"Chief, I never considered that there might be a body in there. I thought you'd find evidence of jade and statuary and other antiquities sorts of things. But a body! My brain never went in that direction."

"Well, neither did ours. The water department guys were the first ones in and, from what Ornick tells me, the first ones out." The chief was laughing so I knew the stories were probably pretty good. And then everything the chief had said started sinking in.

"You said leathery and wrinkled and witchlike. Are you saying it was a woman who still had flesh on her body?"

"Yep! That's exactly what I'm saying. I guess the conditions down there didn't allow the body to fully decompose. Ornick said the place was pretty well sealed, and they had to work hard to get the door off."

"Did they get her out?"

Yeah. They went in through the tunnel the first day. Took a while because they had to reinforce as they went. It wasn't in the best of shape."

"I can't imagine what a job that was," I said, thinking I was glad I wasn't on that crew.

"So, then we had to convince the same three poor devils from the water department to haul a front-end loader out there the next day and dig out the entire area over the bunker. Then they had to cut through the steel plate that covered it and get the body up and out of the way. The Feds arrived just as our deputies were pulling the body out with the help of an EMS crew. So they kind of took over. Anyway, the body is at the crime lab in Charleston, and the Feds and our crime scene unit have thoroughly gone through the bunker to collect any other evidence that was there. And, yes, from early reports there is some evidence of artifacts and maybe jade. Don't know anything for sure yet."

"Any ideas on who she is?"

"None whatsoever! Thought you might know something. You've been way ahead of us on this bunker thing."

"I don't have a clue, Chief. Not even a stray thought."

"Well, I'd tell you to keep quiet, but I think the water department guys have told most of the town. So far today, three people have asked me about the body and the newspaper called while I was out. And, Mrs. Cain, we do appreciate you giving us the info on the bunker. But please remember, we still don't know the extent of what we're dealing with. No more investigating on your own."

"No problem there, Chief. But thank you for telling me what's going on. I guess I'm free to tell Tony?"

"Sure, but he may already know if he's been in the courthouse this morning."

I thanked the chief, went to my car, and called Tony. He was at home putting title files together, and I knew he hadn't been in. Tony was just as surprised by the news as I was.

"Donna, did they say how long the body had been there?"

"No, and I didn't think to ask. The chief said the place was pretty well sealed, so I doubt they could tell just by looking. Why?"

"Because I don't think the people from Louisiana ever had any dealings with local people. I bet they stashed a body from Louisiana there, someone they needed to get rid of."

"That's a good thought, Tony, but I would presume the Feds would go down that road as well."

"Probably, but I might just throw this info Lenai's way and see if she can find anything."

"Tony, isn't she going to get tired of you asking her to research things?"

"Are you kidding? She says this is far more interesting than the stuff she normally works on. In fact, I get an email every few days asking me if anything has developed and if there's anything else she can do."

"Go for it then. She'll love this news, and who knows what she might find."

I was still sitting in the car thinking, after my chat with Tony, when the phone rang. It was Aunt Betty.

"Oh my, I can't imagine how excited you are. I just had coffee after class with Arnold, and he told me everything. He told me why you couldn't tell me, too, and I totally understand. But Joni told Arnold it was okay to tell me. And, knowing Arnold, I really think he wanted to be the first to break the news to me before you did."

Aunt Betty had finally run out of breath, and I couldn't help but say, "Hello to you, too."

She just laughed. "Sorry, I'm just excited about this. You found him! Or at least the former him. And Arnold says Joni has made this change so well, and she's such a nice person. I hope I can meet her sometime."

"Well, the Professor is right about her being a very nice person, and she has made the transition quite well, although I would think it couldn't have been easy and still isn't."

"Arnold told me all about Thea and how they met in class and that Thea now knows."

I spent the rest of the conversation filling her in on the details of my first dinner with Joni and the more recent dinner with Joni and Thea. I explained that Joni was going to call me with, what I supposed would be, some sort of plan for telling the rest of the family, although she really had no obligation to share that with me.

"Aunt Betty, don't forget that you helped with this as well. The rapport you established with Professor Wilson couldn't have hurt in the trust department. And remember, you put me up for a night and traipsed all over Pittsburgh with me looking for people who knew Aunt Maud."

"Oh, but that was such fun. It was like playing detective. And I got a new friend out of it anyway. This has been more than interesting and such a good ending!"

I'm always amazed at just how broad-minded and accepting my aunt is. No one ever has to preach the benefits of diversity to her!

I went back in the courthouse to check a few more details and then headed home to put all my evidence together. On the way, I stopped at a local restaurant with the best salmon salad ever. I'd just pulled into their parking lot when the phone rang again.

The caller ID said it was Miriam Baxter. Oh my! It's so hard keeping secrets.

"Hi, Miriam!"

"Donna, I just got out of bed, which is so unlike me, but I was up until four in the morning and then I just collapsed."

"Miriam, is something wrong?"

"No . . . no . . ."

Her voice was definitely faltering.

"Miriam?"

I heard her take a deep breath. "Donna, at nine thirty last night, Thea drove up the driveway. I knew she was coming in later than usual so when I heard her car it was no big deal. But then I realized there was another car behind her. Just a friend, I thought, but kind of late for a visit."

I knew without asking who was in the second car, but I couldn't believe they did it that quickly.

Miriam continued, "I didn't know it, of course, but before she left Morgantown Thea had called Chris and asked her to come to my house. Chris was expecting the worst and had me dying of cancer by the time she got in the door. Thea and 'her friend' got here first and, after a very quick introduction, they both headed for Thea's room saying they had to check some notes."

"But then, when Chris got here a few minutes later, they both came out and just looked at us. Chris and I were completely confused, but we were also both aware of something very familiar about Joni. I don't think the whole process took more than twenty seconds but, Donna, it felt like twenty minutes. Our minds were moving in slow motion. It was so strange. We knew before we knew we knew."

"You figured it out that fast?"

"Well, Joni began to smile, a very trembling smile, and we could see tears, and we knew."

"And what happened?"

"Hugs, tears, joy, anger. Everything happened all at once!"

The scene was rolling before my eyes like a movie.

"Miriam, are you and Chris okay?"

"Oh my. We're confused, we're ecstatic, we're sad that Joe's gone, and we're mad that all this took twenty years. Really, Donna, we're emotionally exhausted. But it's going to be okay. It's just such a completely new reality. We don't have Joe, but we do have a new sister, and what a great gal she is. I just haven't wrapped my head around it yet. And, Donna, we understand why you didn't tell us. Joni told us about the two dinners."

Miriam's voice was filled with emotion. I could tell she didn't know whether to laugh or cry, and it sounded like she was doing a bit of both.

"Miriam, when I left them last night, I had no idea they were going to your house. I would never have imagined they'd do it so quickly. They said they were headed to Starbucks."

"And they did go there. But then they decided that there was really nothing to wait for and why not get it done and over with, I guess."

"I'm so glad they did. And really, how could you plan for this anyway?"

"Donna, Chris and I are both very thankful that you started this process. I know now that Joe—Joni—was slowly coming our way, but who knows how much longer it would have taken. Joni said when you realized so quickly that she was Joe, she knew she had to go forward. She had no idea if you would keep it a secret or not. She thought you would, but how could she be sure? And it's not that she didn't want to reunite. She said she was just really, really scared to do this. From what she explained, some families never accept people like her. Chris and I learned a lot last night."

"I'm sure you did. I've been on a pretty steep learning curve myself. Miriam, I don't think Joni ever realized that the family would think Joe might be a drug addict or in prison or dead. She seemed really taken aback in our first meeting when I told her those were the outcomes we'd imagined. And Miriam, do you realize now what that letter to Maud was about?"

There was silence as Miriam thought it over.

"Oh, good heavens, Donna, it was his operation, or treatment, or whatever it is that happens. We would never have thought of that!"

"No. It was never on our list of possibilities. But everything that was said in that letter fits the situation. So what happens now?"

I suddenly realized that no one, me included, had said the word "Harold." He was obviously the next step.

"Do you mean what do we do about Harold?" Miriam was chuckling when she said that.

"Donna, we talked about that, and we pretty much came to the conclusion that Harold gets handled like Chris and I did. I mean we can't send him to a class like Thea had to expand his horizons. We can't leave articles around the house hoping he'll read them. I mean, what do you do with Harold?"

Harold, the ever-present question.

"Well, Donna, here's what we decided. Everyone will gather at my house—Chris and I, Joni, Thea, Harold and Kathleen. We definitely need Kathleen, and we're going to tell her beforehand. We need her to be ready to help rather than be in a state of shock. Kathleen has a way of handling Harold. And then, Joni is simply going to introduce herself and tell Harold who she used to be. He may pick up on it first. Chris and I did, but Harold doesn't pay attention like we do. And, if a teary woman looks at him, he'll head the other way!" We both laughed, picturing that.

"Do you think Harold will accept this?"

"No. Not at first anyway. But I think he'll eventually come around. Over the years, we've come to realize that what our brother says and what he does are often two different things. He never wants anyone to notice that, but we do. There are some holes in his suit of armor."

"Well, Miriam, I guess Harold will have to sort it out for himself. And really, what does he gain by not accepting Joni?"

Miriam's voice was sounding stronger and happier the longer our conversation went. I figured talking this stuff out was good. I knew she and Chris both had to be going through a maze of adjustments in their heads trying to come to terms with finding their long-lost sibling and accepting the fact that they now had a sister and not a brother.

"And Donna, we haven't forgotten about the lease. Let us get through the Harold thing and then I promise you, we'll get down to business on the lease. It's not fair to you to put that off."

"Thanks, Miriam. I appreciate that."

I Can Finally Talk

After talking to Miriam I realized I was now free to tell Joanne about Joe, now Joni. And, in addition, the chief had okayed my talking about the bunker and what was going on there. Things were moving fast and, all of a sudden, all the secrets I'd been sworn to keep were out of the bag.

I decided to wait until I got home to make the call to Joanne. Trying to impart so much information while driving just wasn't a good idea. And besides that, I needed to process all this myself.

I pulled out of the restaurant parking lot, deciding to skip the salmon salad in favor of a quicker trip home. I got water and cashews at the local Go-Mart, and proceeded to strew salt and nut pieces all over me as I drove.

I hadn't fully comprehended yet that Miriam and Chris had been reunited with their long-lost sibling. And I was still reeling somewhat from the news that they were going full steam ahead in telling Harold. This was all happening so much faster than I had ever imagined it would.

But it was all good, even though I knew there were still hurdles to cross. Harold was certainly a hurdle. But beyond him, I could only imagine what Miriam and Chris were going through in trying to come to grips with such a sudden end to a two-decade disappearance, not to mention the fact that they now had a sister instead of a brother. I remembered one of my early emotions after realizing that Joni was Joe. It was a sense of mourning because I would never meet Joe as I'd come to know him through his sisters. Miriam and Chris had lived with him, called him family, for eighteen years. That sense of loss had to be much greater in them.

I knew all of this could be, and I was pretty sure would be, overcome, even the hurdle named Harold. Miriam and Chris seemed to be confident that Kathleen would be on board and that meant Harold would be facing three formidable females—five, if you counted Joni and Thea.

From what Kathleen had told me in our phone conversation, Harold desperately needed an end to his brother's disappearance. And Harold was no dummy. He had to have pictured all of the same bad endings his sisters and I had pictured. So the fact that Joe was alive, healthy, accomplished, and a very nice person had to be, on some level, a relief for Harold. The fact that he was a woman would be a little harder for the ex-marine to digest. But given enough time, and a good deal of patience on the part of the family, I had to think Harold would eventually come around.

I was getting close to home and feeling more settled, having thoroughly gone over the events of the last eighteen hours or so. Now to tell Joanne.

I said hello to the dogs and my brother, got a glass of ice water and headed for my desk. It was about one thirty, and I figured Joanne was back from lunch. However, I had a lot to say, so I decided to send her an email and suggest she call me. It was short and to the point: "Major developments with the Tredloes. Call me when you have time to talk. I'm in my office."

The phone rang in under a minute.

"So what's happening, Donna? Did you find Joe?"

It seemed everyone was dispensing with hello today.

"Yes, Joanne, Joe is found. Actually, Joe's been found for a week now. A week and one day, actually. I just couldn't talk about it until certain things happened. Joanne, Joe is now a woman. Her name is Joni Morgan, and she lives in Morgantown and works at the university."

That was met with stone-cold silence, so I figured I should just push on.

"And there's more. A body has been found in an old bunker on the Tredloe oil and gas tract. It's a woman, but she's not been identified yet."

"Donna, I'm putting you on hold while I grab a couple more people, and then I'll put you on speakerphone. Hold on."

It wasn't long before Joanne punched the button and Susan, the project manager, and Carol, the director of land, said hello.

"We hear you have some major developments," Carol said, "but Joanne won't tell us what."

I laughed. "Well, the missing Joe has been found. At least in a manner of speaking. Joe is now Joni Morgan. She lives in Morgantown and works at the university."

A barrage of questions followed so I started at the beginning with my trip to Pittsburgh. I told them how Aunt Betty and Professor Wilson had hit it off and how, from that first meeting, I thought the Professor might know more than he was telling. I told them about "Jill" and my first dinner and the unintended consequences of that. And then, about Joni's call to me for a second dinner and about Thea and the important link she became. And lastly, I explained last night's surprise visit by Thea and Joni to Miriam and Chris.

One of the things I loved about the company I was on contract to was the fact that they had no problem whatsoever putting qualified women in top positions. In most companies, I would have been talking to three men. And, while they would have appreciated the story, they wouldn't have reacted like my three very intent listeners were reacting. Again, I was hearing silence.

"Ladies?" I wasn't sure on speakerphone who was saying what, but the comments started coming.

"That's such an amazing story."

"Makes me teary."

"Wow! And we have to say, good job. For this to happen, you had to have handled it with kid gloves. This was a tough one," Carol said.

"Oh, I don't know. Joni was certainly headed down the path towards at least an attempted reunion with her family. I think the most important thing I did was to assure her in our first dinner that her sisters desperately wanted their brother back. And, while she couldn't quite do that, she could get close. I think that little extra reassurance put her on the fast track."

Joanne was ready to get down to the business end of things. "What about the lease?"

"Miriam told me this morning that once they got Harold out of the way they would sit down and meet with me on the lease. Of course, you have to understand that Harold could get stubborn and say no if he gets really bent out of shape over having a sister instead of a brother."

"Well, that wouldn't make any sense!" Susan commented.

"No, it wouldn't, but Harold being Harold, you just never know. My gut feeling, though, is that I'll be able to pull them all in. Kathleen, Harold's wife, should be for signing, so I don't know that Harold stands much of a chance if he does go negative on me."

Joanne was moving things along again and said, "Okay, now tell them about the body. Did you really tell me there was a body in a bunker?"

"I did, Joanne." Once they heard just a little of this one, they stopped me and brought in the guy in charge of the ground crews as well as the mapper. They always liked to know exactly where things are.

I again went through a long explanation of my and Tony's involvement with the Sheriff's Department. I told them what Lenai had found, and about my meeting with Lester Bolings and our trek to the bunker site, my and Tony's trip there and, finally, the discovery of the body.

Doug, head of ground operations, said, "This sounds like a movie, not a drilling project!"

And you've only heard part of it! With that, Joanne, Susan, and Carol quickly filled the guys in on the Joe to Joni saga and where that stood. And then Carol asked me an obvious question that I had no answer for.

"So what did those three guys at the old Tredloe homeplace get arrested for anyway?"

I had to admit that I didn't know. The chief had never said, and I had never asked.

"I'll ask the chief the next time I see him. He's never said, and I haven't asked too many questions. I think the biggest thing we really want to know is how long the land will be tied up."

Everyone agreed with that, and Doug asked, "But, Donna, the bunker isn't on the drillsite land is it?"

"No, it's not. It's on the tract the Tredloe heirs own the oil and gas on. It's adjacent to the drillsite but, from what I've seen on our maps, it's not a tract that there's likely to be any surface development on. It's south of the coal company property, and it looks like your pipelines are coming in from the north. I know the access roads wouldn't come across this property either, so maybe if all we're doing is drilling horizontally a mile and a half down, maybe they won't hold us up from doing it."

"So, Donna, what about the tract that Earl Crofton owns? He owns the oil and gas on that one, right?" Carol asked.

"Right. Earl owns both the surface and the oil and gas on Barrett Tredloe's original sixteen-acre farm, the old homeplace, and we do have a leg going under that. I would suspicion we'll have to wait until his case is resolved to know what happens there. It may get confiscated."

Skip, the mapper, pointed out that only one leg went through the sixteen acres so we could still do three southern legs if we got the Tredloe heirs. And, since drilling projects take lots and lots of time, by the time we were ready, the courts may have determined if Earl was keeping his land or not.

I noted everyone's questions and promised I would put them to the chief the next time I was in the courthouse. Whether or not he would, or could, answer them all was anyone's guess.

If ever I needed a walk, today was the day. It was only two thirty, but I had people I needed to call in the evening, so I decided to head up the road and clear my head. Bird watching, flower finding, and a warm late spring breeze were just what I needed. I changed my clothes, grabbed my pepper spray in a nod to all of Josh's warnings, and headed up the road.

My first wildlife sighting was not pleasant. It was a muskrat, dead in the road, a victim of somebody's tires. Road kill isn't unusual on our road, but a muskrat carcass is. They're very furtive creatures, living in burrows along the creek bank, and staying either there or in the water most of the time. We'd had a very heavy overnight rain the night before, and I'd noticed this morning that the creek had come up a good bit but was already receding. I suspected he'd been flooded out and was heading to higher ground.

A muskrat is about twice the size of a squirrel with a beautiful coat that, unfortunately, looks like mink when it's dry, making it a target for trappers. It is, though, very definitely a rodent, the most telling part of its body being the tail. Pretty fur, really ugly tail. It's a thick, hairless, triangular appendage, about nine inches long and rubbery looking. This poor guy was yet another meal for the vultures and crows!

The rest of my walk was more pleasant with the usual mallards in the creek, a squawking and diving kingfisher, and a variety of newly blooming "weeds" garnering my attention. I have to say, though, that I wasn't as engaged in my surroundings as I usually was, my mind constantly wandering to the dual dramas our drilling project was immersed in.

It was a half-hour walk that did leave me feeling more settled but, as I got back home and walked in the door, the phone was ringing. I picked it up and said, "Hello."

"Donna, it's Joni. I talked to Miriam so I know you know about last night. Thea and I would have told you what we were going to do but, when we left you, we had no idea that's what we were going to do!"

Yet another helloless phone call. Joni's voice was so upbeat it made me smile.

"Joni, I was totally shocked when Miriam told me, but it was a good shock. And, I have to admit, I can't think of any advantages to waiting to tell them. It would have been very hard for Thea to have kept it a secret anyway. At least it would have been for me if I was her."

"Oh, she was bursting to tell and I couldn't blame her. Donna, do you think Miriam is okay? Could you tell?"

I thought about that question for a second. "You know, Joni, there are three words that Miriam used that I think sum it up pretty well. They were overjoyed, angry, and confused. The anger is normal I would think. The family missed twenty years of your life and that hurts, but they'll work through it. And the confusion is totally understandable, but that will get better with time, too. In the end, the joy of having you back will trump everything else."

"Donna, it doesn't go this way with every family. I'm lucky that my two sisters are on board. And you're right, they'll still have some struggles but they'll be okay. I'm not so sure about Harold, and that's what I wanted to talk to you about. Miriam and Chris have already told Kathleen. She's apparently on the Internet trying to figure out the whole trans thing. She wants information so she can deal with Harold."

Wow, this family was moving fast. It had only been a couple of hours since I'd talked to Miriam. And then I remembered Kathleen's call to me, and I decided to tell Joni. I felt she should know Kathleen's take on things if she didn't already.

"Joni, Kathleen called me a couple of weeks ago. I wasn't supposed to tell anyone, but I think it's probably okay now, and it might help you and your sisters to know this."

I went on to explain the fact that Kathleen felt Joe's disappearance was eating at Harold every day. And that resolving it, no matter the outcome, would be a positive for Harold.

"Donna, Kathleen had that same conversation this morning with Miriam. And, of course, Miriam told me. It made me realize that I should have come forward long ago. I kept telling myself that I would hurt them too much. They would never understand.

They'd be embarrassed at church, yada yada. The bottom line is, I was too scared to do it. A total rejection would have devastated me. Over time, though, I realized I had to try. I know now that my sisters will be okay with it. We still have a lot of talking to do and things to work through, but Miriam and Chris and I are family again. I know that. But now I'm getting greedy, I guess, and I really want my brother back. If I don't get him, it won't be the end of the world, but I'm going to do everything I can to get Harold to understand."

"So what's the plan? Or do you even have one yet?"

"We do. I just talked to Miriam and it's all happening tomorrow evening at her house. Harold comes back tonight from several straight days on a job in central Pennsylvania. He was pulled in to help them out of some kind of problem they ran into. He's off for the next four days, and then he goes back to his regular crew. But here's something else Kathleen has told us. Harold has rheumatoid arthritis, and these jobs are just way too hard on him now. With the Marcellus boom, he wants to start his own company doing pipeline design, consulting, that kind of thing—more of an inside job so he's not out in the weather so much. And he's told Kathleen, 'If they could find that damn Joe, the bonus money from the lease could put me in business.' Well, that damn Joe is found, so we think the money angle will help keep him on board."

Joni had been imitating Harold's voice, and I laughed because her imitation was a pretty good one.

"And you're going to tell him everything tomorrow evening?"

"Here's the plan. Miriam is going to have everyone over for dinner. I'll be there as Thea's friend. We want you to come later."

"What! Me? What am I doing there?"

"We're going to tell Harold that you've asked for a meeting to talk to us about the lease. If Harold questions meeting without Joe being found, Miriam's going to remind him that you might have found Joe and not be able to tell them. That will get Harold there. He's going to be very curious."

"Won't he find it odd that you're there when it's a family meeting to discuss business?"

"We'll say Thea and I are working on her thesis plans, and we're heading to her room after dinner. He'll buy that. Of course, it won't play out that way."

"Joni, you realize that Harold may figure out who you are before you ever tell him. Miriam and Chris did."

"Well, hopefully I won't cry when I see Harold. My face said it all when I saw my sisters. But, if he figures it out, that's okay too. There's no perfect way to break this news to Harold. But Donna, Kathleen says Harold's arthritis is really getting to him. If you're coming, she thinks he'll stay around no matter how unhappy he is over me. The longer we can keep him there and interacting, the better chance we'll have to get him settled down and on board about me, at least a little."

I knew I had that deer-in-the-headlights look again, even though Joni couldn't see me through the phone lines. "Boy, you guys have come up with a plan pretty quick."

"We've kept the phone lines hot this morning. Honestly, Donna, when I picked up the phone to call Miriam, I got all teary. It seems like such a simple thing, but being able to call my sister is a big, big deal."

"I can only imagine. Are you at work?" I was picturing Joni in her office sobbing and coworkers and students wondering what in the world was going on.

"No. I called off for two days. So did Chris, and Miriam said her transcription jobs are kind of slow right now. We wouldn't be very productive anyway. Actually, Chris and Miriam and I are having lunch together tomorrow. It's sort of to plan for tomorrow night, but mostly it's just catch up. I know they're bursting with questions and mostly ones they're afraid to ask. Who wouldn't be? So Donna, can you be there tomorrow evening?"

It was just like our dinner at Amani's two nights before. I shouldn't say yes but, of course, I was going to.

"What time, Joni?"

"About six thirty. We're going to eat a little early so we have time to talk to you. And I promise, we will talk about the lease, with or without Harold."

A Couple More Miscreants

I f I was going to meet with the Tredloe heirs on Thursday night about the lease, I was going to have signable documents in hand. If Harold actually stayed to talk, I knew he would take the lead and want to negotiate, and that was fine. Everyone should negotiate. However, I had been blindsided a couple of times in meetings where I thought we were negotiating and, surprisingly, my lessors were ready to sign.

I began by reviewing the documents I had already given Miriam, Chris, and Harold, and then started filling in a lease for the first time for Joni. The very first blank line is for the lessor's legal name, and I realized, I didn't have that information on Joni. I picked up the phone and called her, explaining what I needed.

"Actually, Donna, on the name change document, it says 'Joni J. Morgan.' And the *J* is just that. In my mind, it stands for Joseph but that would have been kind of odd. So it's just a *J.*"

"Joni, legally I have to include your former name as an 'f/k/a' or 'formerly known as.' You will only sign as Joni J. Morgan, but legally, we have to have that link back to Joe, since that's who legally inherited from your father. Is that okay?"

"Donna, I know the lease will be recorded. But if the cat's out of the bag with my family, I don't really mind if anyone else knows. Doing the f/k/a is fine."

We hung up and I entered "Joni J. Morgan f/k/a Joseph Morgan Tredloe" on my lease header. This was getting so real.

Another wave of emotion swept over me, triggered, I think, by the sheer amazement that after twenty years, Joni and her sisters were together again—and, the big rock in the road was soon to be tackled.

It suddenly hit me that while Tony knew all about the body in the bunker, he knew nothing about Joe being found. And the office didn't yet know about my meeting with the family Thursday night to talk about the lease.

But I was tired of being on the phone. I decided that I would let Thursday night's meeting play out and bring everyone up to speed on Friday. First, I needed to bring Sam up to speed. When he got home, we both set about our dinner duties with me making salad, and Sam whipping up "Chicken Larue," a delicious creamed chicken and mushroom dish over egg noodles. I filled Sam in on the latest details, watching him occasionally shake his head and smile. This drilling project had turned into quite a saga.

I was, though, anxious about the next evening's meeting with the Tredloe heirs. I figured I wouldn't sleep a wink, so I was more than surprised when, the next morning, I awoke from a very deep sleep feeling rested and ready to roll.

I had an early email from Tony asking if I could meet him at the coffee shop near the courthouse around ten. I had a few courthouse details to track down; it worked for me. Tony had several title files that he was finishing, so I figured he would be handing me lots more work.

I was enjoying the last few bites of my breakfast around seven Thursday morning while I finished reading the newspaper. Sam had his laptop open on the island and was digging into a waffle while telling me interesting tidbits from his Facebook page.

He finished and asked, "So what time do you have to meet with the Tredloe clan tonight, Donna?"

"Six thirty."

"I probably won't be home in time to make dinner before you leave."

"That's okay. I don't want to eat much anyway. I figure my stomach will be in somewhat of a knot. I have no idea what I'm going to walk into tonight."

"Think you should take your pistol?" Sam was grinning, knowing my feelings on carrying a gun.

"Sam, the company really frowns on shooting lessors. And besides, Harold might make a scene, but I don't think he'll be a danger to anyone. Well, at least not to me."

We both laughed, and Sam headed for the shower. I cleaned up the kitchen, said good-bye to Sam on his way out, did a few things at my desk, and set off to meet Tony. I had just crossed into Taylor County when my phone rang and the caller ID said Lester Bolings, the guy responsible for all of us knowing about the bunker.

"Good morning, Mr. Bolings."

"There was a hesitation and he said, "I've never got used to people having caller ID."

We both laughed.

"Mrs. Cain, I just watched a car park up the road a ways. There's a right-of-way up there for high-voltage electric lines. It's the same one cuts through not too far from where I showed you the bunker."

I had noticed it when I was at Mr. Bolings's house. I knew it didn't go through the Tredloe property because rights-of-way were prohibited there by the deed. But it might be on Crofton's sixteen acres or at least close.

"Are you saying it would provide a path from your road over to the Tredloe property?"

"It sure would. Well I was out by the road putting a bill in my mailbox when that car went past. It had Louisiana tags, and there was a man and a woman in the car. They both took a good look at me as they went by. Kind of made me uneasy."

"Did you recognize them?"

"Never seen 'em before. I went on back in the house, but I kept watch up that way out my living room window. They drove past the right-of-way and turned around, then parked beside it facing this way. They locked the car and then headed up the path under the wires. They had those things the school kids wear on their backs."

"Backpacks?"

"Yeah. At least that's what it looked like. They kept looking back towards my place, though, I guess to see if they could see me watching them."

"Mr. Bolings, did you call the Sheriff's Department?"

"No, you think I should?"

"Hang up and call now. It's important. Ask for Chief Warner, but if he's not there make sure you get a deputy. Tell them that right-of-way leads to the Crofton and Tredloe tracts. And Mr. Bolings?"

"Yeah?"

"Lock your doors!"

We hung up and I immediately decided to head to the chief's office before I met with Tony. I wanted to make sure Lester Bolings had made the call. However, just as I hit the edge of town, two sheriff's cruisers and an unmarked car passed me going the other way, no lights and sirens, but moving at a pretty good clip. Mr. Bolings had called. I canceled my visit to the chief's office, mostly because I thought I saw him in the passenger seat of the unmarked car.

My curiosity was demanding that I turn around and fall
in line behind them, but I knew that would get me the biggest
lecture yet. So, I shored up my willpower and continued on to the
coffee shop. I was no more in the door when Tony says, "Donna,
Lenai thinks she knows who the body is!"

"You've got to be kidding!"

"Nope! A call girl named Candy Lapoe!"

I burst out laughing, way too loud for a public place. Thank-
fully, at ten o'clock in the morning, we were the only custom-
ers. The girl behind the counter started listening though. Who
wouldn't.

"I'm sorry, Tony, but what a name."

"That was her professional name, Donna. She was born
Ethel Marie Schoop. Not much pizazz in that one. But here's the
scoop."

"Would that be the Schoop scoop?"

I almost slapped myself for that one. Tony just rolled his eyes
and kept going.

"In the late nineties, Renee de la Corte was named a person of
interest in the disappearance of Candy Lapoe. From what Lenai
can gather, Ramone Gagne was a frequent customer of Candy's.
And, it was highly suspected that she entertained William as
well."

"Tony, where does Lenai get all this information?"

"Some of it is from transcripts of actual court proceedings.
Renee de la Corte was eventually brought before the grand jury,
but they didn't feel they had enough evidence so the case never
went to trial. Lenai said some of the other details are on the web
and not nearly so verifiable. But she said several people have
posted their take on it, and the information is pretty consistent."

"So, I'm guessing blackmail, right?"

"That's it. It was believed that Candy was mining William and Ramone for information on the art thefts and where the goods were going. She must not have gotten enough info, though, because after William and Ramone passed away—and she was probably getting a little old for her first chosen profession—she got a job working for Renee's art import business. I'm thinking she did it to learn more about the operation and finally decided she had enough evidence to blackmail Renee."

"But she disappeared, never to be found?"

"According to what Lenai could find, yes."

"Tony, the Feds have to have come across this info already."

"Probably, but they would never tell us. It's fun to be in the know!"

I sure couldn't disagree with that.

Tony handed me three title files, and we both headed to the courthouse with me stowing the files safely in my car on the way. As we walked, I told Tony about the call from Lester Bolings about the man and woman in the car with Louisiana tags.

"Donna, those cruisers could have been going anywhere. You'd better stop in the Sheriff's Department and make sure Lester Bolings called."

I couldn't disagree with that, so Tony and I walked into the outer office, which we knew was quite busy before we ever got in the door. Out in the hall we could hear the radio traffic going crazy, and someone was giving Elaine a list of things to do stat! She looked at us like we were the last thing she needed.

I waited for a break and said, "Elaine, I just wanted to make sure Lester Bolings called in with his information."

"Oh, yeah, he called. All hell's breaking loose out there, but I can't say anything."

"That's okay, Elaine. Just wanted to make sure."

That's when Tony piped up. "And tell the chief we already know who the body is. That will save him filling us in."

Elaine was feverishly punching numbers into the phone on orders from the field, but on Tony's revelation, she slammed the phone down and we got her full attention. "You know who the body is?" she exclaimed.

"Well, we're pretty sure!"

Tony was puffed up like a peacock. I knew exactly what he'd done, and I was more than impressed. My old boss at the radio station called it dragging a bare hook. You might catch something, you might not, but sometimes it pays to drag the hook and see what you get.

Elaine was barking into the radio. "Chief. Call in. It's important. Now!"

I was guessing Elaine had been with the department longer than the chief. She obviously swung some weight. The phone rang in the time it took to punch speed dial.

"Chief! Donna Cain and . . ."

"Tony," Tony said.

". . . Tony are in the office, and they say they know who the body is."

We could clearly hear the chief on the other end say, "Well, for God's sake!"

Elaine handed the phone to Tony, and he relayed the facts in as few words as possible. I could hear the chief say he needed filled in on a few things like how William and Ramone fit into the whole thing as well as Renee de la Corte. We figured he'd turned all the info we'd given him over to the Feds and needed a refresher course. He said he'd be back in the office in about an hour and a half and to wait for him.

I gave Elaine my cell number, and she said she'd call when

the chief got back. It was ten thirty so it would probably be right around lunchtime.

Tony and I headed to the record room to work, both knowing it was going to be hard to concentrate on the mundane tasks at hand when we had such drama playing out. But work we did. I had to run down a few facts, which turned out to be rather mindless tasks. But Tony was actually running title, something that takes a fair degree of concentration. I figured he'd review everything when he was in a more settled state of mind.

At about ten until twelve my cell rang and Elaine, ever brief and to the point, said, "Chief's here." And with that she hung up.

We put our work in files, stowed our satchels in the copy room, and headed to the chief's office.

"How'd you figure this out?"

Geez. Nobody said hello anymore.

"Well, sir, my friend in Louisiana is a library research specialist, and she works for the State. She has access to quite a lot of material. But," Tony was quick to add, "everything she's told us is from documents available to the public."

"And you're saying it's a call girl named Carly?"

"Candy, sir, Candy Lapoe, real name Ethel Marie Schoop."

It was the chief's turn to roll his eyes.

"And she was blackmailing Renee what's her name, who supposedly murdered her?"

"It appeared that way, sir. At least there was enough evidence to take Renee de la Corte before the grand jury but not enough to go to trial."

"Well, I'm guessing the Feds know all this, and they just haven't told us yet. Happens a lot." The chief leaned forward in his chair and yelled into the outer office, "Elaine, call the State Medical Examiner's Office and tell them we probably have an ID on the body. See if it sounds like they already know."

He leaned back, turning his attention to us, but then yelled out one more thing. "Elaine, if they don't know, don't tell them. Say I'm tied up, and I'll call them later. I want them to dangle a while."

He turned back to us.

"And now, since you correctly told Lester Bolings to call us, Mrs. Cain, I'll tell you two what went on out there. It's going to break by tomorrow anyway."

The chief was looking pretty satisfied with things, and I was thinking they must be getting to the end of the line. He leaned back in his chair and said, "We realized that if those two people were sneaking in on the right-of-way, there was something out there they needed to get out. It's about a mile and a quarter from Lester's road to the Tredloe place, and the first part is a heck of a climb. That gave us time to get in there and get in position to observe with binoculars. By the time we saw them coming down the hill on the right-of-way, we could tell they were pretty tuckered out. Neither one looked like they were in great shape for a hike." The chief looked like a man telling a good yarn with a good ending.

"Their first stop was an old water pump in the backyard. It still works. They pumped and drank, sat down to rest, and then got in a heck of an argument. She kept saying, 'I should have divorced you long ago!' so we knew they were married. He kept harping on her sister and saying they wouldn't be in this fix if it wasn't for the fact that her family preferred a life of crime to going straight."

"I bet it was Renee de la Corte's sister and brother-in-law," I said, desperately trying to remember their names. "They were listed in Helena Vanscoy's obituary. Helena's other daughter."

The chief agreed that was a good possibility and continued with his story.

"Finally, they headed downhill a ways and stopped at a pole on the edge of the property that has a dusk-to-dawn light on it. We've kind of wondered before about that light being so far from the house."

The chief's radio came to life, but it was just a deputy reporting that the car parked near Lester Bolings's house was now on the impound lot.

"Anyway, the guy took a pocketknife and popped a little metal plate open on the pole. He reached in and apparently flipped a switch. The next thing we knew, they walked into an old shed that's close by, tossed out four or five bales of hay, and closed the door behind them. We moved in quietly, didn't hear anything in the shed, so we opened the door. We were looking at about a three-by-five-foot piece of the floor that was hinged and propped open. The bales of hay had apparently been covering it. There was a set of concrete steps going down to a tunnel that we could see was well lit. The switch on the pole controlled the lights."

"So, Chief," I asked, "this was another tunnel going to the bunker with the body?"

"Nope, new tunnel, new bunker."

Tony and I were all ears. The chief continued.

"Well, we didn't think they'd stay down there long, so we backed out, closed the door and got on either side of the shed. Sure enough, in a few minutes we could hear them coming. They were cussing and complaining all the way up those stairs about the weight of what they were carrying and how they were ever going to get it over that damned hill and into the car." The chief was enjoying every minute of this tale!

"I gotta tell you, that was one of the best takedowns I've ever seen. They came out of that shed, each with backpacks that looked heavy. She was first and was holding the front end of a statue about three feet long. She had it in the crook of her elbow gripping it around the neck, and he had the other end by the feet. They were just getting ready to set it down and close everything up when Bauer yelled freeze! They both jumped and yelled, and that statue dropped right on her foot as she spun around." Tony and I were both wishing we could have been there!

"So, Mrs. Cain, who'd you just say you thought they were? 'Cause they were smart and didn't have any ID on them. Nothing in the car either. They both gave us names, but we don't think they were real. They're running the tags on the car now, but it could be stolen or rented. They're both in a holding cell as John Does, and we want names before we send them to regional."

"Chief, Helena Vanscoy's other daughter was listed in her obituary. And she and her husband both come up on the Louisiana Secretary of State's records as officers in Renee de la Corte's business. I don't remember the name. But if you google Helena Vanscoy's obituary, it should come up."

The chief did, and in under thirty seconds we had the names. Michelle and Arthur Lyon.

"That's them," the chief said. "I remember now that she called him Art once when they were arguing by the well."

The chief leaned forward in his chair to yell at Elaine and give her the info, but she'd been listening the whole time.

"Got it, Chief!"

We heard her getting the names to the deputies to run through the system. No grass grew under Elaine's feet.

I was still in need of more details. "So, Chief, there was another bunker?"

"Oh, yeah. And this one was climate-controlled. Had heat and dehumidifiers. Pretty expensive operation."

"Was the statue okay? The one they dropped?" Tony asked.

The chief told us it fell on grass, and feet, of course, and there didn't appear to be any damage to it from the fall. He said the statue was primitive, definitely from another culture and possibly portrayed a mythical figure. That fit right in with the theft of antiquities in Central America.

"The backpacks were filled with small, stone carvings and a good bit of jade. I sure wouldn't have wanted to get back over that hill carrying all of that. I figure those two would have been in a real battle by the time they got to Lester's road." The chief was chuckling thinking about that.

"But there was a lot more down in the bunker," Chief Warner continued. "We found several paintings, all carefully wrapped and actually hanging on two walls made of pegboard. And there was still some jade there, mostly figurines. At least we think they were jade. Art theft isn't something we ever deal with here."

I had a million questions in my head but could only get them out so fast.

The chief was patient, telling us they left everything in the bunker figuring that was the best environment for it. They had secured it with padlocks, and the FBI had already been notified. They were sending in specialists who would run the paintings and statuary through the National Stolen Art File. Tony and I were absolutely spellbound.

But then I remembered, one more very important question.

"Chief, can you tell us why Earl Crofton and the other two guys at his place were arrested in the first place?"

"One of the guys was wanted for murder in Louisiana. The other was thought to be an accessory. When the federal marshals first got on their trail, they thought the murder was tied to an active drug investigation and that they'd find a big drug operation here. They didn't. But they did have enough to hold both of them on charges related to murder, and Earl just got hauled in because he was hiding them.

My head was spinning, and I could tell Tony was deep in thought as well.

"So those guys are charged with murdering Candy Lapoe?"

"No, it was a man they murdered. They shot him as he walked out of an apartment house in New Orleans and, apparently, there were witnesses, but the suspects got away. The victim was a drug dealer so that's why it was initially a drug investigation. The shooters had fled the state so the marshals were brought in and started getting leads that pointed towards here and the Crofton tract. And then when you two gave us the information on the ownership history of the land and the whole Guatemala–Honduras thing and the possibility of art theft, the marshals called in the FBI. They're the ones with the knowledge to do that kind of investigation. And, once they started going down that road, it led somewhere."

"So," Tony asked, "there were actually two murders? Candy Lapoe and the drug dealer?"

"It sure looks that way," the chief said.

By this time, we were all sitting there feeling rather smug and self-satisfied. And just then, Elaine came to the door and told the chief that Detective Bauer was on the phone. It was a short call that left the chief laughing.

"Bauer says he asked those two what they knew about the woman's body in the other bunker, and he said they turned white. Obviously, couldn't believe we'd found her. And then they both started spilling the beans on Renee de la Corte. I think they better get her in custody down in Louisiana before she skips town. I figure she was supposed to hear back from these two and she hasn't, so she may get a little antsy."

Tony and I gave the chief a little refresher course on the lineage of the Gagnes, Helena Vanscoy, and Renee de la Corte. All stuff we'd told him before, but it was really too much to remember.

Just then Elaine stuck her head in the door again. "Chief, I just got the M-E, and she seemed totally clueless. She said the Feds hadn't called her with any names yet. Said they usually did."

"Well, well. I'm going to have lots of fun with this one. It appears I know who the body is and they don't."

"Whoa, Chief!" Tony was looking uncomfortable. "This is just my friend Lenai putting two and two together. It does seem logical though."

"I'd put money on it, but I'll go easy, Tony. I'll just tell them it's a lead."

The chief was smiling from ear to ear. But, it was his next statement that made me smile.

"Donna!"

Wow, he called me Donna rather than Mrs. Cain.

"We know your company needs things wrapped up so you can go forward with the well. I'll do my best to make sure it's in high gear."

"Thanks, Chief. We appreciate it."

Harold Meets Fritz

ony and I walked back to the copy room, both feeling really good that we'd helped unravel such an amazing tale.

"Tony, it was your knowledge of history and the Banana Wars that really started this whole thing. Without that, this would be a puzzle with a lot of missing pieces."

"Well, I think we both knew there was a story in this. Never thought it would be this big of a story though!"

I got my satchel, said good-bye to Tony, and headed for home. What should have been a routine morning had turned into something much bigger, and I still had to get ready for an evening meeting with the Tredloe heirs. I had a feeling this day was going to be well marked in my memory!

When I got home, I considered calling Joanne but decided I'd just wait until tomorrow when I could tell her everything at once. I knew it would be another speakerphone-in-the-conference-room session because there were quite a few people at the company who couldn't move forward on this particular well until I got the Tredloe leases and the land was out of the clutches of the various police agencies who now had a grip on it.

I had already printed out each of the siblings' leases for the meeting on the hopes that the family would be ready to talk. I gave that about a fifty–fifty chance and that may have been my optimism talking. But I looked over everything again making sure there were no mistakes. I finally gave up on doing anything productive and played solitaire on my iPad. Total waste of time, but it always calmed my nerves.

I made half a sandwich with some leftover meatloaf, ate that and a few grapes, and then got in the car. My brain was finally beginning to comprehend the fact that I was going to meet with all four Tredloe siblings at once. At least that was the plan.

And, as all plans have the potential to do, this one went awry—a lot faster than I had anticipated. The trouble started when I made the turn into Miriam's long driveway and came within inches of mowing down Harold who was striding towards the road with a stormy look on his face!

I leaped from the car shouting, "Mr. Tredloe, are you okay?" He'd fallen down when he tried to jump out of my way, and I was envisioning broken bones, concussions, and God knows what else. And what was he doing walking out of Miriam's driveway, anyway?

Harold, meanwhile, was picking himself up and heading towards me in a way that could only be called menacing.

"So, now can you see what you've done! Couldn't let well enough alone. Had to find a scab and pick at it. And, yes, I know my sisters encouraged you. Fine mess you've got this family into now!"

My mouth had been open to apologize to Harold for almost running him over. But in the time it took him to lecture me, I realized that he'd walked out of the house in anger and stomped off! He wasn't concerned about falling in the road; rather, he was ranting about Joni. And he was blaming me!

My mother died in 2003. She was a wee little woman with a hair trigger when it came to anger, but that had never been me. I took after my father, easygoing and deliberate. However, after Mom died, I noticed that I occasionally would react quickly and forcefully and say things that surprised me as much as anyone else. Her nickname was Fritz, and I would always say to myself, "Okay, Fritz, enough of that!"

Poor Harold. He'd never met Fritz, but he was about to. My mouth opened, and a dressing down came out that I had no idea was in me.

"Harold, your family was a mess. It was broken and hurting and certainly not whole. Joni was coming back to you, and it would have happened with or without me. I speeded it up, and I will forever be proud of that. And, if you think for one minute that Joni is something to be ashamed of, you need help and a lot of it. That's your sister. She's a very nice woman, she's educated, and she's successful. And, you know what Harold, she's making a real difference in this world! Harold, you never had a brother. Joe was fiction. You had a sister from the day she was born. She was a female in the wrong body."

The whole time I was talking I was walking towards Harold, and he was backing up. I suddenly snapped out of it and was totally aghast at what I'd just done.

Harold was looking at me in disbelief. I'd backed him towards a low wall at the side of Miriam's driveway, and he sat down on it and started to cry.

Good grief! "Harold, I'm so sorry!"

He just looked at me and blubbered, "I had a brother. But now, he's gone!"

I dove in the car for a box of Kleenex and gave Harold a handful.

"Harold, when I first figured it out, I felt like I was mourning Joe, and I only knew him through Miriam and Chris. But it was a sense of loss. And it has to be a whole lot more intense for you."

"I will never see my brother again, Mrs. Cain. Never!"

I sat down on the wall next to Harold, handing him tissues from time to time. I didn't think there was much I could say that would help.

Little by little, Harold got control and started talking. "Mrs. Cain, I'm a very simple man. I work hard, I pray hard; life has its rules and I've lived by them. But it just seems to me like the rules keep changing. Not just with things like this, with everything. I'm playing the game I learned as a young man, but I'm not winning anymore."

"It is a world that's changing fast, Mr. Tredloe. I agree."

"Mrs. Cain, everyone thinks I'm the bad guy, well Dad and I, but Dad's gone. We were at the house the night Joe left so, of course, we caused the whole thing. Well, we didn't. Do you know what Dad and I walked in on that night, Mrs. Cain?"

I'd done a lot of reading on transgender and the habits and patterns that go with it. I suspected that I did know what they'd walked in on, and I understood them being totally freaked out and angry.

"I'm going to guess that you found Joe in your mother's clothing, Mr. Tredloe."

Harold's stunned look confirmed I was right.

"Mr. Tredloe, I've done a lot of reading trying to understand more about this. Apparently, that's common. If you feel like a female, but you have to wear male clothing all the time, when you think it's safe you put on female clothing."

Harold just sat, shaking his head. I knew he was running scenes from that night through his mind. It couldn't have been easy, especially for a guy fresh from the testosterone-filled atmosphere of the marines.

Neither of us had any idea that anyone else was around. We both jumped about a foot off the wall when Kathleen put a hand on each of our shoulders from behind us.

"Kathleen, we didn't see you coming," I practically shrieked.

Harold had gotten the tears under control, and I could tell he was trying to hide any evidence of them from Kathleen. She wasn't buying it.

"Mrs. Cain is trying to talk some sense into me, Kathleen."

"Is she having any luck?"

"Maybe a little, but I thought I was going to have to shoot her at one point. She can get pretty mean."

I was off the wall and smiling, glad that Harold was making a joke out of my bad behavior. Kathleen was looking a little confused, but had sat down where I'd been, and put her arm around Harold saying, "I'm glad you ran into Donna."

Harold gave me a knowing look and said, "Donna ran into me, Kathleen."

Suddenly, a diversionary tactic hit me.

"You know, I'd like to get everyone together to tell you what's been happening on your great-grandfather's old farm and on the land you own the minerals on. It involves dead bodies in bunkers, art theft, and a big arrest today."

I could tell I had their attention.

"You're talking about Earl Crofton and his buddies?" Harold asked.

"Earl, his buddies, and now two more."

"How about I give you both a ride up the hill so I don't have to tell this tale twice."

Kathleen climbed in the front, Harold got in the back, and I put it in drive quickly, absolutely flabbergasted that Harold was letting me take him back up the hill and into Miriam's house. Given the looks on everyone's faces when we entered, they were just as surprised.

One More Surprise

nce we were all in the house, the ex-marine took control, and we all had the good sense to let him.

"Listen up everybody. Mrs. Cain has a report on everything that's been happening on Great-Grandpap Tredloe's farm and that tract we own the oil and gas on."

I took a seat at the table and Miriam handed me a glass of iced tea, but refrained from asking me if I wanted the last piece of the apple pie on the table. She'd had a dessert plate in her hand ready to serve it to me, but she decided to follow Harold's orders since he'd seen fit to come back.

I launched into the whole story, not leaving out a detail. If I could keep Harold and Joni in the same room with a good yarn, I figured that was progress. The lease could be divisive, and I didn't want to get into any negotiations just yet. As much as we needed their signatures, I knew I had to go slowly.

The tale I was telling was a good one, and there were questions and comments along the way. We were all around the table with Harold at one end and me at the other. That put Joni in Harold's line of sight when he was looking at me. I could see his eyes wander to her on occasion.

I had the feeling that everyone in the room was on board with the process, that they knew as long as we were talking about this bizarre story, they were sharing something. And the important thing was, they were sharing something other than the Joe to Joni saga.

I kept seeing smiles that weren't in response to the story I was telling. They were smiles of relief, smiles of surprise, smiles of contentment. Joni smiled because she was with her siblings at long last. Miriam and Chris and Thea and Kathleen occasionally smiled, I think, solely because they were surprised and happy that Harold was still in the room. Harold, on the other hand, tried to maintain a face devoid of emotion. He lost that battle, but Harold did stay seated. And when my tale was done, he demanded another piece of pie from Miriam, and she jumped up to give him the last piece. Oh, Harold.

And One More Surprise

I t was Friday morning. When I'd gotten home Thursday night, I spent a full hour telling Sam about my meeting as well as all that had happened that morning with the two people sneaking into the Tredloe property. By the time I went to bed, I was exhausted.

I hadn't set the alarm, telling Sam to let me sleep in if I could. But I still woke up at the normal five thirty, and Sam and I rehashed the previous day's events over breakfast.

"So, Donna, do you think they'll sign the lease?"

"I think so. I knew that last night was not the time to negotiate. I didn't want to do anything that could put Harold and Joni on opposite sides of any issues that might come up. And really, it was never realistic that we could discuss the lease so soon after Harold finding out. Everyone was just emotionally spent. A good story was what was needed."

As expected, I was on speakerphone with the office for a long, long time going over all of the events of the previous day. I explained that the night before, as I was leaving, everyone promised me that we would get together on the lease as soon as their schedules allowed. They said they'd work it out and let me know. I was very confident that it would happen, and I told everyone listening in the conference room that I had every expectation of having the leases within a couple of weeks.

I hung up with the office, and within thirty seconds, the

phone rang. It was Joni.

"Donna, I just want to say thanks again for the role you've played in this. Harold is going to be okay. It will take a little time, but he's coming around. I don't know what you said to him at the bottom of the driveway, Donna, but he warned us all before he left that we should be a little cautious of you. Something about 'that woman must think she's about three times the size she really is!' But he kind of grinned when he said it."

"Long story, Joni, but that was my mother, Fritz, talking down by the road. Sometimes she takes possession of me, and I have to beat her back with a stick before she gets me in too much trouble."

Joni was laughing.

"Donna, Thea is going with me to Pittsburgh this afternoon. We're staying until Sunday. And then, next weekend, someone who is very special in my life will be coming down here for the weekend."

Joni had my full attention, and I was thinking a love interest. Joni had a boyfriend.

"I have a daughter, Donna. She's twelve years old. You know, I was a functioning man, and for a while I tried very hard to play the role. I even got married. It got very complicated between my ex and me, but once we got it sorted out, she simply became a good friend. Other than Aunt Maud and my cousin Jill, my family was just an empty space to my daughter and my wife. I can fill that space in now. Thea will be the first and then, next weekend, my family is in for another surprise."

Oh my! I wasn't family, but I was surprised. I was confused. I was kind of speechless. But . . . I was smiling. And in the final analysis, isn't that what really counts.

Acknowledgments

What an adventure this has been. I want to thank my husband, Roland, for his encouragement and critiques. A big thanks to my beta readers, Lois Tobin, Carole Klepfel, and Sheri Ruland, all of whom gave me valuable input. Also a huge thank you to Sam and Alexandra. They very candidly shared information with me on my journey from knowing little to, at the very least, a reasonable knowledge of a very complex subject. And, along the way, they turned me into an advocate. I am truly grateful for the education. My thanks to fellow Rotary members Hal Reed and Gordon Keyes who included me in their dental trips to Guatemala. I was forever changed by those opportunities. My never-ending gratitude to Belinda Miles, a daughter in our heart and a very talented lady, who gave me a cover design I love. Finally, I want to thank Populore Publishing staff for the careful editing and page layout, the insightful comments on content, and, most of all, for the miscellaneous explanations and words to the wise.